EPILOGUE

RICHARD ROSS

For Carol, my dream that came true.

PART ONE

PROLOGUE

ABOUT 10 YEARS AGO

Victor Penlick was well into his 60s, but his drives off the tee were only a few yards short of what they had been 40 years earlier.

"You're buying," he said to his golfing pal as he dropped a birdie in the 18th hole.

"Hell, I don't know why I still do this. I should just give you my wallet and get it over with." Roger chuckled.

"That works, too," Penlick said.

Roger Skarlyle had been his friend for decades. An oil magnate, the press accused him of owning half the politicians in Texas. He said they were dead wrong. That the number was closer to two-thirds.

In the clubhouse, they each ordered a ribeye steak sandwich and an iced tea. Victor's phone rang.

"Hello, Senator," he answered. "I just so happen to be at Meadow Park having lunch with Roger. That sounds mighty fine. I'll see you then, Pierce."

The waiter delivered the teas. It was springtime, and the two men sported polo shirts and golf shorts. They were both clean shaven and wore their hair cropped short, but that was where the comparisons stopped. Victor was tall and slim, and Roger was fat and bald.

"Pierce is flying in from DC," Victor said. "He recruited another."

The sandwiches were delivered. "Well, that's good news," Roger said, and he took a bite.

"He wants to talk about it tonight. He said the man sits on the highest court in the land."

CHAPTER 1

PRESENT DAY

The stadium was sold out, all 70,000 seats. On the stage, Derrick Romano's eyes were filled with laughter as he rapped the chorus,

> To the fire, in the fire,
> All aflame
> Ain't no shame.
> To the light, in the darkness,
> Where it burns
> Everything turns to ash, baby.

Derrick's hair was cut short, colored black, and combed forward, framing his almost ghost-white complexion. His eyes were black and piercing, and his lips, heart-shaped and sensual. He and his bandmates —guitar, bass, and drums—were all dressed in black jeans and tees.

The song he sang was the last number for the evening. It was a new piece, and everyone was filled with anticipation. The final song at Romano's concerts always included a surprise ending.

Five thousand groupies had crammed themselves into the pit at the foot of the stage. The lyrics of the song were on a giant screen behind the rapper, and his fans screamed every word with him. The surprise came as they sang the last line of the chorus the fourth time through, "Everything turns to ash, baby," when there was a burst of light; it was flames modulating orange, red, and blue as they consumed a man in the middle of the pit.

All the voices became a single shrill siren of horror. Those who were close to the man on fire pushed outward. But the people on the edge of the fenced pit had nowhere to go. They pushed inward.

The smell of burning flesh filled the air of the stadium. People were throwing up, fainting, and scrambling for the exits. Some were unable to move, paralyzed with fear. The drummer finished the song with a cymbal crash, Derrick pumped his fist, and the band left the stage.

359 BC – MACEDONIA

The stone-built hall was cavernous, large enough to host hundreds of guests. This night, candles and hanging oil lamps lit the hall for the dozens of commanders of the Macedonian army who gathered there. They reclined on couches throughout the hall, drinking mead from deep cups, and satisfying their hunger with the roasted and sauced beef, goat, chicken, and wild boar that was piled high on platters. A flutist filled the room with music.

Perdiccas III, the king, and his brother, Philip II, reclined side by side.

Perdiccas gestured with a shank of roasted goat. "I'm proud to lead these men in battle," he said. He tore off a mouthful of meat.

"No further attempts for a treaty?"

"We have exhausted all such measures. Over the past weeks the Illyrians have swept up a dozen villages inside our borders, leaving behind nothing but corpses." He took a swig of mead and stood. After he cleared his throat, he shouted, "Men of Macedonia!"

The flutist stopped playing and the men became silent.

"The barbarians stand on our very doorstep in the north," he said. The men roared with curses. "Tomorrow, we'll color the border with their blood!" The hall began to rumble with shouts of approval. "I stand in the company of the world's greatest warriors, men born to fight for their women and children, for their homes and farms, men who will never bow down to another man, men who were ordained before the beginning of time to be victors!" Perdiccas could hardly hear his own voice with the cheering, but he continued: "The Illyrians are not worthy of the expense to sharpen our swords! They are insects to be crushed and swept away; we will put them under our feet!"

The men stood and shouted, "Hoorah!" And they lifted their cups, and they drank.

"In my absence, I leave my brother, Philip, with my signet ring," Perdiccas said.

Philip stood and held up his right hand.

"I declare him regent until my return." Perdiccas slipped the ring from his finger and put it on the ring finger of his brother's extended hand.

Holding their cups above their heads, the men shouted their consent, and they drank again.

Perdiccas and Philip reclined on the couches again. Perdiccas sighed as he grabbed the remaining shank of goat and took another bite.

"When will you return?" Philip asked.

"When the Illyrians bend the knee."

"May Goddess Tyche go with you."

"Yes, and many strong and brave men."

PRESENT DAY

All was gray and the drizzle constant; it was a usual fall afternoon in Queens, New York. They were in Glen Cemetery, and a priest read Psalm 23 over Linda M. Lange's casket.

She had been widowed at a relatively young age, but she never remarried. For over fifty years she had lived in the same two-story brick house in Bayside, Queens. The one hundred people who stood in the rain for her interment were her neighbors, fellow parishioners, or family.

Clayton, her only child, sat under the canopy with his mom's brother, two sisters, and other relations. He had sandy blond hair, a cleft chin, and baby blue eyes.

Sprinkling a handful of dirt on the casket, the priest said, "We now commit Linda's body to the ground—earth to earth, ashes to ashes, dust to dust, in the sure and certain hope of the resurrection to eternal life through our Lord Jesus Christ."

She was such a cheerful person, Clayton thought. *A sunshiny day would've been better for her sending off.*

With the invitation to say a final goodbye, Clayton led the procession and placed a rose on the casket, after which he knelt and touched the names of his grandparents' headstone that was next to his parents'. Someday, he would be buried here, too.

The reception was at Mom's house. Her sisters had organized it. Clayton thanked God for his aunts. They were just like Mom—thrifty, industrious, and cheery—stereotypical German women, who had prepared countless plates of food and welcomed all comers with their indomitable smiles.

Making a beeline through the house with many thank yous, hugs, and handshakes, Clayton got to his mom's bedroom. He shut the door behind him. There was a queen-sized bed covered with a white down comforter. A closet was across from it, which he looked at with a sense of apprehension. He did not like the idea of rummaging around in it now. But this was for her.

He opened the closet door. *Mom, didn't you ever throw anything away?* It was packed so tight he was sure there was no need for hangers. There was a cardboard box on the top shelf in the lefthand corner. That was what he had come for. It was one of the last things she had told him about before she died.

What kind of secrets did you hide, Mom?

Shaking his head, he stood on his toes and coaxed the box off the shelf with the tips of his fingers. It fell into his hands, and he read out loud the words she had written in block letters across the top: "CLAYTON LANGE – CONFIDENTIAL."

With the box under one arm, he made his way back through the house and outside to the car. His phone rang, and he put it on his shoulder to answer as he put the box in the car. Hey, Elliot," he said. "I'm good. No problem." He chuckled. "I didn't want to come to the reception myself. Please tell Sarah thank you for coming to the gravesite. I appreciate you guys. Yeah, sure, in a couple weeks. See you then."

Elliot wanted to talk about his next novel.

He went back to the reception and stayed until his aunts shooed him out the door with the assurance they had everything under control.

After snaking through snarled traffic into the heart of Manhattan for what seemed an eternity, he finally pulled into the underground parking lot of his building in Greenwich Village.

He pushed open the door of his condo on the fourth floor; Herodotus greeted him with a lolling tongue. The French bulldog had a black coat and a white face and chest.

Clayton stooped and scratched him around the ears and rubbed his back. "How're you doing, pal? Mom's gone and life's pretty sad for me right now."

The condo had an open design with a vaulted ceiling with a sofa and armchairs that were upholstered with creamy black leather. Lamps, end tables, and a coffee table were Modernist with black metal and glass. A set of shelves against an inside wall displayed his collection of knickknacks from his travels around the world. Authentic Persian throws were scattered on the hardwood floor. There was an enclosed bookcase with his collection of original documents, papers, and books, all of which centered on his love of ancient Mediterranean history.

Paintings by local artists—mostly impressionist oils—hung on the walls.

It was nice, but for an inside glimpse at Clayton Lange's vibrant mind, one had to visit his office, crammed with books, journals, and notebooks on shelves and in stacks on the floor. There was a row of filing cabinets crushed against one wall and stacked with documents. A computer monitor, printer, legal pad, and cup filled with pens and pencils were organized on top of a long plank desk that was shoved up beside the cabinets. There was a loveseat on the opposite wall, and under the window on the outside wall was an antique oak and wrought-iron typing desk, on top of which sat a manual typewriter with the word, "Underwood," scrawled across the paper rest.

He set the box down on the loveseat. "Later for that," he said to the dog. "Let's get ourselves something to eat."

CHAPTER 2

PRESENT DAY

"Man, you know I'm with you in everything. But last night?" TJ said as he shook his head. "The dude burning up? And then the people getting crushed in the pit? It wasn't right, bro."

TJ had played bass with Derrick since a pickup gig at the club on 126th Street four years ago. He was tall, black, and gangly. Drinking an IPA, he sat with the others around a table in the Gulfstream as it flew steady at 30,000 feet.

Derrick sipped from a can of Monster Energy black cherry. He snorted. "That dude felt no pain. I saw him smile through the flames. And, besides, everyone who goes into the pit knows they're there at their own risk."

The lead guitarist's name was Rex. He scrunched up his nose. "Who can die like that and be happy about it?" He was hungover and drinking seltzer water. Though he was a redhead with fair skin, he had grown up in Camden, New Jersey, and the brothers assured him his soul was as black as theirs.

Dazzle finished a whiskey neat and tapped out a rhythm on his legs with his sticks, his eyes jumping from one band member to another until they settled on Derrick. "I saw the smile," he said. He wore his fro high and tight.

"Listen, if you boys want to go to the man's funeral, go for it," Derrick said. "That'd be dope. But something you all got to understand is that this thing you got in your heads about living forever is nonsense. We live, and we die, and when we do, we can either go out in a flame of glory, sometimes literally, or in a puff of smoke. Period. And besides, the fire marshal said the man had doused himself with gasoline. I didn't even know who he was. All I did was reach out anonymously and persuade a man to do what he would've done someday on his own anyway."

———

Amelia Irons sat at her desk, reading *The New York Times*. Floor-to-ceiling windows in the corner office on the 36th floor of the tower gave her a view of Central Park and the skyline.

She was tall and slim, and her full-length black dress made her look even taller and slimmer, an appearance she accented with a string of pearls around her neck and her gray hair in a bun. No one knew her age—she had always looked old. Rarely had anyone shown a romantic interest in her, and she liked it that way. She was married to her work, and she wore a ten-carat step cut emerald on her ring finger to show that.

Derrick Romano had caught Amelia's interest at a concert at the Rose Bowl in Pasadena, California, a couple of years before, singing a song about his love for redheads when every single redheaded woman in the stadium took off her shirt, exposing her breasts. There were nearly 3,000 redheaded women. It was remarkable. But the thing that got Amelia's attention was Derrick's remark, "All you girls just made my dream come true."

Dreams: That was one of the clues for a legendary power she had been looking for. Her phone rang. It was her secretary. "Send them in," she said.

The door swung open, and two women and two men entered. "Have a seat," she said.

She seemed to glide as she moved across the office to the captain's chair at the head of a polished conference table. The black ops team sat around table. "Let's begin by brainstorming our observations of Derrick Romano's concert last night," she said.

"No one has died at one of his concerts until now," Penelope Savage began. She wore jeans and a long-sleeved white t-shirt. Her freckles gave her the deceiving appearance of innocence.

"That's not exactly true," Raven Creed countered. "There was the man who had a heart attack during a mosh pit fight who later died at the hospital." Creed was six feet tall like Amelia, but that was the only characteristic they shared. Her skin was black velvet, and she wore wax print skirts and blouses in the bright yellows, blues, greens, and reds loved by her West African sisters. She had big, round, green eyes, and her lips were full.

"I said, '*at* one of his concerts,'" Penelope scorned. "There's a difference."

"You're pedantic."

"You're pathetic."

"Ladies," Amelia intervened.

"May I say something?" Tarek Nasr asked. He continued without waiting for permission. "Regardless of who died when, I think it goes without saying the level of violence at this concert was without precedent." He was a naturalized citizen as were his parents and siblings, who had immigrated from Jordan when he was in high school. He wore a blue-and-white striped short-sleeved button-up with chinos.

"You're right," Jake Silva said. "When Romano began, the things that happened were more like pranks, like the concert where he finished the set with 'Prey' and some five hundred eagles and hawks perched on banners and speakers on the stage."

Jake's blond mop looked like it had never seen a comb. He wore cargo pants and a t-shirt. In college he had majored in forensic science.

"Or the time he sang about his love of redheads," said Raven.

"Keep going," Amelia said.

Tarek flipped open a file folder. "Romano's actions seem to be characteristic of this power we're trying to unmask," he said. "But we still have a question: Does he possess a physical object, like an amulet, that somehow connects him to this power? The fragments of Ptolemy I's third century BCE diary suggests there was such a thing."

<hr>

Clayton sat at his desk with the box his mom had left him in front of him. Herodotus was at his feet as he cut through the tape that sealed the lid with a boxcutter. He opened it. Inside, there was an envelope with his name scrawled across it in his mother's hand. He tore it open and pulled out a card.

It began, "Dear Son, I'm so sorry I could not bring myself to give you these things before I died." He sighed and wiped a tear from an eye.

He continued reading:

They belonged to your grandfather, Karl. He was a good man, a hard worker and a devoted husband and father. But as you will see, he was involved in some activities which are better left unsaid. Your father insisted we keep these mementos. We argued about it a lot. It is unfortunate he died before we resolved anything.

Absentmindedly, Clayton drew a finger through a chain made of white gold he wore around his neck, which his mom had given to him. He read on:

I probably should've thrown all this out and spared you the trouble of dealing with it. But I couldn't do it. It didn't seem honest. Perhaps you can use it in your writing. It's up to you, dear.

Someday we will meet again, but until that time I trust you will do the right thing for yourself and your family. I love you very much.

Your mother,

He set the card down on the desk and took from the box a plaque that read, "Lange's Chemical Company—Best Medium-Sized Business of the Year. Better Business Bureau, Queens, NY." He smiled. Dad and Grandpa had run one of the fastest growing businesses in the city, and the BBB had honored them. They said Grandpa and Dad's product development was innovative, their means of production was cutting edge, and their employees gushed about how the men had created a great place to work.

"Well, that's harmless," Clayton said, and he set the plaque on the desk next to the card.

In the bottom of the box was a polished black hardwood jewelry case. "This is a nice piece," he murmured. He took it out and set it on the desk.

Opening it, he saw there was lots of gold: watches and diamond rings; bracelets, chains, and cufflinks. He had seen in photo albums that the old man loved to wear stuff like this. He lifted the tray out; there was a square envelope underneath with the word "PHOTOGRAPHS" printed across it. He set the tray down and took out the envelope and underneath that there was a medallion. He began to hyperventilate. The pendant was made of gold and silver, and in its center was a symbol painted with glossy black enamel.

"You've got to be kidding me," he gasped.

His hands shook as he put the tray back in its place. He closed the jewelry box lid and rested his elbows on his knees. Looking at Herodotus, he said, "My heart's about to beat out of my chest."

He opened the envelope with the photos. They were black-and-white snapshots, 4-inches square. The first three pictures were of his grandpa with what appeared to be his soldier buddies. They all wore German army uniforms. They had armbands with swastikas, and there were SS insignias on their collars.

Oh my God, Clayton thought.

Grandpa stood next to Adolf Hitler in the fourth photo, showing a medallion on Grandpa's right chest pocket with an eight-pointed star around its outside edge, a stylized laurel wreath inside the star which was wrapped around a black swastika: one of the highest awards for valor in Nazi Germany—exactly the medallion that lay in the bottom of the jewelry box.

Clayton's hands shook as he put the jewelry box and photos back into their cardboard hiding place.

Mom, you should've told me. I have a thousand questions, but now you're gone. He rolled his shoulders a couple times. *Maybe I should do what she did and hide this stuff for another generation to find. Or better yet, maybe I should throw it all into the Hudson River.*

CHAPTER 3

A warrior-king must be a master horseman, for conducting war and ruling a people require the use of the great beast. But riding was also a pleasure for Philip. He thanked Zeus for making him as he had and for his friend, Alekos, alongside whom he had just raced from the rolling hill country where they lived into the plains—a 20-minute gallop. They slowed the horses to a trot.

"Excellent form," Philip said.

"Thank you," Alekos said. "You as well. It won't be long before we ride with your brother and the other men of war."

"I live in anticipation of that day."

In the distance, from the north, another rider came into view. Alekos pointed.

"I see him," Philip said. As he neared, his features became clear. "It's Joacheim."

"This is not a good sign," Alekos said. "An army's lead scout never retreats from a battle short of imminent defeat."

"I know," Philip said.

Joacheim rode hard.

The two men reined their horses to a stop as the scout settled his mount before them. "Master Philip," Joacheim said, "I have tragic news."

"Tell me," Philip said.

"Perdiccas is dead."

PRESENT DAY

"It's been rough," Clayton said. He sat in Elliot Berkowitz's office in Midtown Manhattan. "I'd always thought my dad's parents had immigrated from Germany to the US in nineteen thirty-nine or 'forty because they hated Hitler. My grandma told me that when I was in middle school, I think. But lo and behold, Grandpa was a bona fide Nazi."

"Let me think about this for a second," Elliot said.

Elliot's gray hair was thin, his nose hooked very slightly, and his eyes were hazel. He had been working with Clayton since he wrote his first book.

"I'm really sorry about this, Elliot. I feel terrible. And if I go public—"

"Slow down, Clayton. Let me begin by saying we are not in conflict as far as I'm concerned because I'm a Jew and there was a Nazi in your family. You have nothing to feel sorry for. And I think most people, especially your fans, will feel the same way. But what you're talking about could become a distraction very quickly. *60 Minutes* will want to do an interview. Nazi hunters will be knocking on your door, trying to figure out how they never caught up with your grandfather. The ICC might want to poke around to find out if you inherited anything which could be linked to the Nazi lootings. And so forth."

"Are you thinking I should do as my mom did and just keep this on the QT?"

"For now."

"Okay. That's good. You've given me some perspective."

"Are you sure?"

"Yeah. I'm good," Clayton insisted.

"Want to talk about your next work?"

"It should be done in about six weeks."

"That's perfect. In the meanwhile, I've got a personal project I'm working on, and I'd like your input."

"Shoot."

"You'll remember the non-fiction piece I wrote about writing fiction?"

Clayton nodded. "*How to Be a Bestseller*?"

"That's it. I want to do a sequel. One of the chapters I'm writing will be about what makes Clayton Lange tick."

"Good luck with that, Elliot." He shook his head with a chuckle. "I'm just like everyone else."

"You write two or three bestsellers a year. There must be something you can share that will be inspirational or technically helpful."

"Maybe my one piece of advice to other writers is for them to be disciplined and to treat writing like they would any other job."

"That's good, but it doesn't get at the quality and creativity of your work. That's what I'm really itching to explore," Elliot said, sincerely.

"Honestly, I don't know how to describe that except to say I let my imagination run free, and I write. I don't have any secrets. I just write."

"'I just write.' That's cute."

"One of my advantages is that I have few outside responsibilities: I don't have another job and I'm not married. And I'm an introvert. I read somewhere that introverts are usually faster writers than extroverts."

"You're not telling me anything I haven't written about before."

"I do have a dog." He raised his eyebrows, smiled.

"I've known you all these years, and I never knew you had a dog. What kind?"

"French bulldog."

"I love him already. What's his name?"

"Herodotus."

"Cute. So am I supposed to believe he's your secret weapon?"

"He takes dictation, and he types."

"Your punctuation gives that away."

"Nice retort. But now you understand the run-on sentences."

"I would've expected more from a Frenchie. But back to topic: There is something else we haven't talked about. It concerns your genre. Have you been watching social media?"

"It's against my religion, and Herodotus refuses to monitor it."

"Your fans are calling it 'immediate futurism.'"

"That's oxymoronic."

"It means that what you write happens not long after you write it. It's as though you anticipate certain things happening as you write about them. Some believe you're actually causing things to happen. Don't tell me you haven't read about this."

Deep breath. "Okay, yes, I have. But I'm not a prophet and there's no causal relationship between what I write and what happens elsewhere. Do you know why?"

"Why?"

"Because that would require godlike powers."

"So what's your explanation?"

"It's life imitating art, or coincidence. The world is a very big place, and stuff happens."

"You're making sweeping generalizations that don't take into account the precise fulfillment of your supposed fictional stories."

Clayton frowned. "I don't see it."

"Then I'll show you." There was a wall full of books behind Elliot's desk. A whole shelf was filled with Clayton's novels. Elliot grabbed *The Cry*. He held it up for Clayton to see the cover, and he flipped it open. "For example, on page two-sixty-seven, you wrote:"

She thrust the blade into his chest, but its tip snapped off on a rib. Surprise, horror, and pain: Those were the words she would later use to describe what she saw in her husband's eyes as he awoke. And she threw her body on top of the butt of the knife nearly impaling herself as the blade pierced his heart.

"Your point?"

Elliot chuckled. "That was exactly how Jennifer Houser described her murder of her drunken, cheating husband a month after your book hit the shelves."

"Like I said, it's life imitating art."

"Okay. Here's another example." He pulled the book, *For Love,* from the shelf. He said, "page one eighty-eight," and read,

I had known the signs since I was three: the dizziness and the breathing. But I didn't care anymore, and I fell. Coco knew the signs, too. How many times had she seen me scramble for an EpiPen? The last thing I remember before I passed out was the dog holding the damn thing in her mouth and diving for my leg.

"That was the real story of Jackie Vander two months after you gave me your manuscript!"

"A pure coincidence," Clayton said.

"A Chihuahua miraculously saving the life of a woman having anaphylactic shock? The only thing you got wrong was the name of the dog."

"What was it?"

"Lucy."

"Someone must've leaked the story. The woman is probably a nutjob who just wanted attention."

"There was no leak. And the only thing about the woman that was nutty was her allergy."

"It's a matter of statistical probability. I write a lot. It's inevitable that something in my fantasy world would come true."

"You see it especially in your epilogues."

"What?"

"You explain what has happened to your principal characters—"

"I know what an epilogue is."

"I have found some of the most dramatic examples of your imme-diate futurism in those summaries."

"But what about the sixteen-year-old boy who cured leukemia, or the discovery that Elvis lived to be eighty and died in Canada?"

"For every case I can't prove, I can show you a dozen others which have come true."

"Well, my friend, I wish it were true I could write what I want into reality. But, honestly, these things in my books are all just fragments of inspiration from a conversation, an observation, or a dream."

CHAPTER 4

359 BC – MACEDONIA

Candles lined the ledges of the cave walls. There were two men whose shadows were long and deep. One of the men was a priest who wore a purple robe which enveloped him but for his face, which was defined by a long nose, thin lips, and small eyes that glistened in the candle-light. He stood next to a stone altar, on top of which was a sheep that bleated as it struggled against its restraints. And there was Philip, who stood next to the priest wearing only a simple white tunic.

"What is your petition?" the priest asked.

"I desire to be the king of Macedonia."

"But other men have already laid claim to this throne."

"They are imposters or as is the case with my nephew, too young to take the position. The lad is under the guardianship of old men. But we are at war, and I must take charge. If I do not, I am certain we will lose everything because of these fools who claim the right to rule until the boy comes of age."

"I will query Lord Hades," the priest said. He raised his hands above his head and closed his eyes. His lips moved. After a few moments, he dropped his hands to his sides, and he gazed at Philip. "My lord will give you what you desire if you pledge your eternal soul to him."

"I do so pledge, if he will show me his favor."

Unsheathing a knife from his belt with his right hand, the priest said, "You give your life for this covenant which we will seal with blood?"

"I do."

A wide-mouthed bronze cup rested on the altar next to the sheep. The priest took it in his left hand, and with a single swipe of the blade, he opened the animal's neck and filled the cup with its blood. He lifted the cup to his lips and drank a deep draught. And then he gave the cup to Philip, who also drank.

The priest said, "Lord Hades gives you a power which will guarantee your success and the success of the one who follows you."

He took the cup from Philip and returned it to the altar.

"My firstborn?"

"Indeed, and his soul will also belong to Lord Hades." He placed a leather pouch in Philip's right hand. "There is a charm in this purse. Protect it and fear it, for it is as powerful as many lives in one."

"How does it work?"

"When it touches your flesh and you express your heart's desire in music, or with words, or in images, and then when you dream that wish, the lord of the underworld will give that thing to you."

"And what of my heir?"

"For as long as you bear this amulet, he also will wield this power."

"But what if he does evil?"

"The blood he sheds will be on your head, for you are the source of his power. However, whenever you remove the amulet from your person, he will be powerless."

"And what if he chooses the priesthood and takes a vow of poverty?"

"He may abdicate the power of the amulet with such a vow."

Without another word, the priest turned and retreated into the darkness of the cave. Philip pulled the charm from the pouch, a stone delicately woven with silver wire with a loop which was attached to a leather cord, and he gazed at it in wonder.

PRESENT DAY

Clayton had not been entirely honest with Elliot. He knew about his fans who had convinced themselves he was a mutant superhero. The tourists who wandered around Lower Manhattan were the worst. They literally hunted for celebrities. A few had trapped him a couple of times. They had memorized long passages from his books, which for some reason they felt compelled to recite to him. And after the recital, they would beg him for miracles for themselves or their friends and relatives in future books.

Clayton's disguise this morning was a Yankees' cap and sunglasses. Carrying a newspaper under an arm, he pulled the door open on a '50s-style diner. He let go of Herodotus' leash, and the dog led the way to their table.

"Good morning, Mr. Lange," a waitress behind the counter said. She was forty-something and wore a white blouse and skirt with a red apron. Her dark brown hair was pulled back in a ponytail.

"Good morning, Carmen."

It was late and there was only a handful of people in the restaurant —an elderly man at the counter and a middle-aged couple at a table near the door. Clayton went to a booth against a window at the end of the restaurant. The dog jumped up onto the bench across from him. Carmen carried a steaming pot of coffee, and she asked Clayton if he would like a cup.

"That would be great. Thanks." He turned over his cup and she filled it.

"The usual?"

"Yes, please. Has your son heard from NYU yet?"

"That is so sweet you remembered. Bobby got his acceptance letter last Friday."

"Congratulations. I bet he's excited."

"Yeah, except the grant money available is based on a family's net wealth. We have no cash, but the value of our house in Brooklyn makes us look rich."

Clayton sipped his coffee.

"So we're thinking he could go to community college for a couple of years and then transfer. It won't kill him." She paused and refilled his cup. "Sorry to blab so much. Let me put your order in."

Clayton opened the newspaper. The headline was in giant letters: "High School Student Discovers Cure For Cancer." The hair on his arms stood on end, and he read on. A few minutes later Carmen returned. He pushed the paper to the side, and she set a plate with scrambled eggs and a piece of rye toast in front of him.

"Isn't that something?" she commented.

He looked up at her. His face was white.

"That a kid would somehow figure out the cure for cancer in his science class?"

"Yeah. It's a miracle."

"It truly is." She turned and left him to his meal.

It happened just as he had written in *No Other Way*. The plot was simple: A man who had been estranged from his family was diagnosed with leukemia. But his 16-year-old son still loved him. In his science class, he did a project on leukemia, first reading everything he could get his hands on about DNA, gene mutation, and bone marrow. And then he conducted a series of experiments which led him to a new chemotherapy that killed mutant cells with nearly 100 percent success. His dad was healed with the new therapy, and the family was reconciled. The end.

Clayton's hand shook as he picked up the fork for his eggs. He set it back down and stood. He set money on the table and grabbed the dog's leash.

"Hey, Carmen," he said, "I forgot an appointment, and I've got to run."

She waved, and they were on the street. Clayton slipped his shades down over his eyes, and he and the dog walked fast until they reached the condo.

Anna Kravets was in the kitchen. "Good morning, Mr. Lange," she said as she heard the door open.

Her short-sleeved gray dress fell just below her knees. It had a wide white collar, and she wore a full-length white apron. She had been with Clayton for almost ten years. She reminded him a lot of his mom

—forever blond, happy blue eyes, a great cook, and she had always been an encouragement to him.

"Good morning, Anna. Whatever you're making smells delicious," Clayton said.

"Thank you. It's chicken marsala."

He went into the office. Herodotus followed him. He knelt before the bookshelves; his journals were on the bottom. He had recorded his thoughts almost daily from the time he could complete a sentence. He scratched the dog's head and grabbed one of his first journals; he would've been about six.

He found July 17: "There's nobody to hang out with. Brian and Chad are on vacation. I wish I had a dog, and I told Mom and Dad. They argued about it for a long time. Father Francis told me to pray about it. I did that, and now we'll see if God heard me." He had made a crayon drawing underneath the entry of what appeared to be a very rough rendition of a furry orange creature, his attempt at a Golden Retriever.

He chuckled. An artist he would never be. He flipped through several pages of the journal to July 28. The entry read,

God heard my prayer! Dad bought me a dog! He looks exactly like what I saw in my dream!

Buddy was a great dog, his best friend through high school. Clayton grabbed another journal. He would've been about 15 years old. He opened it to April 22:

I wrote to the borough president of Queens and told him we need skateparks. Everyone's mad at us because we're on the sidewalks, in parks, and in parking lots. But where are we supposed to go?

I explained to him that skating is great for our health, and it keeps us out of trouble. I even sent him some pictures of parks in California that the borough could copy.

I got a letter from him today, and I'm not kidding when I say he's an SOB! He said skaters have created dangerous conditions for pedestrians and vehicular traffic, and as of May 1st we will only be permitted to skate in our driveways and on residential streets. That's ridiculous! He wrote we have to stay off sidewalks and out of parking lots, that public and private open spaces are also off limits, and "skaters are absolutely prohibited from using arterials, highways, throughways, and any other road that is not in an area that is exclusively zoned residential." Nice guy.

And to top it all off, he threatened us. He wrote, "Do not interfere with traffic or you will be fined. And be careful not to injure pedestrians or you may be incarcerated." Oh gosh, thanks for the heads-up, otherwise I might've gone out and maimed someone today. A-hole! He didn't even say anything about the pictures I sent to him. He's a double A-hole!

He flipped forward to August 12. He had written, "Our first skatepark just opened! I've been dreaming about this park, literally. It has stairs, rails, and ledges just as I imagined, and it's less than a half-mile from my house! Yay!"

He could do this all day. There were dozens of accounts of good fortune or good luck or whatever you wanted to call it that ran through his journals from the beginning until the present: from the Christmas gifts he received, to the jobs he had had as a young man; from his success on the high school football team, to his adventures traveling Europe. His imagination had created all of this. The logical side of his brain had refused to acknowledge that this was possible, but there it was. He put the journals back on the shelf and sat at the desk.

"Herodotus, let's write." The dog was looking at him intently, his tongue hanging out of his pug face. "This feels like an Underwood story, doesn't it?" he said as he rolled his chair over to the ancient type-writer under the window. He pulled a sheet of paper from a stack on the desk, inserted it into the carriage, rolled it in, centered for the title, and typed, "The Italian Miracle."

He typed for several hours. It was not an award winner, but it was a solid short story with a beginning, middle, and a tear-jerking conclusion. He finished with "The End" and rolled the last page out of the machine.

"Are you ready for dinner, Mr. Lange?" Anna asked from the doorway.

"I'm famished," Clayton said, and he and the dog followed her into the dining room.

CHAPTER 5

PRESENT DAY

Victor Penlick thought himself a self-made man. He had often quipped, "I wasn't raised with a silver spoon. But I was raised *up* with a leather belt, daily." That drew chuckles from men who shared similar memories.

Victor had three older brothers, and Daddy's punishments were pretty much evenly divided among them and Mother. So it was all manageable. But when his brothers started moving out, Victor knew it was just a matter of time before someone got badly hurt.

It was Victor's brother, Luke: He lay unconscious on the kitchen floor. After twenty-plus years of silence, Mother finally spoke up. Standing over her son, she cried, "Lee! Stop! Or you'll kill him!"

That stopped the beating, but Mother got a black eye for her trouble. That was when Victor knew it was up to him to take his family's survival into his own hands.

Daddy was a hunter, and Victor had easily taken to the sport. The tracking, the shooting, the dressing, everything—he enjoyed it all. Spring was when they traditionally hog-hunted in East Texas. Victor had just turned 16 years old, and it was his turn to hunt with Daddy alone. It was something of an initiation into manhood Daddy had done for each one of his sons. He was in a good mood, and he told Victor so as they loaded the truck with gear.

It was in the morning on the second day of the expedition when Victor and his dad sighted a 300-pound hog wading in a river about 50 yards from the wooded patch where they knelt. Daddy was about 20 feet away from Victor when he nodded at him to take his shot.

Peering through his rifle's scope, Victor saw the detail in Daddy's face. An eyebrow raised. Mouth open. His lips formed the word, "No." Fear—Victor had never seen that expression on Daddy's face before. It gave him goosebumps. The exchange lasted about two seconds before the .308 entered Daddy's skull and his head exploded like a can of tomatoes.

The D.A. wrote off the death as a hunting accident. Victor's punishment was a browbeating by the judge and an assignment to take a gun safety course.

Lee's funeral was a closed casket graveside service, a sad affair with only the cemetery chaplain, Mother, and Victor. When the preacher was done, Victor held his mother's hand as they watched a backhoe dump dirt into the grave. He thought he heard her breathe a sigh of relief. Neither of them ever said a word to the other about the shooting, but Victor was certain she knew that what had happened was not accidental. Himself, he wanted to dance on the bastard's grave. He had saved the family from further torment, and, unexpectedly, he had received the gift of self-understanding. It was as he watched Daddy die, he realized the one thing that would forever inspire him was power, mortal power, the power to decide who lives and who does not.

Victor went on to study law, finishing at the top of his class. Despite an offer to fast-track at a leading firm with the promise of partnership, he chose to go out on his own. The power he had tasted earlier had become an ache, a craving in his belly that he knew he could not satisfy working for someone else.

In his undergraduate course work, he had taken an interest in Western Civilization, especially the stories of the emperors, from Alexander the Great to the Habsburgs. It was in those stories where his goals crystalized and gave shape to what had only been a feeling before. His hunger for power became a lust for absolute power, for an autocracy to reshape the political and economic landscape of the world.

As an independent lawyer with laser-like focus, he used his wit and charm to get introductions to people who lived in that place where he wanted to live. The prophets and poets said that place was close to the sun, and it was dangerous. But he knew what he wanted was worth any risk and, in the end, only fools got burned.

As he pursued his dream, he discovered that the people he wanted to be close to came from a variety of backgrounds and followed all kinds of career paths: They were politicians, CEOs, military officers, financial tycoons, real estate investors, and entrepreneurs. But they all had one thing in common: An unquenchable thirst for power, just like him.

In less than ten years of shaking hands and rubbing elbows at dinner parties, in courtrooms, and on the golf course, Victor created what he called a gentlemen's club. Anyone else would've called it a cabal: Together, the seven men guessed they might control what would amount to the twelfth largest GDP in the world. And they shared a single vision for world domination.

During one of their dinners, one of their members laughingly remarked, "I don't know if you guys are listening to yourselves, but our conversation has digressed to a game I'm calling, Drop That Name." They all laughed self-consciously. He continued, "Kidding aside, I have just realized there's probably no more than two degrees of separation between our little group and any seat of power in the world."

Besides Victor Penlick, the group's membership was Roger Skarlyle, the oil magnate; Pierce Cockler, the US senator from Texas; and the supreme court justice, whom the senator recruited, Jay J. Orden. He was a tall, wiry man. He had had his share of run-ins with Congress over supposed ethics violations. But they all had to do with money. And no one likes the green stuff more than the people who launch investigations, which had all disappeared.

There was US Army general, Bud Hammerman. Everyone called

him by his surname with a subtle twist: "Hammer Man." He liked the title, supposing it came from his reputation for the work he had done in Iraq and Afghanistan. His square jaw and barrel chest completed the picture.

The youngest member of the group was Adam Stone, a venture capitalist. He was average in appearance. Easy to forget. But that was the only average thing about him. He was a master investor in all forms of trading and currency exchange, and he had used that skill to make himself one of the five richest men in the world before he was 30 years old.

Benjamin Greenbaugh retired when he was 50, leaving an auto company he had saved from bankruptcy and built up, multiplying its profitability many times over. He was bored only a week into his withdrawal from the daily grind. He bought a struggling machine shop that manufactured aftermarket car parts, and today, 20 years later, that shop was now only a footnote in the history of the world's largest manufacturing conglomerate. With plants in a dozen countries, Greenbaugh's company manufactured a host of things including microchips, cosmetics, and textiles.

The personalities of the seven men ranged from sanguine to melancholy. There was one who was a devout Catholic and another who was a self-declared atheist. But they all shared Victor's passion to acquire that one thing they believed had empowered past empires, that object which would catapult them from the shadows into the light, that thing which Amelia Irons and her black ops team now searched for.

"She said she's FBI," Dazzle said, holding the telephone receiver. His body lay across an armchair with his legs draped over the side.

"So what?" Derrick asked.

He was on a couch, and the others were slung across other pieces of furniture in the presidential suite at the Four Seasons in Miami. A bottle of whiskey was going around, passed from hand to hand.

"Said she wants to ask a few questions."

"Does she sound sexy?"

"She sounds old. There's another agent with her. A guy."

"Tell her it's her lucky day."

After inviting the agents to the suite, Dazzle hung up the phone.

"Let's get some girls up here after this little meeting," Derrick said. He pointed out the window with the bottle of whiskey at a rooftop pool. "For some fun in the sun."

"I'm down with that," TJ said.

There was a knock on the door. Rex answered it, and Amelia and Tarek came in, flashing fake FBI ID. Amelia wore her usual black dress —sans pearls, and Tarek wore a black suit and tie with a white shirt.

"I'm Special Agent Amelia Williams. And this is my partner, Special Agent Tarek Ali."

Derrick still lay on the couch. "Whassup?"

"May we sit?" Amelia asked.

"Feel free," Derrick said as he swung his feet around to the floor. "Want a drink?" He took a swig from the bottle and held it out to her and Tarek.

"No thanks," Amelia said, and Tarek shook his head no. They sat on a loveseat across from Derrick. "We want to ask you a few questions about the strange occurrences that have been taking place during your concerts."

He handed the bottle to Dazzle. "That's what I figured," he said. "Go for it."

"What's your explanation?"

"I don't have one. They just happen. A bunch of girls get naked, birds appear, a man bursts into flames, and I get laid. Weird stuff just happens." He grinned and looked around at the other guys.

"Were those things intentional?"

"What's this worth to you?"

"You've got it backward, Mr. Romano. We could take you in for questioning, have a press conference, maybe hold you for a night. So my question is, what is this worth to you?"

"Okay, fair enough. This is my story: I write songs, and then I dream them. They're usually set in performances, often as the last piece. And they just happen."

"Besides performances, at what other times have your dreams come true?"

"At home with personal stuff."

"Give me an example."

"A few weeks ago a neighbor's terrier barked all night, and I made up a dumb song."

"It was hilarious," TJ said,

"Yeah, it was," Derrick said. "It went like this:

> Little skittle bitch dog
> Screams all night.
> But that's all right
> Coyote's holding tight
> With a nibble, then a bite
> A chomp and a chew
> And it's over for you,
> Little skittle bitch dog."

"Funny as hell." Dazzle laughed.

"And?" Amelia asked.

"The only thing that was left of it the next morning was its tail," Derrick said.

"Do you have any artifacts which you wear frequently?"

"Artifacts?" he tittered. "Like my cock ring?" The other guys sniggered. "No, I don't wear no fucking artifacts. Are we done? I'm kind of busy." The bottle came back around to him, and he took another swig.

"Tell me about your childhood," she said.

"What's to tell? Everyone who's interviewed me has written about it."

"I'd like to hear it from you personally," Amelia said.

He rolled his eyes. "Okay. One more time: Poor white kid raised by crackhead mother in the Detroit projects gets a break singing rap. He drops out of school and makes a fortune. End of story."

"What happened to your dad?"

"That piece of shit? He was a lawyer with an alcohol problem who left my mom for some slut when I was six."

"And he's dead."

"I heard he had an encounter with a bus, and he lost."

"Tragic."

"For him."

"And you and your mom."

"Don't talk about my mom. It's not her fault. He screwed her up."

"Has she ever had experiences like you've had with the paranormal?"

"If she had, do you think she'd be where she is today?"

"How about your father?"

"How the hell would I know?"

"Did you inherit anything from him?"

"This is getting old. I don't know anything about that dick, and no he didn't leave us shit."

"One last question."

"Good."

"Are you familiar with the legends of other people who've had special powers like yours?"

"Besides Jesus and David Blaine?"

She stared at him.

"No. Are we done?"

"Yes, we are, Mr. Romano," Amelia said. She and Tarek stood. "Thank you for your time." They turned to leave.

"Hey, Tarek," Derrick said.

He turned back.

"If you like girls and drink, quit that dumb job and make some real money as one of my bodyguards. We could use a Muslim brother on staff. Join us this afternoon."

"I'll pass, but thanks."

In the elevator Tarek asked, "Do you think he told the truth about his father?"

"The story's consistent with what he's said previously and what his mother reported initially after the accident. But that was fifteen years ago. Maybe it's time to pay Serenity Romano a visit."

352 BC - MACEDONIA

"I dreamed it last night," Philip said.

He and Alekos admired a terracotta vase he held in his hands—it was big enough to hold two liters of wine. The artist had painted the mythological war between Zeus of the Olympians and Cronus of the Titans in gold and red against a black background. The scene was familiar to all God-fearing people as it had been replicated innumerable times by artists on pottery and in murals. But this piece was strikingly different from the others: Zeus' likeness had been replaced with that of Philip's, and Cronus' resembled Onomarchus, the commander of the Phocians.

"We will crush them in Crocus Field," Philip said.

He set the vase down on a table and they went out double doors to the balcony, where they looked over the property below. Hardly a stone's throw away was a corral of horses and a great shade tree under which children played.

"Will you ever reveal to me how this works, where your power comes from, and why?" Alekos asked.

"I cannot say, even to my dearest friend. But I will tell you this: For as long as my kingdom stands, you will stand."

"I am grateful for that, and I shall not nag you again with questions. Whatever this power's origin, you have used it to serve Macedonia faithfully. With every victory we are one step closer to ruling the whole land."

The leafy branches of the tree below created a luxurious canopy of shade under which a class of young boys played soldier with wooden swords. Philip's son, Alexander, was among them. "Do they not look like miniature versions of us in their tunics?" Philip asked.

"Indeed, they do." Alekos chuckled.

"I have married many women, but only Olympias gave me a son."

"A philosopher once said, 'A single son who is wise, strong, and loyal is worth more than a hundred foolish ones.' Alexander's mentor tells me that even at the tender age of four years, the boy has shown a remarkable keenness for learning, is very persuasive in his speech, and has a high level of skill—his grip is sure and his swing, precise."

"I suppose, then, I should start praying for his wisdom and loyalty," Philip said.

CHAPTER 6

PRESENT DAY

"Mr. Lange?" Anna asked, as she gently shook his shoulder.

Sitting on the condo's balcony in the late afternoon sun, Clayton opened his eyes. "I was having the weirdest dream," he said.

"I'm leaving now. Your dinner's on the table."

"Great. Thanks."

"Don't let it get cold. And don't forget, you still need to take Herodotus for a walk."

"You're a dog's best friend. Have a great weekend."

"Thanks. I'll try."

He found the dog at his bowl in the kitchen. "She loves you, doesn't she?"

Herodotus glanced at him and went back to eating.

Clayton poured himself a glass of white wine and sat down. He took a bite. It was one of Anna's specialties: chicken thigh marinade with a side of asparagus. He felt a little out of it, like he was still in the dream. It was about his short story, "The Italian Miracle." It was so real, he felt like he was still there. So weird. He took a drink of wine.

When he was finished, he went to the door for his leather bomber's jacket and whistled. Herodotus appeared, his tongue hanging out in anticipation.

"Let's go pick up some music," Clayton said.

It was getting dark and in the upper 40s outside. But it was a short walk, and the Yankees cap and jacket would suffice.

Carlyle's was a jazz club he frequented. He took a table in the back not far from the small stage where a band played.

A waiter greeted him, "Hi, Mr. Lange. How're you tonight?"

"I'm good. How about yourself?"

"I'm good. What do you think of this band? They're new."

"They have a nice groove. Who are they?"

"Elowen and the Hurricanes."

"Are they living up to their name?"

"Blowing everyone away."

"Good one."

"They told me to say that."

"Hilarious."

"What're you drinking?"

"A stout."

The waiter left for the beer, and Clayton watched the band play. Elowen was singing "Cheek to Cheek." Her hair was ink black and it hung below her shoulders. She reminded him a little of Joan Jett. She wore a short, black strapless cocktail dress.

"Do you like her?" he asked the dog who lay at his feet. "Yeah, me, too."

She was accompanied by two female vocalists, a guitar, string bass, piano, and drums.

The waiter returned with the beer. Clayton nodded toward the band. "What're they drinking?"

"The singers are drinking wine. And the others are drinking beer."

"When they break, set 'em up on me."

"You bet."

After another song, Elowen said, "We'll be back in twenty minutes. Don't go anywhere!" She and the others stepped down to tables below the stage. She sat with the other vocalists. The waiter came with the wine and beer, and after he spoke to them, Elowen waved Clayton over.

"We have an invitation, Herodotus," Clayton said. "What do you think?" The dog stood and looked at him with his head cocked to the side. "Who's dreaming now?" Clayton chuckled.

He grabbed his beer, and they went to Elowen's table. The two background singers introduced themselves as Abby, a blonde, and Jocelyn, an African-American. Their dresses were the same style as Elowen's, but red.

"Thanks for the wine," Elowen said, and she held up her glass as did the others.

"It's the least I could do. Your voice reminds me of Ella's, but it's still your own."

"I think that's the highest compliment I've ever gotten. Would you like to join us?"

"Sure," he said, and he went around both tables and shook every-one's hand.

He sat down with the vocalists, and Elowen said, "This is not a random invitation to a fan. You're the novelist, Clayton Lange, right?"

"Yep."

"We're all big fans of yours. But I will confess that we buy one book and pass it around. Sorry."

He smiled. "I think that's the highest compliment *I've* ever gotten."

They chatted through the break until the band returned to the stage. After playing jazz covers, the musicians returned to the tables.

"Is this the first time you've played this venue?" Clayton asked.

"Yeah," Elowen said. "But we're going to be here on the second and fourth Fridays for a few months."

"Congratulations."

"Thanks. Incidentally, Jocelyn is an aspiring writer."

Jocelyn looked at Elowen, mortified.

"No kidding?" Clayton said.

"But she's shy," Elowen added, "and she wouldn't have dared say anything to you."

"That's okay. What're you writing, Jocelyn?"

"It's a romance novel set in Chicago's 'sixty's music culture. My parents are musicians, and it's based on stories I've heard them tell over the years."

"I love it already," he said. They talked for a few moments, and he gave her some tips for honing her work. "And when you're done, send it to me. I'll give it a read."

"That would be wonderful, Mr. Lange. Thank you."

"It's nothing," he said. "If you write the way you sing, you've got a great future ahead of you."

"You haven't introduced us to your girl magnet yet," Elowen said as she bent down to pet Herodotus.

"This guy? His name is Herodotus."

"There must be a story behind that."

"I love Greek history. His namesake was an ancient Greek historian."

She rubbed under his chin. "Can I have him?"

"Well, we are a package."

As the morning sun crawled up the bed, it revealed a human body wrapped up in rust-colored linen bedsheets. Clayton peeked out from under a pillow. "Hey," he said.

Elowen was struggling to button her dress. "Hey," she said.

"Work?"

"Yeah. I'm going to be late."

"This is kind of early for band practice, isn't it?"

"I have a day job, too. It's temp work at a bank."

"Sorry."

"It's not your fault."

"Herodotus, did you hear that?" The dog barked. "I have a witness."

"I've got to go."

"Call me."

"You call me."

"I had fun."

At the door she turned and smiled. "I had fun, too."

The front door clicked shut, and he pulled the pillow back over his head.

"Good morning," Clayton said. He stood at the edge of the kitchen in a thick blue terrycloth bathrobe.

Anna looked at the clock on the wall over the doorway. It was nearly 1:00 p.m. "Morning?"

"Someplace in the world it's morning." He grinned and went to the counter.

Anna poured him a cup of coffee. "A lady friend last night?"

"We're not really friends yet." He took the coffee.

"Mr. Lange, that's terrible!"

"But I do like her."

"What's her name?"

"*Ummm*, let me think about that for a second. It's a hard one."

Anna *tsked, tsked*.

"Elowen of Elowen and the Hurricanes."

"I'm sorry?"

"She's the leader of a jazz band I met last night."

"You'd be happier, Mr. Lange, if you got married."

"You left your husband."

"He cheated on me."

"Maybe I'd be a cheater, too."

"You wouldn't be a cheater, Mr. Lange. I can tell. Haven't you ever met someone you thought you might like to share your life with?"

"Back in college. But that was a long time ago. The coffee's perfect. Thanks."

"You're welcome."

"Don't worry about lunch. I'm going to take the dog for a walk in a minute, and I think I'm going to stop by the diner and have a bite to eat."

"No problem, Mr. Lange."

A half an hour later, Clayton and Herodotus emerged from the condominium. There was a breeze coming off the river, and he wore a heavy coat, a beanie, and sunglasses. He was well camouflaged from head to toe, but some art students recognized the dog—he had become a social media sensation—and Clayton spent several minutes talking with them. At the restaurant, he took his regular booth by the window.

"Hi, Mr. Lange." It was Amanda. She and Carmen usually worked the breakfast-lunch shift together. She was blond and in her forties.

"How're you?"

"I'm well. You know the manager doesn't really care, but if a customer says something about the dog, I'm going to have to ask you to tie him up outside."

"Herodotus? Outside? He's my service dog."

She folded her arms and shook her head.

"My typist."

"Come on, Mr. Lange. I'm serious."

"I was just talking to my agent about his run-on sentences."

"Why do I try?" she asked herself. "What would you like, Mr. Smarty Pants?"

He grinned. "The club sandwich and a bowl of soup."

"How about the medley of vegetables for your side dish?"

"Chips would be better, and I'll have a Diet Coke, too."

"You got it."

"Is Carmen working?"

"She left right after breakfast."

"Sick?"

"Nope. NYU called her about her son. They told her if they wanted a scholarship for him, they had to sign up for it before the end of the day."

He stared at her.

"It's for Sicilian Italians from Brooklyn who're majoring in engineering."

"That's amazing."

"It's a miracle, a scholarship designed just for him. Let me get that sandwich and soup going for you."

CHAPTER 7

The amphitheater was filled with people; it was standing room only. A parody of a royal wedding was playing, and the crowd thundered with applause between acts. The king's daughter had married just the day before.

"The people are so happy, Father," Alexander said as they approached the theater on foot with his new brother-in-law, also Alexander.

"They love a wedding, but they love to have a laugh even more," Philip said.

"It is all for fun," said the second Alexander.

They passed through the gate into the amphitheater. Philip gestured at box seats across from the stage where his wife, Olympias sat. "There is your mother."

"Indeed," Alexander said.

The people stood and cheered as the king and his two sons entered the stadium. Philip raised his arms to the people in gratitude. Olympias remained seated. Her black hair and piercing green eyes had always reminded Philip of Alexander.

"You should speak with her, son," Philip said, continuing his smile for the crowd. "I know she is jealous of my other wives, but you and I are at peace since I have confirmed publicly that you are my rightful heir. She should be pleased with this."

"I will talk to her, Father."

"Pausanias is joining us," the son-in-law said.

The elder warrior and bodyguard of the king approached them quickly as though he had an urgent message.

"What is it, my dear friend?" Philip asked.

Pausanias came in close, and he kissed and embraced the king. But when he pulled back, the handle of a knife protruded from Philip's chest. Pausanias raced to the exit, and Philip's white tunic exploded with blood. His eyes were filled with disbelief as he crumpled to the ground.

Alexander bent down over his father, kissed his forehead, and snatched from his neck the thing on a leather strap the priest had given him many years earlier. He looked up to where his mother had been seated and saw her just as she left the theater. There was a great rumbling all around—it was the beginning of a riot.

"Come," said the brother-in-law, "we must leave immediately."

One week following Philip's assassination, Alexander stood with the royal family's artist in the great room of the palace.

"Vases were your father's preference," the artist said, pointing at the shelves lined with them. "All his victories—in Crocus Field and in Chaerones, over the Scythians, and the Greeks—he anticipated on terracotta vases."

"As I have trained, I have immersed myself in poetry," Alexander said. "But now I would like to do something different, something grand, something the people can enjoy and celebrate with their king."

"Perhaps mosaics?"

"Mosaics would be perfect. But can you do it? You know how I devise my plans with haste."

"Yes, my king, for your purposes I will paint on wood in detail a mosaic exactly as it will appear when it is later finished with cut stone and glass. It will be an exact prototype of the final work."

"Very good. Here, then, is what I envision for our first battle against the Persians: We will meet them on the edge of Asia, facing off across a river. I will lead my men across the water by horseback...."

PRESENT DAY

"Stunned" was the first word that came to mind for Clayton to describe it. Or maybe a better word was "shocked," or "surprised," or "startled." *The alliteration is getting in the way of my thinking,* he reflected.

He had just woken up after a long, restless night. The revelation of the power he possessed had turned his sense of equilibrium upside down. His ability to make things in his imagination come true had been present for as long as he could remember, but he had subconsciously held his acceptance of it at bay. But now there was no denying it.

As he watched the morning light fill the walls from the bed, his thoughts raced: *It was one thing to fantasize or idealize or conceptualize... Stop it!* he thought. *This is scary as hell. Am I like a superhero?* He mused over the thought for a moment. *I have to test this power one more time.*

If anyone deserved a miracle it was his housekeeper, Anna. Born in the Ukraine, she had come to the States as a child with parents who had only their prayers and the clothes they wore. Anna had married and had children young and committed herself to work hard for her family's future. But just as she and Charlie were beginning to enjoy a little financial security, he had cheated on her. After all the hardships and challenges she had weathered over the years, this guy trashed their marriage for a fling with a girl twenty years younger than himself.

Clayton sat at the island in the kitchen as Anna chopped veggies for a salad. He took a sip of coffee. "Has Charlie come crawling back yet?" he asked.

She shook her head and sighed. "Not yet. But it's just a matter of time. That girl is hardly an adult, and I can't help but think she'll tire of him soon."

"How're you doing?"

"I don't like the separation. I'm lonely."

"Will you take him back when he comes?"

"I don't know, Mr. Lange. He hurt me when he left. The things he said were really cruel."

Amelia and two from her team had picked up an SUV at the Detroit Metro Airport, and Jake parked it in front of one of many brick duplexes in the East Detroit housing project. The mortar crumbled, bars covered the windows, the paint on the wooden porches peeled, and trash filled the gutters. The postage stamp yards were dirt and weeds. This part of Detroit had been one of the poorest and most dangerous neighborhoods in the nation for years.

Tarek got out of the SUV and opened Amelia's door for her. He gave her his hand, and she stepped down into the street. "Do you want me to come with you?"

"She's not dangerous. You'll be more valuable to me out here, keeping an eye on things."

Once on the porch, Amelia pressed the doorbell. It was dead. She banged on the metal screen. As it rattled, a dog barked inside. She banged again. "I'm a friend of your son's!" she shouted.

The door opened a couple inches against a chain. Cigarette smoke billowed out. "Did he die?" a woman asked through the crack.

"No," Amelia said. "He's very much alive."

She snorted. "You look like a mortician. What do you want?"

"Are you Serenity Romano?"

"Who wants to know?"

"I'm Amelia Williams, a private investigator."

"Are you law enforcement or the press? You have to tell me."

"No, I'm not law enforcement or the press."

"What's in it for me?"

"I can tell you about your son."

"I can read about him in every gossip magazine."

"And I can pay you for your time."

"How much?"

"Hundred dollars an hour."

"Two hundred."

"Deal."

The door clicked shut, and there was the sound of the chain sliding across its track. The woman pulled the door open and pushed open the screen. Looking at her face-to-face, Amelia recognized where Derrick Romano had gotten his high cheekbones, dark eyes, and sensuous lips. Serenity was not pretty anymore, but she had been at another time in her life.

A strong odor permeated the house, like ammonia—it was dog pee—and it was mixed with secondhand smoke. Serenity threw herself into a recliner and gestured around the room for Amelia to find a seat.

"Wherever you like," she said.

Ash from her cigarette fell into the carpet. There were empty beer cans and candles that had burned down to nothing on the coffee table. The dog barked and pawed the door of a room where he had been confined.

Amelia grabbed a straight-back chair from a table in the kitchen and set it across from Serenity.

"Okay, now that we're all comfy, what do you want to talk about?" Serenity asked, and she took a long draw on her cigarette.

Sitting at the Underwood, Clayton typed, "A Story of True Love." Herodotus lay at his feet. "Dog, this second test will either confirm or disprove everything we've been thinking about this thing."

But despite multiple attempts over many hours, everything Clayton had typed had ended up in a wastebasket. It was getting late. He had let Anna go home early because he was planning on taking Elowen out for dinner. "Damn it, Herodotus. Why can't I get this one out?"

The dog stood and whined.

"What are you saying, pal?" He scratched behind his ears. "You want to go for a walk, don't you?"

He folded his arms and stared out the window for a long moment. "Let's try a poem," he said, and he rolled another sheet of paper into the typewriter. After the title, he typed,

> Shattered
> A vow broken
> A heart pierced
> The circle goes round
>
> Shattered
> The man—the woman
> A hope—a dream
> The circle goes round
>
> Shattered
> Lives changed
> As the wheels turn
> The circle goes round
>
> Shattered
> The body
> The spirit
> The circle goes round
>
> Shattered
> Humility for hope
> Pride for love
> And the circle goes round

He looked at the dog. "What? It's only a start. I'll finish it later. Let's get out of here."

On the street, they went underground to the subway. They would make one connection to Brooklyn. In a little less than an hour they would be at the restaurant Elowen had chosen.

CHAPTER 8

334 BC – ANATOLIA

It was just as the artist had rendered in his painting and as Alexander had dreamed: The Persians were there, armed for battle on the other side of the Granicus River. But their formation was not right—their cavalry was in front of their infantry instead of its flanks.

Alexander's men faced the Persians. His infantry was in phalanx formation in the center, with cavalry on the right and on the left. He rode with those on the righthand side. Lifting his lance, he shouted, "Zeus shall prevail!" And the infantry plunged into the river shouting the same.

Javelins and arrows rained down on them, but to no effect as the men deflected them with their shields. Their war cry carried over the banks of the river into the ears of their enemy: "Zeus shall prevail!"

Alexander led the horsemen across the water. A giant white plume on top of his helmet whipped in the wind as he charged. He could not help but grin for his taunt of his enemy.

Alexander recognized Mithridates, King Darius' son-in-law, and he set upon him, plunging his lance into his face, killing him instantly. When the nobleman-warrior Rhosaces saw it, he attacked Alexander only to succeed in slicing off a part of the plume and cracking his helmet. Alexander sneered at the man as he drove his broadsword into his gut.

In less than an hour the battle was done: The Persian loss was over 5,000 men. Alexander's loss was 120.

The sun settled on the horizon as the Macedonian troops burned the dead. Alexander watched with his generals not far from the river.

His close friend and the head of his personal cavalry, broad-shouldered Hephaestion, sat at his side. "Darius himself did not come," he remarked.

"Nor did I expect him to," Alexander said. "He knew me only as the son of Philip. However, he knows me now as the king who killed his son-in-law and routed his army. He will come next time."

PRESENT DAY

Elowen sat in the bedroom bay window as she watched the early sun begin to illumine the edifices of downtown Manhattan. Clayton was sound asleep. She had always been a morning person. Welcoming the day with the sunrise was a source of joy for her.

She gazed across the room at Clayton's face. He had a high forehead, a distinguished nose, and cleft chin. Noble features. And he had nice lips—very nice lips. He was a great author, and, as it turned out, an excellent lover. And he was a good man. She had thought she might go bi; it was a very real possibility after her experience with a girl in college. But she did prefer the other species. However, her experiences until now had begun to persuade her that the probability of finding a man who was not only physically attractive but intellectually interesting and not a narcissist seemed impossibly small. But here he was, Clayton Lange—never married, deliciously handsome, only two years older than she, and rich. But most importantly, he was a nice guy.

He opened one eye. "Hey, gorgeous."

"You need glasses."

He opened the other eye. "Oh my gosh, you might be right."

"I was just having pleasant thoughts about you."

"What time is it?" he asked.

"Six-thirty."

"I'm not familiar with that time. Is that like thirty minutes before seven?"

"You are adorable."

"Have you been awake for a while?"

"About half an hour."

"Are you hungry?"

"For what?" she said.

"Exactly what I was thinking." He stretched an arm out and she jumped back in bed.

It was thirty minutes later when she said she was still hungry.

"We have three choices," he said. "We could hit the diner, or wait for Anna, who will be here in an hour and a half, or we could have Cheerios."

"I haven't had Cheerios since I left home for college, but let's go to the diner. That sounds like more fun."

After she had taken a shower, Clayton got in, and she put on his terrycloth bathrobe and snooped around the apartment. The living room furnishings were somewhat stark but for mementos from his travels. And there was an old bookcase filled with what looked like histories. There were lots of original pieces of art hanging on the walls. But the peaceful sensation the space gave her was much different from what she experienced when she stepped into his crowded office. It was as though there was a storm of ideas waiting to break loose from the piles of paper and file folders and shelves filled with journals and books. There was an ancient typewriter under the window, with a piece of paper in it. She looked at it and read out loud,

> Shattered
> A vow broken
> A heart pierced
> The circle goes round....

A little before eight when they left the condo with Herodotus in tow, it was 50 degrees, and Elowen wore an oversized wool sweater with boyfriend jeans and UGGs. Clayton wore jeans, a turtleneck, his

Yankees' cap, shades, and a bomber's jacket. It was Saturday and the streets were already busy with tourists on the prowl.

"I read your poem," she said.

"Tell me you didn't."

"I love it."

"It's not done."

"It's beautiful."

Clayton let go of the dog's leash at the diner, and Herodotus went to their table and jumped up on a bench.

"I see you two are regulars," Elowen said.

"I don't know what he's going to do if there's ever someone else sitting at that table."

They sat down across from the dog.

Melody came with a pot of coffee and filled their cups. "What can I bring you?" she asked.

"I'll have my usual, scrambled eggs and rye toast," Clayton said.

"I'll have the same with a fruit cup," Elowen said.

While Melody was still at the table, a couple in their early sixties came up. They wore matching burnt orange fleece-lined jackets. "We're the Hansons," the woman said. "Are you Mr. Clayton Lange, the author?"

"I am," Clayton said, and he stood. "It's good to meet you." He held out his hand, and they shook.

"We're great fans," the woman said, "and we were wondering if we could take a selfie with you?"

Clayton invited them to squeeze onto the bench with him and Elowen. Melody took the photo. The couple thanked Clayton as they scooted out.

"May I ask you a question, Mr. Lange?" the man asked.

"Sure."

"Do you know if the things that happen in your books are going to happen in real life before they do, or are they as much a surprise to you as they are to everyone else?"

"It's always a surprise to me, Mr. Hanson."

They thanked him again, and he thanked them for reading his books.

"That was nice of you," Elowen said.

"It's nothing really. I try to avoid being mobbed by fans on the street because it's overwhelming. But I am doing well because of people like the Hansons. They seemed like nice people."

"The girls and I have talked a lot about Mr. Hanson's question."

"About things coming true?"

"Yeah. I've heard it called immediate futurism. Have you heard that, too?"

Melody came with their breakfasts. As they dug in, Clayton asked Elowen if she would like to go for a walk to the park when they finished.

"That'd be nice," she said.

They ate in silence for a few moments until Elowen asked, "Well, are you going to answer my question?"

"Huh?"

"Clayton?" she said, lowering her voice.

"Oh, about immediate futurism?"

She nodded as she took a bite from the fruit cup.

He put his fork down, and she stopped eating. "I kind of lied to the Hansons. But honestly, I hadn't given it a second thought until Elliot—he's my agent—pointed it out. I don't read reviews of my work. I just put words on paper and go about my life. I've always had good luck, which I attributed more to my parentage, white privilege, and being a pretty good scribbler. But after that meeting with Elliot, I looked at some of my old journals. You wouldn't believe how many of the wishes I made ever since I was a little boy came true after I wrote them down."

"Really?"

"Pets, presents, work, a skate park—all kinds of things."

"I don't know what to say."

He sighed. "It's messing with my mind."

"What are you going to do?"

"I did an experiment with a story, and it came true." He told her about the scholarship for Carmen's son, and her jaw dropped. "I'm giving it one more test before I take it seriously, though."

"And if the test is affirmative?"

"Then I want to figure out, why me?"

They finished breakfast and paid the bill. Central Park was about two miles away and they began their trek north. A lowrider pulled up to an intersection where they waited. Its subwoofers pounded out a rap song.

"That's a nineteen-ninety Chevrolet Caprice," Clayton yelled over the music.

"You know your cars," Elowen shouted.

Before the light changed, they listened to the lyrics:

> He got no creed
> And I let him bleed
> Let 'em bleed
> Cuz I gotta feed

With the green light, the car's roar drowned out the song.

"That's that death rapper, Derrick Romano," Elowen said.

"I've never heard of him, though the last name sounds familiar for some reason."

"Cheese?"

"Sorry?"

"Romano cheese?"

"Oh, yeah."

"There're some pretty crazy things that happen at his concerts, which you may've read about," she said. "A couple weeks ago a man burst into flames."

"Yeah, I read about that."

"It's a huge scandal."

"You know your musicians."

"I don't know a lot about him. As a musician I just try to keep up on who's who. About your poem?"

He responded tepidly, "Yeah?"

"Is that a part of your second experiment?"

"It is. But it's kind of weak. I need to work on it some more."

CHAPTER 9

Alexander ate with his generals, all of whom were drunk.

General Cassander said to Alexander, "Your affections for this young wife of yours have driven you mad."

Alexander had boasted of his good fortune for months, having married the Persian noblewoman, Roxana. She had raven black hair, sultry eyes, and a beguiling smile.

"I highly recommend the Persians," Alexander said. "You should marry one of their women, Cassander, and raise up a family."

The general slammed his fist on the table. "I will do no such thing," he exclaimed. "I and mine are nothing if we are not pure Macedonian."

"And a tired old man," Alexander shot back with a laugh.

The others laughed with him.

Hephaestion sat on Alexander's right side, and another general sat on his left. He was General Perdiccas, an imposing and grave character. "I have another subject to discuss, if I may?" he said.

Alexander gave him a short nod.

"I'm a little concerned about this new title you have adopted."

"'King of Kings'?"

"For the Persians it is a reference to a deity."

"And what is the harm in that? I have not lost a single battle, and the people seem pleased with my new status as an explanation for this." He ran a finger along the leather cord he wore around his neck.

"But the title includes the Persian custom of kneeling and kissing your hand before speaking to you. I fear this will create an itch where there was not one before among our own men."

"It is just a game, General. It is a part of the culture we have adopted."

"But it is not familiar to the Macedonians. They hate it. Kissing a man's hand is how a servant shows deference to his master."

"Did I ever give these men permission to feel anything? They have only one responsibility—only one—and that is to obey my orders without question." He lifted his cup for more wine, and the steward refilled it. Standing, Alexander declared, "My brothers, I salute you. Tomorrow, we will open up a new frontier on the continent of Asia." The men cheered. "As we move across the land, we will experience many things which none of us has ever yet imagined. Even so, I do not fear that we will lose anything, as others seem to believe." As he said this he gazed at General Cassander and smiled. "Rather, we will be enlightened," he continued. "And we will continue to enjoy victory after victory, personally and professionally, as individuals and as a community. We are Macedonian—this cannot be changed. It is a truth that has preserved us until now, and it will be the thing in our hearts that carries us forth to the very ends of the Earth.

"One day the time will come when you will retire from the battle-field. Some of you will return to Macedonia, others will settle in Asia, some will return to Persia, and still others will go to other parts of the world which have captured their hearts. Wherever you go, you will build your homes and your families, and you will succeed in whatever you do, for you are Macedonian. Nothing can take your heritage away from you. Nothing can rob you of the genius that flows through your veins. Wherever you go, you will be the papa of a new generation of Macedonians. My friends, through our victories, one day the world will be one Macedonia. Let us drink to our future success and the success of all Macedonians wherever we find ourselves in this world."

The men applauded and they drank.

The next morning, Alexander emerged from his tent wrapped in fur. His face was pasty white, and his gait, unsteady. Hephaestion sat on a rock near the campfire. Alexander joined him.

"I had too much to drink last night," Alexander said.

"But nice speech," Hephaestion said.

Alexander laughed. "I suppose it was, if you say so."

"Did you dream?"

"No, but it doesn't matter. I didn't commission a mosaic for this battle." He shrugged his shoulders. "Our success does not depend on dreams."

"Shall we advance as planned?"

"We shall proceed, and we will prevail."

Over the following days Alexander's engagement at the Hydaspes River against the forces of King Porus of Paurava was a near disaster: Hundreds of warships—armored elephants with towers on their backs filled with archers—rolled over his army. His losses were greater than anything he had ever experienced before, and his victory was only by a small margin. And Bucephalus, his beloved stallion, was injured, dying shortly after the battle.

On the night the conflict ended, Alexander lay in his tent, alone, contemplating the cost of staking a foothold in Asia. What he had said to Hephaestion about the dreams had been wishful thinking. *I must use the charm just as Father taught me,* he thought.

PRESENT DAY

It was dark but for a single lightbulb far away. And there was a sound; it was the distant echo of an electric motor and metal on metal. The wheels go round.

The sounds grew louder, and the light got brighter. It was not a lightbulb; it was a headlight. And it was bearing down on him. The wheels go round.

Light shown all around. He was in a tunnel; it was the subway. Metal screeched on metal. And a woman's voice screamed, "No!" The wheels go round.

From a subway car expressionless faces stared down on him. The wheels go round.

Clayton yelled himself awake. Sitting up, he shook his head. It was only a nightmare. Herodotus was on the floor, looking up at him. Clayton looked at the clock. It was just after five, and he lay back down.

The phone rang. He rolled over. Slowly the clock came into focus. It was seven. He looked at the caller ID and picked up the phone. "Good morning, Anna. How're you?"

"Hello, Mr. Lange. I'm not so good. I'm at the hospital. Charlie has had an accident."

Fifteen minutes later, Clayton was outside and making his way to the subway platform for the next car to Brooklyn. "What have I done?" he muttered to himself. The car squealed to a stop, and he got on.

For the next hour he thought about his poem, about how he had caused this. What happened was his fault.

The subway stopped under the hospital, and he ran from the underground into the hospital building.

He found Anna in the surgery waiting area with a dozen other people. Her face was buried in her hands. She was sobbing.

Clayton sat next to her. "Anna," he whispered, and he put his arm around her.

She looked up. Her eyes were red and filled with confusion, like those of a bewildered child.

He did not have to ask—he knew what had happened. "I'm so sorry," he said, and her sobs turned into convulsions.

As they waited, Clayton glanced around at the other people. They were like mirrors. They looked like how he felt and how he knew Anna felt—afraid, anxious, and sad.

A doctor emerged from behind Staff Only doors. "Mrs. Anna Kravets?" he called.

Clayton stood with her. "I'm Mrs. Kravets," she said.

"Your husband just came out of surgery."

She covered her mouth with one of her hands.

"He's stable."

She released a sigh of relief.

"He'll be in recovery for a couple hours. You'll be able to see him then."

"How are his legs?"

"I'm sorry, Mrs. Kravets, but he lost both of them," he said, and he turned and disappeared behind the doors.

Anna's eyes rolled back, and she fainted. Clayton caught her in his arms, and he lay her down on the white tile. He pushed her hair back. After a few moments, she opened her eyes.

"Are you okay?" he asked. With tears, she said she was, and slowly she got to her feet. "How about a cup of coffee?" Clayton asked.

She nodded, and they went to the cafeteria. With their cups in hand they found a table and sat across from each other. "When did it happen?" Clayton asked.

"They said it was at about five. He was on his way to work at the warehouse." She sipped her coffee. "I feel so bad. It's my fault. He called me last night and asked if he could come home. I told him no. I'm so upset, Mr. Lange. He wouldn't have jumped if I'd let him come back."

"It's not your fault, Anna, it's mine," Clayton said.

"What?"

He muttered to himself and gazed over her shoulder for a moment. After releasing a sigh, he said, "I mean we're all in this together. Why do you think he jumped?"

"The police said several people witnessed it. You know how busy the subway is at that hour. They said he was standing really close to the edge of the platform, and as the first car was about to pass by he stepped off the platform in front of it."

For the next couple of hours, they drank coffee and shared their thoughts and fears. Anna said, "It's times like this that make you think about what's really important."

"You're right," Clayton said. After refilling their cups, he said he wanted to help.

"We have insurance," Anna said.

"Yeah, but I bet there'll be expenses that aren't covered. I'll take care of it."

"Mr. Lange, you don't have to."

"I know, but I want to. And I also want you to take some time off. It'll be paid leave. Under no circumstances will you be allowed to work for me until Charlie is well on the road to recovery. Okay?"

"Are you sure?"

"I'm positive."

It was almost 10:30 a.m. when they were permitted to visit Charlie. Bedside, Anna took one of his hands. He opened his eyes.

"Hey, Charlie."

"Hey, Anna. What happened?"

"You don't remember?"

"All I remember is being underground. The subway was coming."

"You jumped, Charlie."

"What? No. I couldn't."

"And you lost your legs."

He looked down at the end of the bed, and his mouth fell open. Squeezing her hand hard, he groaned, "Oh, no."

"But you're alive," she said.

He wept. "What am I going to do?"

"You're coming home."

———

Three days after Charlie's accident, Clayton had not left the condo except to let Herodotus do his business. Man and dog sat together brooding in the front room. The only calls he had taken were Anna's. They would keep Charlie under observation for at least two weeks as an attempted suicide. It would be three to four months before he was ready to be evaluated for prosthetics. Life would never be the same.

Clayton sat in the front room on the couch with its view of the Hudson. It was a dreary afternoon, raining and sleeting. It was going to be a desolate Christmas. Maybe he should see a therapist for depression. But not yet. He deserved to be depressed, to be sad, to be filled with shame.

Elowen had left messages for him several times. She knew what had happened from a text he had sent her on the day of the accident, which reminded him of how he had told her the poem was weak.

This is so incredibly bad, he thought. *What am I going to do?*

He was obsessed with trying to figure out how he could fix this thing with Charlie. But the best he could conjure up was a story about the donation of two legs from a car accident fatality. But would that make him responsible for another accident, plus a death?

Thoughts about taking his own life had entered his mind, but he wanted to figure this out first. If there was something he could do to control this weird power he had, maybe he could do something to make amends for this evil he was responsible for.

He got up and went out onto the balcony. It was wet and cold. He had to get out of the city. He found Elliot's number on his cell and called it. Elliot picked up. "Hey, Clayton. What's going on, my friend?"

"Hi, Elliot. I'm sorry I've been out of the loop. My housekeeper, Anna—you met her at the funeral?"

"Yeah, I remember. Nice lady."

"Her husband had an accident in the subway. He lost both his legs."

"Was he the jumper in Brooklyn I read about?"

"Yeah, but I don't really believe he jumped. He's not the type. Anyway, we're all very close. She's been like my second mom. I'm kind of depressed and I'm going to take some time off."

"This weather is miserable and doesn't help."

"That's what I'm thinking."

"Are you going to travel?"

"Yeah, I could really use some sun."

"Bon voyage, Clayton. Give me a call when you're ready to get back to work."

"Thanks, Elliot." He disconnected and looked at the dog. "What am I going to do about Elowen?" Herodotus whined. "Yeah, that's how I feel."

He speed-dialed her number: As he had hoped, she was working, and her phone went straight to voicemail. He left a message: "Hi. It's me. Sorry I haven't returned your calls. I'm in a really bad state right now, and I need to unplug for a while. Take care." He disconnected. "I am so lame," he said out loud.

It was afternoon the next day when he and Herodotus stood outside the terminal of the Rio De Janeiro International Airport waiting for a taxi. The sky was clear blue, it was hot, and it was humid. In half an hour he would be poolside drinking a piña colada.

CHAPTER 10

300 BC – EGYPT

Ptolemy I Soter reclined in the great hall of the palace. He wore the usual costume of a pharaoh—the blue-and-gold-striped headdress and ornamental robes. A scribe sat cross-legged on the floor next to him. He wore only a white tunic. A writing board with a sheet of papyrus lay on his lap.

Ptolemy dictated, "Alexander revealed his secret only to Hephaestion. But we all suspected it. It was in the mosaics he commissioned of actual scenes from the battles we ourselves beheld. A clue to understanding Alexander's unique power is to know the mosaics were completed before the battles ever happened.

"At first, we thought the images were premonitions, that Alexander saw things in his mind's eye which were destined to happen. But there were other clues, like the times he would tell the troop physician to concoct a potion to help him dream after his artist had presented him with the image he had commissioned for an intended mosaic. I, myself, witnessed such an exchange before the War of Gaugamela, and I shared it with General Seleucus. He told me he had overheard a similar conversation before the Battle of Issus.

"In addition to these things, there was the amulet which Alexander always wore. It was the one his father had worn until his death, and like his father it hung to the middle of his chest. He could not help but touch it whenever he spoke about a coming engagement with an enemy."

Pausing, Ptolemy gave the scribe time to catch up. He gazed at the great walls of the hall as he fondled the charm he had acquired from Alexander posthumously. Ptolemy admired the genius of the Egyptian engineers, how they had created this building and so many others, stacking such enormous carved stones one on top of the other. It was the same technique they had used with the pyramids thousands of years before. The stone-built palace reflected strength and power, but with the statues of previous pharaohs on pedestals and the tapestries on the walls and Alexander's mosaics in the floors, there was an element of nobility and elegance.

Ptolemy fixed his eyes on the mosaic of the Battle of Issus: Darius rode his chariot hard. But his eyes, they were filled with fear. In the background there was a dead tree, which was a hint of what would become of the Persians. Across from Darius was Alexander on his great steed, which reared up with so much power. The king did not wear a helmet, often his practice after his victory at the Granicus River, for he thought himself invincible.

The Persians—such awesome warriors of antiquity with so many crowns—were portrayed in the mosaic as confused and afraid. That Alexander could imagine such a catastrophe in the ranks of his enemy's army despite the number of voices that were in his ear saying otherwise, was an inspiration from the gods. But for his illness he would have continued his campaigns and put the entire world under his feet.

The scribe said he was ready for further dictation. "I think that's enough for today," Ptolemy said. "Let us continue tomorrow."

With a bow, the scribe backed out of the room. The pharaoh smiled to himself. *Someday my story will be read by my heirs,* he thought. He wanted them to understand how he had acquired the amulet from Alexander. But it was a story they would not hear until after he was gone. If it got out while he was still pharaoh, his status as a living deity among the Egyptians might be put in jeopardy. But that would not dissuade him from having the scribe record in detail exactly what had happened for later generations, a tale he enjoyed remembering.

He closed his eyes, and he recited in his mind the story: After Alexander died, General Perdiccas insisted he lie in state in Babylon for two years. This made Ptolemy angry. But when he heard that the charm had never left Alexander's neck, he realized Perdiccas did not know what it was, and it was there for him to take! But how?

Perdiccas himself provided the answer. He built a mausoleum for Alexander's body. It was made of marble and gold and Greek columns; it was beautiful, and it was monstrously heavy. He then announced he would transport the mausoleum back to Macedonia. The people believed that living or dead Alexander's body possessed special powers and that wherever he was there would be prosperity and security. And who deserved such a blessing but Alexander's own people?

These ideas about Alexander's body were nothing but pure superstition. But when it comes to politics, faith is half the battle, and Ptolemy knew that if he brought the king's body back to Egypt, he would hold the heart of the people in his hand.

Engineers designed a carriage for the mausoleum, which would carry it from Persia all the way back to Macedonia under the tow of sixty-four mules. To ensure its safe arrival, mercenaries would accompany it. But, alas, Perdiccas should have sent soldiers, for the loyalty of mercenaries can only be measured in gold.

Ptolemy's envoy caught up to the carriage before it even left Asia, and his men paid the mercenaries three times what Perdiccas had paid them. Thus without spilling a single drop of blood, the whole caravan turned to Egypt.

The pharaoh was sitting in the portico of the palace in Memphis when the carriage with the mausoleum arrived. He watched his hand shake. How he longed to know whether or not the charm still hung around the king's neck.

Once the mausoleum was unloaded from the carriage in the palace square, he stationed a unit of armed troops to watch over it. And he waited, but only a few hours. At the deepest hour of the night he strode to the square with his guards. Standing before the mausoleum, he ordered the troops to open it for him that he might venerate the king. They did so without hesitation. However, when he commanded them to remove the lid of the sarcophagus, they turned white. But they could not refuse the order, and they did it. Not surprisingly, they left him alone with the king's body without any reluctance when he told them to go.

Alexander was wrapped in layers of linen, but the charm hung around his neck on a leather strap outside the linens. Gently, Ptolemy pulled the strap over his head. And he remembered the next moment as though it had happened yesterday: When he had hung the medallion around his own neck, there had been a flash of light behind his eyes, and, falling to his knees, he cried out, "The face of Alexander!"

That was Ptolemy's story, and he knew when the people heard it and realized how much he and the great king had depended on the talisman, they might think less of their skills as strategists and army commanders. But things such as these did not concern him as much as the need for the dynasty to continue to possess and use the amulet in perpetuity. For with it they would govern with success the vast stretches of territory in the north, including Libya, Palestine, and Syria. These acquisitions had prospered Egypt far beyond anyone's wildest dreams.

Ptolemy's son, Ceraunus, was eighteen years old. Ever since he was a young man, he had possessed the same power he had, so he had figured the charm was for the succession of a dynasty. He imagined that it all began with Alexander's father, Philip II. Alexander must have taken it from him when he was assassinated by his bodyguard, Pausanias, in the amphitheater the day after his daughter's wedding.

Alexander's son was born after his death, so the child was always powerless. To add to the misery of it all, the baby and his mother, Roxana, suffered a miserable end at the hand of that wicked creature, General Cassander.

Ptolemy discovered how the power of the charm worked through experimentation, using what he knew about Alexander and the mosaics. Himself, he would draw an image of an idea he had or of a physical object he desired. And if he dreamed the image, what he had drawn would come true. The same had been true for Ceraunus.

When Ceraunus was very young, Ptolemy conducted an experiment with him; he had wanted to discover how the power flowed between generations. He put the charm around the boy's neck, and then he told him to draw a picture of something he wanted, something that had been on his heart. He drew an elephant, that great creature which had captured his imagination ever since he had heard the stories about the Battle of Hydaspes. And then he told him to meditate on those things before he slept that night. Ptolemy also drew an image. But his was of a woman whom he had seen in the market the day before. She was the most beautiful he had ever set eyes on. The next morning there was a great trumpeting outside the palace. It awakened everyone. And there, underneath Ceraunus' window, was an elephant!

To this day, the elephant's origin remains unknown. And as for the woman Ptolemy imagined, she never appeared. That was how he discovered the charm works for both generations but only from the oldest to the youngest, just as one's last will and testament would work.

It was only last year when Ptolemy transported Alexander's body to his namesake city, Alexandria. His remains now resided in an underground tomb suitable for a son of a god. And the people believe their prosperity flowed from that place.

Ptolemy touched the amulet with his forefinger, and he smiled.

CHAPTER 11

Amelia looked over the conference table at her team as she talked on the speaker phone. "This is remarkable, Dr. Rachid."

"It is a once in a lifetime discovery," the Egyptologist said. "I am pretty certain it will be helpful for the work you're doing."

"Can you sit on it until I've seen it?"

"For a short time. When can you come?"

She looked at Tarek, who sat across from her with his tablet open, typing. He said, "There's a flight in three hours."

"We'll be on a plane in three hours. That puts us in Alexandria in time for dinner tomorrow evening, Dr. Rachid," she said. "Tarek's coming with me."

As Amelia and Tarek prepared for their flight, Dr. Ahmed Rachid, professor of Egyptology at Alexandria University, was booking a car and driver. The discovery he and his team had made would turn the world of Ptolemy Studies on its head. And the information he would share with this cabal would make him rich.

A flight attendant served Amelia and Tarek hot tea. "What do you think this will mean for our work?" Tarek asked.

Amelia took a sip of the tea. "Without knowing what exactly we were looking for, we've been tracing the path of this power backward, looking for its cause. The artifact Dr. Rachid has found could be the clue that will finally remove our blinders."

Amelia looked out the window. The sun was just beginning to slip underneath the horizon of the Mediterranean Sea. "Beneath us is Turkey, ancient Anatolia," Tarek said.

"This is where Alexander the Great launched his Eastern campaign," Amelia said, "ultimately planting his flag in the Levant, Egypt, and the Middle East. If he hadn't died, he would have taken India, too. What he did reveals how awesome this power is when it's coupled with genius."

"Perhaps we'll finish what Alexander started."

"That is what the director hopes." She always called Victor "the director."

Clayton lay in a chaise lounge under a canopy, alongside the hotel's pool; Herodotus rested in the shade next to him.

Clayton had drunk a lot of rum. The booze had shut down his dreams. But his thoughts ran wild: *The dreams that came true were from the stories I wrote. The images were so vivid, I cannot not see them. Will the dreams stop, if I stop writing? How is this possible, and why is this happening to me? Has anyone else ever experienced this?*

He ordered another piña colada.

Tarek had been to Egypt many times on holiday. Sharm El-Sheikh was his favorite place to go for the beaches and clubs. But this tour was for an entirely different purpose. He and Amelia were passing through security at a lab on the site of the ancient Temple of Serapis in Alexandria with Dr. Rachid. The Egyptian was dressed in a dark suit and bowtie.

"This artifact is a granite tile, roughly a half-meter square," the Egyptologist said. "On it is a painted portrait of a pharaoh. The head is approximately five inches high. Below the head is an inscription chiseled into the stone."

They entered the room where the granite lay on a viewing table. Amelia, Tarek, and the doctor gazed at it. "This piece is one of the most remarkable discoveries we've had in a long time," Rachid said. "We date it, two hundred thirty BCE. It is a dedication of the temple by the man who commissioned it."

"Pharoah Ptolemy III Euergetes," Tarek said.

"Correct. The inscription reads, 'I, Ptolemy III Euergetes, devote this temple to Serapis, god of gods and lord of lords. May he forever hold our kingdom in his hands.'"

"This pharaoh was only a couple of generations removed from Alexander the Great," Amelia said.

"About a hundred years," Rachid said. "And this brings me to that which will be of special interest to you." He held a magnifying glass to the painting, revealing a neckless with a pendant around the pharaoh's neck. "Roughly speaking," he said, "that ornament would have been two inches long and a half-inch wide. A colleague who is a geologist thinks it may have been a black tourmaline crystal. They're still very common. People have always believed they are good luck charms."

"Why's this one special?" Tarek asked.

"Alexander the Great wore something similar if, indeed, it wasn't the same crystal," Rachid said. He pulled an 8x10" glossy color photo from a manila envelope and handed it to Amelia. "This is a close-up from Alexander's mosaic for the Battle of Issus."

Amelia examined it, and Tarek looked at the picture with her.

Rashid continued: "As you have read in the fragments of Ptolemy I Soter's diary, we believe there was an amulet. But it was never described with enough detail for anyone besides the user and perhaps his closest confidents to know exactly what it was. These two images are the only visual evidence we have. For me, it would be more surprising if they were two different objects than if they were one and the same. Which is to say, if you find someone with similar powers wearing a tourmaline crystal, I'm certain you'll be looking at the original amulet."

"What do you think, Amelia?" Tarek asked.

"I think this might be the nexus for more than two thousand years of history."

222 BC – EGYPT

"Father and Grandfather used the amulet for good just as I have," said Ptolemy III Euergetes. He was sick, and he lay in bed. It was night, and despite a cool draft off the Mediterranean, his fever persisted, and a bead of sweat formed across his forehead.

Aegeas, the high priest of Serapis, sat at his side. His features were sharp and angular, accented as they were by candlelight that flickered. He had listened to the pharaoh's soliloquy many times before, but tonight it was his last will and testament.

"That my uncle abdicated the Egyptian throne and his powers to my father was a blessing for all the people," Euergetes continued. "Surely, Ceraunus would have driven it all into the ground for his madness and lust for power. But we have built an army and a navy superior to anything the world has ever seen. We have taken possession of every port on the Mediterranean and Red Sea. And we are renowned for our art and literature; we have multiplied the harvests of the fields tenfold; and, with mathematics, we have unlocked the mysteries of the sea and the stars.

"But, as you know, Aegeas, my son, is a sadist. He is craven. His enchantment with the sacred prostitutes is to excess. And he is filled with bloodlust. Even as a young boy he was cruel and without remorse. First, he tortured his animals, and then people against whom he held nothing more than a grudge. Do you understand?"

"Indeed, my lord. Even his name is a mockery."

Euergetes nodded his head. "'Philopator'? Yes, it is as you have said. My son shed so much blood in the palace, I had no other choice but to put the crystal away for long periods of time. I was so afraid he would bring the whole house down on our heads! Why did the gods give me this mad child?" He stared into the eyes of the priest. "There is no answer, is there?"

"My lord, this is a mystery even to me."

"You and I shall visit the tomb tonight."

"Shall I call a guard to accompany us?"

"No, for what we will do will be for your eyes only. Hereafter, you will share what you know with the high priest who will assume your office when you die, and he shall do likewise until a righteous heir of the throne comes forth."

"How will we know who he is?"

"He will be chosen by Serapis, who will reveal him to your successor."

With the priest's help, Euergetes slipped into a tunic and the cloak of a court servant. He finished the disguise with a scarf around his face. The pharaoh leaned into the priest who was not a big man himself, who nearly fell supporting his weight.

"Come now, Aegeas, call on Serapis to strengthen you for the both of us," Euergetes said.

Together, they went from the pharaoh's room, through a secret passageway, and into the courtyard where Aegeas called for two horses. With the guard's help, Euergetes climbed onto his horse. Aegeas mounted his, and he ordered the gates to be opened.

The tomb of Alexander was not far from the palace, and the two men were there in minutes. A unit of troops stood at the entrance. It was a permanent post, partly ceremonial but also necessary for security. The authorities knew there was always the risk of losing the complex to the peasants who worshipped the dead king.

Euergetes pulled back his scarf and showed the guards his signet ring—it was engraved with an eagle gripping a thunderbolt in its talons. The guards stepped to the side, and the two men rode into the courtyard of the tomb. They dismounted their horses before the burial chamber. It was built with Doric columns and a portico. Three images were engraved on its façade: Alexander the Great, the royal eagle, and the god, Serapis. The pharaoh produced a key and unlocked the great door, which swung open easily. Aegeas took a torch that was at the door and led the way down the staircase into the tomb. It was a large area, and he lit torches on the walls.

A long, narrow marble table rested in the middle of the space. Across it lay a stone sarcophagus. Painted on its lid was the image of the deified king. The priest stood at the head of the sarcophagus with his arms raised, and he prayed, "Serapis and all gods, those in the heavens and those in the underworld, save us from all calamities, for our intentions are pure and our devotion is single-minded, imbued with your light and grace."

He and the pharaoh lifted the lid off the sarcophagus and set it onto the floor.

The 100-year-old mummified body of the king was wrapped in layer upon layer of linen. "We shall not disturb it," Euergetes said.

He took the black tourmaline crystal by its leather strap from a small satchel he carried and placed it on the king's chest. For a moment, the two men gazed at it in the stillness. Then they picked up the lid of the sarcophagus and slowly lowered it back into place.

"I will pray again," the priest said. He raised his arms. After a moment of silence, he whispered, "Serapis and all gods, those in the heavens and those in the underworld, let this tomb be sealed by your power until a righteous king comes forth for the complete redemption and restoration of your people."

CHAPTER 12

After his two-week drunk in Rio, Clayton had only more questions about why and how his stories and dreams came true. Stepping out of arrivals at LaGuardia with his bag over a shoulder and Herodotus on a leash, he swore, "Damn it's cold," as the icy air slapped him in the face. He jumped into a cab and sat back with his cell phone to his ear, waiting with a sense of trepidation.

"This is going to be interesting," Elowen answered.

"How're you?"

"I'm torn. I want to yell at you, but I'm also relieved to hear your voice."

"Do you want to get together?"

"Carlyle's at seven." She hung up.

Closing his eyes, he put his head back, settling in for the slow drive home. His mind wandered: *Did Grandpa have this same power? If he did, why didn't Dad or Mom ever say anything about it? And what about Dad? If he had the power, did it have something to do with how he and Grandpa died?*

And he thought about the rapper, Derrick Romano—*Damn, that name sounds familiar.* He had performed some outrageous stunts that were very difficult to explain short of true magic. But what Romano had done was so different from what he had done.... It was probably nothing.

While he had been in Rio, one afternoon after lying in the sun too long—getting cooked like a convenience store hotdog, he mused—he had awoken with an idea: He would research the great generals, dictators, and emperors, men like Attila the Hun, Constantine, and General Patton. Perhaps one of them had had this power, too, and he could learn more about it through them. He would start reading about them when he got home.

"We're here," the driver said.

Clayton opened his eyes. "Thanks," he said, and he paid for the ride and got out with the Frenchie. "We're home, my friend." Herodotus tugged on the leash toward the building. They took the elevator up, and Anna met them at the door.

"Hello, Mr. Lange," she said.

"Hi, Anna. What're you doing here? I told you—"

"I love Charlie, but I can't stand being in the house with him all day long."

Clayton sat at the kitchen table. "I hear you."

"You look sunburned. Would you like some water?"

"That would be great. How're you doing? How's Charlie?"

She gave him a bottle of water and sat down across from him. "I'm fine. Charlie starts physical therapy next week."

He took a long drink. "Has his disability insurance kicked in?"

"We're supposed to start getting checks next week. I hope you don't mind if I ask, but have you talked to your girlfriend recently?"

"Elowen? I talked to her on the way home from the airport. Why?"

"Because she's come by several times since you left."

"Oh, my gosh."

"The next time you decide to unplug, Mr. Lange, it would be helpful if you gave me a message for your lady friends."

"You're right. But hopefully there won't be a next time."

He got up with the water and went outside onto balcony. The wind off the river threw back his hair. There was a black SUV on the other side of the street, four stories below. The driver was looking up at him with binoculars. "Hey, Anna, check this out." She joined him just as the vehicle pulled off the curb. "Ever seen that SUV before? It looks like an Escalade."

"It's been parked out there off and on ever since you left."

"Probably the paparazzi. That's the nice thing about going somewhere where you're entirely unknown. You can be truly anonymous."

After a nap, Clayton showered, shaved, dressed, and out the door with the dog. Already, he was missing Rio's laidback vibe. When he was offline, he was able to ignore his reality, especially his fear that he might accidentally do something like what he had done to Charlie again. But he could not be shitfaced poolside all the time. His German heritage would not permit it.

At the entrance to Carlyle's, the hostess pointed him to a small, square table near the back of the restaurant. Elowen was there, tapping something into her cell.

"You didn't chicken out," she said.

He sat next to her. "I know what's good for me."

A waiter came and got their drink order. "Why didn't you call me sooner?" Elowen asked.

"No segue?"

"Nope."

"I'm sorry. I thought about you constantly. But I didn't know what to say. I was so frustrated about this thing I'm going through right now, and I wanted to figure it out before I talked to you."

"Did you?"

"No."

"But you decided to call anyway."

The waiter returned with the drinks.

"I had to. Herodotus pestered me as soon as we landed."

"Frenchies are known for their love of human companionship," she said. "I'm glad you're following his lead."

"Me, too."

"I need to be serious with you for a second, Clayton. If we're going to keep seeing each other, I have certain conditions."

"Okay."

"If you ever disappear like that again, I won't let you back into my life. I have abandonment issues. What you did threatens the health of my spirit, and I can't be with a man who treats me like that."

"I understand. I respect that. For the record, I didn't leave because of you or because of us. I left because of a crisis I'm having with this thing that took away the legs of a man whom I consider a friend."

"Let me help you. Let's put our heads together to figure this out."

Over dinner, he told her about how he had been thinking he wanted to research emperors and warriors who had possessed incredible powers. "And how about adventurers?" she said. "Why not Ferdinand Magellan, Francis Drake, and Leif Erickson?"

"That's really good."

"There've been so many incredible people who've done amazing things," she continued. Her eyes opened wide, she said, "And what about religious luminaries, people like Confucius and Buddha, Moses and Jesus?"

"Can you imagine? If any of these people used this thing it would be like pulling back the curtain on the Wizard of Oz."

204 BC – EGYPT

Flames engulfed Ptolemy IV Philopator's bedroom. Clearly, this was the work of Horwennefer, who had usurped his power upon persuading the masses. The pharaoh reflected sardonically, *There was a time when I summoned the gods just as my father had, and they served me. But he died, and they left me. Why? My son is only six years old, and his caretakers will succumb to that fake pharaoh with his forked tongue.* He released a dark laugh. *Is it because I gorged myself with the love of too many women that the gods have cursed me? Tonight, my flesh will be consumed, and I will go to that other place, and I will know.*

There was no way he could escape the fire—which even now lapped at his garments—and he would not compromise his dignity by screaming and thrashing about. No, he, the fourth Ptolemy, would die with honor, forever remembered as a martyr.

CHAPTER 13

PRESENT DAY

Derrick held a tablet in his lap and typed as he sat cross-legged on a couch. Miami's Biscayne Bay lay several stories below the penthouse. It was a windless day, and the water was still. The other guys from the band sat around watching the big screen TV as Derrick clicked the remote, channel-surfed, and typed.

Dazzle handed him an open bottle of whiskey. "Are you looking for inspiration for the final piece tomorrow?" he asked.

"Yeah. We're going to do something a little different." Derrick took a swig from the bottle and passed it back.

"You think any of this is going to get in the way of the tour?" TJ asked.

"Doesn't really matter, does it? They always come back."

"Any hints?" Rex asked. He took the bottle from Dazzle and drank.

"I'm experimenting. I want to see how far this magic stretches. We're going political. Why don't you guys disappear and give me some space to work this out?"

"Party later?" Dazzle asked.

"Yeah, around midnight. And bring girls back with you."

Derrick identified four politicians from the news. Two of them were from other countries, and the other two were from the US. All were scum. He typed the title of his new rap, "My New Religion."

30 BC – EGYPT

Buffeted by the winds, the sand seas of Egypt tirelessly formed and reformed mountainous dunes shaped like pyramids. Each one was original, and each one was swept away in an instant by the next wind. The hearts of the Egyptians shifted just as frequently as the terrain did.

Contrary to his last thoughts, Pharaoh Ptolemy IV Philopator was never remembered as a martyr, and his nemesis, Horwennefer, was never more than a despotic king over a small province in Egypt. But the late pharaoh would have been pleased to know that his son went on to rule for 25 years and his grandson for 35 years. The empire itself would survive for almost 175 years after his passing until it was swallowed up by Rome, following Cleopatra and her lover, Marcus Antony's, suicides.

Hundreds of troops stood in formation inside the walls that framed Alexander the Great's tomb in the city of Alexandria, and the high priest of Serapis faced Octavian and two of his servants in front of the entrance to the chamber. One of servants carried an armful of flowers and the other, a small hardwood chest.

The priest bowed deeply. "We have waited for you for generations," he said.

"Why are you so sure I am the one?" Octavian asked.

"Serapis revealed this to the council of prophets." He looked up at the image of his god carved on the marble façade of the tomb with the royal eagle and the profile of Alexander the Great.

"So be it."

"Follow me, my lord," the priest said.

He turned, pushing open the door of the tomb and stepping onto the landing. The stairwell was lined with torches, which lit their way down into the vault. The priest said a prayer not unlike that of the high priest who had prayed with Ptolemy III Euergetes so long ago, closing with the words, "Great and awesome Serapis, we beg you to be with this king. Raise him up as a god that he may lead us, your people, to complete redemption and renewal." Then he directed the soldiers to remove the lid from the sarcophagus.

Octavian and the priest stood side by side as they peered at the mummy. Wearing gloves, the priest plucked the black tourmaline crystal from its chest. As he did so, its leather strap fell away, disintegrating into dust. He showed no surprise as he took from a pocket in his cloak a rope chain of white gold.

As he strung the chain through the silver wire that was wound around the crystal, he said, "Octavian Caesar Augustus, this chain is unique as it was woven by a master artisan for the crystal. As you wear it, your firstborn will share with you the crystal's powers. Unless you abdicate the crystal's power, your souls will belong to Lord Hades, the Greek god of the underworld. Do you understand?"

"We call that god Pluto. And, yes, I do understand," Octavian said.

The priest hung the crystal around the emperor's neck, saying, "Emperor Augustus, the power in this crystal is pernicious. Beware!"

As the crystal touched his flesh, Octavian's knees wobbled, and he gulped for a breath of air. Upon regaining his composure, he directed the servant who held the hardwood chest to open it. Inside lay a diadem made of solid gold. It was a simple band that would sit on the brow. Augustus took the crown and placed it on the ancient king's linen-covered head.

"Now you may replace the lid of the sarcophagus," Augustus said.

After the soldiers had done as they were commanded, the second servant set the flowers on top of the sarcophagus.

PRESENT DAY

Derrick and his band had played for three hours, but they were not done. They stood behind stage drinking and reveling in their fans' chant: "Derrik! Derrick! Derrick!"

They came back out, and 65,000 Floridians and groupies from all around the country, screamed, "Derr us! Derr us!"

Dazzle opened the number, whipping out a lightning rhythm on the snare. Someone shouted from the pit, "Dazzle Be Dazzle!" The drummer grinned as he added the toms and high hat. TJ came in heavy on the bass.

Everyone was standing, pumping their fists in the air and stomping their feet. The whole place rumbled like there was an earthquake.

Rex's guitar rang out with a heavy strum, and with the flash of a spotlight, Derrick took a mic at center stage, and his voice pounded down on them,

> When you look in the mirror, you see that
>   sorry face
> You want to puke; you want to die
> It be easy peasy with a bomb from the sky
> To end you.
>
> If you die like that, it be a delight
> For a party's underway all through the night
> As we celebrate a new religion.
>
> You're rich but you're poor; a star all alone
> With the water at your neck in the tub you
>   make a wish
> To have a new life and you breathe like a fish
> And that ends you.
>
> If you die like that, it be a delight
> For a party's underway all through the night
> As we celebrate a new religion.

Amelia watched monitors set in rows on a wall in her living room, from an overstuffed armchair. Her place was a two-story, brick townhouse on the west side of Manhattan. She had a cat. He was a giant

Manx with the markings of a leopard. His name was Gus, and he lay in her lap.

One of the monitors featured Derrick Romano's concert live. He was singing his new song, "My New Religion."

She watched her team on another monitor as they listened to Romano. Some were taking notes. The other monitors were tuned to the different news channels with closed captions and volumes muted.

Less than a minute into Derrick's song, all the news channels flashed banners across their screens: "Breaking News: Presidential Palace In Turkey Bombed."

Derrick sang,

> You're the shit in your limo, but you know it's
>   all a lie
> Your life's a horror; your heart's full of shame
> The shooter'll fix that with a laser-sighted aim.
> And end you.
>
> If you die like that, it be a delight
> For a party's underway all through the night
> As we celebrate a new religion.

The people rapped with him, "As we celebrate a new religion!"

Amelia saw disbelief and horror in the faces of her team members as the news channels flashed more headlines of tragedy at the highest levels: "California Congressman Discovered Drowned In His Own Bathtub." And then, "President of Bolivia Killed by Drive-By Shooter."

Amelia spoke to the team: "This is all we need to confirm everything we've believed about Romano. Jake, Raven, pick him up tomorrow morning." They gave thumbs up. "Penelope and Tarek, meet me at my place tomorrow. It's time to introduce ourselves to Clayton Lange. We will meet at the farm."

As she talked, they watched Derrick rap another verse:

You're a whore to the rich cats—you knew it
    all along
But you wore a disguise, the mask of a pillar
But she got you, and she shot you, a real
    whore was your killer
And she ends you.

If you die like that, it be a delight
For a party's underway all through the night
As we celebrate a new religion.

Within minutes the news channels all flashed another banner: "South Carolina Governor Found Dead At Massage Parlor."

25 BC – ROME

Tiberius' mind wandered as he listened to the politicians in the Roman Senate House argue over their pet projects in their respective districts. He was thinking about how he had come here and where it all might lead and how he would have his scribe write it:

Even as a young boy I understood the cost of war. Growing up in the home of the most powerful man on earth educates one in all matters of life. I was especially afraid for my stepfather in his war against Marcus Antony. It was the battle of the ages, and the victor would be declared Augustus of the whole civilized world. And the loser would die. But Mother assured me. "Tiberius," she said, "do not be afraid. Octavian will be the winner as surely as the sky is blue. For he has been chosen by the gods."

Indeed, after more than two years of war at sea against his last enemy, Octavian was victorious and would thereafter be called Caesar Augustus. I remember hearing this good news before going to bed one night. I was elated, and I could not sleep! I threw off my bedsheets, jumped to my feet, and I roamed the halls of the palace for hours filled with a sense of anticipation, trying to imagine what this might mean.

When at last Augustus returned home, I rode with him in his char-

iot, in his triumphal procession through the city. I was only eleven years old. The people cheered wildly, and he said into my ear, "There is great political theater which will play out in the years ahead, but already I see it all. Someday, my young Tiberius, I will explain this and many other things to you."

I was speechless, and I looked at him in awe. He patted me on the shoulder. "Now I will tell you this one thing. But it must remain our secret." And he pulled from around his neck a black crystal that hung on a white gold rope chain, the beauty of which I had never before seen. He said, "Son, this is the amulet of Alexander which I inherited. With it, we will complete the work he began."

Yes, and now, barely seventeen years old, I am the youngest elected official to ever serve on the military board. Not yet old enough to fight, I am a quaestor. But one day I will fight, and I shall fulfill my childhood dream of being a general in the army. I will expand our nation's borders, pursuing the work of my father, Caesar Augustus, who continues the work of the father of us all, Alexander.

CHAPTER 14

The jet landed early in the morning in Columbus, Ohio. Jake and Raven deboarded onto the tarmac. They wore their usual FBI costumes: black suits and white shirts. Jake wore a tie.

Derrick's limo arrived at the airport within the hour.

Jake and Raven met the band at the foot of the stairs of the band's plane.

Raven said, "We're FBI, and you're under arrest for the murder of four people over the past twenty-four hours."

"Whassup with that? How can you arrest an innocent man?" Derrick asked as Jake cuffed him. "Is this about last night? If it is, will you please tell me how I could've been in Turkey, Brazil, California, and South Carolina simultaneously?"

"Tell it to the judge," Raven said.

"Come on, sister, I know you believe in my music."

She glared at him as she grabbed his arm and walked him to the plane. Jake followed them. The band watched in silence.

The aircraft was a Dassault Falcon. As they neared it, Derrick said, "This is a pretty fancy plane for the US government."

"Just get in," Jake said.

In the plane seated and shackled, Derrick tugged on his restraints.

"Do you really think this is necessary? I mean, where am I going to go?"

"Better safe than sorry," Raven said.

He shook his head. "I never touched anyone."

"We're not concerned with 'touching,'" Jake said, who stood over him.

"Boo!" Derrick taunted, but Jake didn't flinch. He held up a syringe and flicked the barrel a couple times. "What's that?" the rapper asked with a hint of protest.

"Propofol," he said, and he stuck him in the arm.

"Why?" He glared.

"To keep you from dreaming."

Clayton was lying on his couch in the living room, paging through a book.

"Mr. Lange," Anna called from the balcony.

He glanced up.

"Come, take a look," she said.

He had pulled a stack of biographies and histories from the shelves of the old bookcase to review the lives of the greats—renowned emperors and kings; composers and artists; athletes, inventors, engineers, and mathematicians. There had been a lot of people who had done a lot of amazing things. He joined Anna at the rail.

"There's that car again. It's in the fire zone."

It was the black Escalade.

"Did it just pull up?"

Three doors opened as he asked. Two women and a man got out and walked across the sidewalk and into the building.

"Yes, it did."

"I have a weird feeling about this, Anna. Dollars for donuts they're paying me a visit. And if they are, you don't need to be here."

"But—"

"No buts. Charlie needs you, and you don't owe me that kind of loyalty. Will you be okay taking the stairs down?"

She nodded.

The phone rang, he picked it up, and security told him what he had expected. After he hung up, he told Anna they said they were FBI. "But let's not take any chances," he said. He shuffled her out the door, and just as she disappeared into the emergency exit stairwell the elevator door slid open, and the three agents stepped into the corridor.

"Mr. Clayton Lange?" a tall, elderly woman asked.

"Yes. How may I help you?"

"I'm Special Agent Amelia Williams. I'm with the FBI. These are my associates." Penelope and Tarek nodded their heads. "May we have a word?"

"Sure. Come in."

Inside, he waved for them to take a seat. He sat in an armchair with his back against the window. Amelia sat next to Tarek on the couch behind the coffee table across from Clayton. Amelia set a briefcase across her lap. Penelope sat in an overstuffed chair alongside Clayton.

They looked FBI. But Williams was different—a person her age should have been tucked away in an office somewhere doing administrative stuff—at least that was the way it was dramatized on TV. And there were the pearls—the old gal wore a double string of them—they were delicate, flawless, and they were real; they were worth a fortune. FBI?

"How can I help you, Special Agent Williams?" Clayton asked.

"First, thank you for opening your home to us, Mr. Lange. We know this is an imposition."

"I'd be happy to help in whatever way I might."

"We're investigating a case which may involve you and your family."

"I don't know of any wrongdoing."

"Don't worry. To my knowledge, there's nothing that would directly implicate you for a crime."

"Go ahead."

"I'd like to begin by revisiting your college days."

"Wow. That's a long time ago. But I'm listening."

"On April seventeenth of your senior year there was a party at the

Alpha Epsilon Alpha sorority house. You were dating a woman who belonged to that sorority." She opened the briefcase and took out a color 8"x10" photograph and placed it on the coffee table. "The woman's name was Serenity Johansson."

Clayton pulled his chair up close and stared at the photo for a long moment. The girl's hair was long, dark brown, and parted down the middle; her eyes sparkled; and her teeth were the pride of a wealthy orthodontist. She stood between two other girls. They all wore hip-hugger jeans and halter tops. They were laughing for whoever took the picture.

"Yep," Clayton said, "that's Serenity, the love of my life when I was twenty-one."

Amelia set another photo on the table. It was him and Serenity with their arms around each other's waists. Her clothing and the setting hinted that the photo was taken on the same day, at the same party as the other photo.

"What can you tell us about the party?" Amelia asked.

"It was an absolute blowout. Alcohol, coke, weed, everything. The music went all night." He sighed. "But it was probably the worst night of my life."

They waited.

"But I recovered." He chuckled. "Is this why you're here, to hear about my college heartbreak? Did something happen to Serenity?"

"We'll get to her in a moment," Amelia said. "But please go on. We're interested in everything you can tell us about that night."

"Okay. It was our senior year when we met, and by the time of that party we had been going out for about three months. I was totally enthralled with her, and she liked me too, probably not as much as I liked her, but we had started talking about what we wanted in a marriage." He sighed again.

"Please continue, Mr. Lange," Amelia said.

"At the party, she told me she wanted to break up. I was devasted, to say the least. She said she had spent a lot of time trying to imagine our future together, and that if I continued to insist on writing for a living, all she could envision was being in an apartment in the city with threadbare furniture, empty cupboards, and screaming babies. She said she wanted more than that."

"What did you tell her?"

"Well, I had been writing for a couple of magazines human interest stuff. It wasn't much—just enough to pay the bills and get me through school. I didn't have any hot job offers yet, and so I felt like I had to be honest with Serenity and tell her the only thing I knew was true, that I would do my best for her and our children. She said that wasn't good enough. But—and this is the weird part—we went back to her apartment, and we made love. I always thought of it as her going away present to me."

"Is that all you remember from that night? Did you wear protection?"

"I've never told anyone this before, but I guess it's not really an issue now, twenty-plus years later. I was wearing protection. But I was losing my mind—my heart was broken—so I punctured it. I thought if I got her pregnant, she would marry me by default. Crazy, right? But it didn't work, and that was that."

"Did you ever see her again?"

"I saw her briefly at graduation. We said goodbye and she gave me a kiss on the cheek." He leaned back in the chair. "So are you going to tell me what happened to her?"

"Mr. Lange, I'm sorry to be the one to tell you this, but you did get Serenity Johansson pregnant."

His jaw went slack. "How—"

"We interviewed her last week, and she told us the whole story, including the part about the going away present. Apparently, she had been giving presents to other men as well."

"I find that hard to believe."

"She said she'd been fishing for a husband the whole year, that she was particularly interested in an attorney, engineer, or doctor. She loved you the most, she said, but she had zero confidence in your ability to deliver the standard of living she had always hoped for. By graduation she knew she was pregnant. She wasn't showing but she had missed her period. She had been sleeping with two other men, but she was pretty sure it was yours. She propositioned the guy who was the engineer first. But he told her he wasn't interested, and she should get an abortion. Number two was a law student. His name was Joseph Romano."

"Joe Romano? That guy was a scab on humanity."

"But he had what she was looking for, and he didn't ask for a paternity test."

"I just threw up in my mouth."

"The marriage only lasted six years. He left her for another woman."

"I wish I could say I'm sorry, but—"

"Three months later, he was killed when he stepped in front of a bus."

"This is totally freaking me out. The suspense is killing me. What happened to Serenity?"

"Unfortunately, she got lost on drugs. Crystal meth. She lives in Detroit."

"This is getting sadder by the moment. Did she have the kid?"

"Yes, he—"

"Hold it, you said she married Joe Romano? That's where I heard the name before. Is her son the rapper Derrick Romano?"

"Yes, Mr. Lange, that's right."

"Derrick Romano is my son?"

"Yes, Mr. Lange."

Clayton ran his finger along the chain that hung around his neck.

"Mr. Lange, may I ask you about that necklace you're wearing?"

"Oh, this?" He squeezed the chain between his thumb and forefinger. "It's a family heirloom. I don't think I've ever seen a rope chain like it." He pulled it out from under his shirt, revealing a six-sided polished black stone wrapped in silver wire. "Grandpa Karl used to wear it. My mom gave it to me when he died."

Amelia cleared her throat. "Do you know what kind of stone that is?"

"I do not. It's supposed to be lucky, though it didn't seem to work for my grandpa."

Amelia took out two more 8"x10" prints from her briefcase, which she set on the coffee table side by side. One was of the enlarged section of the mosaic of Alexander the Great the Egyptologist had shared with them. The other photo was of the third century BC rock painting with the inscription by Pharaoh Ptolemy III Euergetes. Names and dates were on both prints.

"You'll notice the crystal each one wore," she said.

Clayton pulled the chain and crystal over his head, compare his crystal to the crystals in the photos. "This is that?"

"I believe it is," Amelia said.

"What is it?"

"It's a black tourmaline crystal that was somehow infused with a special power. It may've originated with Philip II, the father of Alexander the Great. He might've used it to build his empire, and Alexander may've inherited it and done the same."

"Why do you think this is the same crystal?"

"We've observed what you've done in your writing and what Derrick's done with his music, and we've compared these things with what these rulers and the early pharaohs did. There are many parallels."

"This is crazy," Clayton said.

"Let me share with you some of our findings."

"Okay."

"First, the holder of the crystal—whom I'll call the primary— shares power with his heir, which we believe is his firstborn. Second, the crystal's power is exercised by means of some form of imagining. They used mosaics, paintings, drawings, art on pottery, and poetry, in antiquity. You and Derrick have used stories and music, respectively. Third, after the imagining, there's the dreaming. Both of you have talked about the power of your dreams in your creative processes. Next, it seems that the crystal's power enables one to manifest his will in many different ways, especially in the lives of other people. For example, after the man burst into flames at Derrick's concert, we discovered he had doused himself with gasoline, which he had smuggled into the pit, something Derrick had apparently persuaded him to do subconsciously. And finally, we believe that a person can only use the crystal's power when it has contact with the flesh of the primary. Can you confirm that?"

"That's a lot to swallow."

"Have you ever taken it off?"

"Sure, but rarely. It gives me a strong sense of connection to my dad and grandpa. I lost them when I was very young." He gazed at the crystal for a moment, put it back around his neck, and tucked it into his shirt.

"Do you know how your grandfather acquired the crystal?" Amelia asked.

"I have no idea."

"Perhaps it was a family heirloom from an earlier generation?"

"I don't know."

"Have you ever thought your grandfather's success and death may've been related to the crystal?"

"Not until now."

"As you might guess, Mr. Lange, the crystal is an object of great interest to the federal government. I dare say your life would be at risk if a leader of any one of a number of terrorist organizations or pariah countries knew you had it."

"But I guess that as long as I'm wearing it, I don't have to worry about that."

"Mr. Lange, this is not just about you. Consider the violence your son, Derrick Romano, has committed. You are implicated because his power is related to your possession of the crystal."

"That's a stretch."

"Another team is picking him up as we speak. As a matter of national security, Mr. Lange, I'm asking you to give us the crystal." She opened the briefcase again, took out a black jewelry box, opened it, and held it out for Clayton to deposit the crystal.

"I'm not going to do that," he said. "This crystal is private property, and you can't prove that it is what you say it is, at least not here. If you want to go to court over it, that's on you."

Penelope and Tarek had been still through the entire exchange, but with a nod from Amelia, they opened their jackets and put their hands on the butts of guns in their shoulder holsters.

Amelia said, "I'm sorry that it has come to this, Mr. Lange, but—"

The front door burst open. "There they are, Officers," Anna said.

Two very large specimens of New York City's finest stepped into the living room. One of the policemen was of Asian descent and the other one African.

"Mr. Lange," the black cop said, "your housekeeper reported that these people are holding you against your will."

"They say they're FBI, but I think they're phonies. They were going to steal from me, and I think my life may've been in danger. They are armed."

The cops drew their weapons.

"I'm sorry, Mr. Lange," Amelia said, "there seems to be a misunderstanding—"

"I need for all three of you to put your hands on your heads and get on your knees," the Asian cop said.

Clayton and Anna watched from the balcony as the police loaded Amelia, Penelope, and Tarek in their cruiser and a tow truck hitched up the Escalade.

"How did you know?" he asked Anna.

"I thought the Escalade was a little much for the FBI, and it didn't have government plates. So I figured it would be better to crash the meeting with the cops and be wrong, than to let something bad happen to you because I was too cautious."

"Good call."

"Do you know what they were trying to do?"

He pulled the crystal out of his shirt. "They wanted this. I told them it was only a family heirloom. But they had this absurd idea about its value."

"That's funny. I never thought it was that nice myself, though the chain is beautiful."

He laughed. "Same here."

CHAPTER 15

It was just seven years ago when Augustus held the amulet in his hand for the first time.

He remembered the moment like it was yesterday. Everything in him was enhanced. His hearing, his sight, and his sense of taste exploded with life. It was as though he could perceive and understand people's intentions more deeply than he ever had before. He grasped the breadth of his kingdom as if he soared over it with eagle's wings. Managing the institutions of government had always come naturally to him, but with the crystal his grasp of its organization was magnified a hundredfold. But all that would come to an end tonight. He had lain in bed with a fever for two weeks now. Despite all his physician's efforts—even now he sat by his side—his condition remained undiagnosed.

Nausea was always present, and he was unable to keep anything down. His body had withered from dramatic weight loss; he did not have enough strength to carry himself to the latrine. He was at death's door, and it would be up to Agrippa to carry on.

Agrippa had been his closest confidante and second in charge for years. He was intelligent, wise, and courageous. Augustus had no doubt he could successfully lead the empire. He found some comfort reminiscing over their years together as fellow warriors and administrators of the greatest nation in the world.

Augustus coughed hard. He moaned from deep inside his belly.

"My dear emperor," the physician said, "do not resist Mors' call. She is ready to receive you."

Again, Augustus moaned, and he hollered, "Help me!"

"Emperor, release your spirit that you may pass peacefully into the underworld to join other sons of god."

Augustus sucked in deeply, and he slapped his hand to his chest against the crystal. And he opened his eyes with a startled expression.

"Emperor, what have you seen?"

"I have seen Pluto and Mors. They stand side by side!"

"Do they beckon you to join them?"

"No, but they say I will recover, that I will continue my work in this world for many years to come."

The doctor placed his hand on Augustus' forehead. "Your fever is gone."

Augustus pushed his covers away, sat up, and hung his legs over the side of the bed.

"Careful, careful," the doctor warned.

Augustus stood, stretched his arms, held his hands out on top of each other as if he held a broadsword, and he swept his arms left and right. "I am well," he said, and he smiled.

PRESENT DAY

Half asleep, half conscious, Derrick remembered: He was six years old. He stood in the hallway in his PJs on his way from the bathroom to his bed. Dad had just come home. He could see him in the kitchen, standing just inside the back door. He wore that dumb sheepish expression on his face he had seen so many times before. Mom was furious.

Do you know what time it is? she said with a muffled yell.

It's ten o'clock. I told you I had to work late on this case.

That's not what your secretary told me.

You called my secretary? What kind of—
She was actually working late. She told me you left at five.
Bullshit. I was working—
You smell like you just had sex.
What's that supposed to—
You're disgusting! Get out!

And then she was crying on the phone to a friend, *He's a good for nothing bastard!*

In his dream, Derrick groaned: Mom had just told him Dad had to leave them because of his work, and things would be different.

Overnight, their world was turned upside down. Mom had to go to work full time, and they had to leave the nice neighborhood with the trees and the schools that had computers for every student and go to the housing projects with the drug dealers and the schools that had more rats than children.

Derrick was afraid. And he was angry. He was in first grade, and it was a Thursday, the day when they had art.

Close your eyes, said the teacher. *What do you see? Your parents or grandparents, your pets, our toys, perhaps other things? What is happening? Is it good or is it bad? Now open your eyes and draw what you saw.*

He had drawn a big yellow rectangle on black wheels. It had windows on its side. Above the windows he wrote, "SCHOOL BUS." Standing in front of the bus was a person, whose identity was indiscernible except it appeared to be a man wearing a suit with a scribble of black crayon for dark hair. He heard his teacher's voice:

What's happening in your picture, Derrick?
That's my daddy getting runover by a bus.
What? the teacher asked, startled.
My mom said he's a good for nothing bastard.

Two days later Joe Romano was killed instantly when he stepped in front of a school bus.

Why am I having this dream, Derrick wondered. *Where am I?*

The dream continued: It was ten years in the future:

The house in the projects was a wreck: Empty beer bottles and syringes lay on the coffee table. Dirty clothes covered the furniture. Dishes with caked-on food filled the kitchen sink. The drapes were closed. There was the smell of stale milk, coffee grounds, and cigarette smoke.

Mom was screaming at him: *If you don't like it, clean it up! You're a bum!*

I'm a bum? I give you money for rent and I'm only sixteen!

You call that money? You have no idea what it takes to pay the bills around here.

The only bills you pay are to your dealer.

Bullshit. All you do is screw and sing that nasty music!

That's where we're different: I get paid for singing, but you get paid for screwing!

You just leach off your poor mother. You don't know nothing about my life. You don't know my pain.

You don't care about anyone but your stupid self.

Go to hell and leave me alone!

You're nothing but a skanky whore!

Get out! Get out of my house, you son of a bitch!

You said it, he said.

As he turned to the door her slipper flew past his head, slapping against the wall. Laughing, he gave her the finger and stepped out onto the porch. It was early afternoon, and the air was fresh after a spring rain. A sense of new beginnings was possible even in the East Detroit projects.

A Cadillac Eldorado pulled up in front of the house. It was all red with a white vinyl top. Its stereo thundered with rap. The driver turned the music down and shouted out the window, *Hey, Derrick, what's shakin', what's breakin'?*

What ain't, Mel? He came down to the curb and poked his head into the open window, resting his arms on the door.

Mel wore a black t-shirt that was at least one size too small, showing off his ripped arms and pecks. Gold chains hung like a thick coil of snakes around his neck, fat, diamond-studded rings were on every finger, and a giant gold Rolex watch was strapped to his left wrist.

Little man, I gotcha a job tonight. It be big; it be tight. Whatcha say?

I say that be all right.

And Derrick climbed into the car.

That was the day when Derrick decided two things: Number one, he was done with his mom. She was a complete fail, and he had to let her go. And number two, he was putting everything into his music career. He had had some ideas about how to integrate his dreams with the songs, and now there was nothing holding him back.

After the show that night, Mel gave him five Benjamins with the promise of more to come. These days he was making a thousand times that for every concert, only six years later.

He opened his eyes, and a fluorescent light in the ceiling came slowly into focus. He was lying on a plastic mattress in a small room. There were no windows. He sat up. He had been stripped of his jeans and t-shirt, he wore navy-blue sweatpants, a matching sweatshirt, and white socks.

On the floor next to the cot there was a bottle of water.

"Mighty kind of y'all," he said. He held the bottle up to a camera mounted above the door. He unscrewed the lid and gave the finger to the camera as he took a drink.

CHAPTER 16

PRESENT DAY

"This thing is dangerous," Elowen insisted. She sat next to Clayton on the couch. "I mean, that there are fake FBI agents roaming around looking for it."

"It's worse than that," he said. He stood, and walked across the living room to the window, and looked out over the city. "It smells like a cabal to me."

"A secret political organization?"

"Yeah. Given all the research they had to do to put two and two together, it seems like they've been looking for this thing for a long time. That kind of effort requires lots of resources. That and the fact that this thing can be used, and, in fact, has been used to build empires, leads me to the conclusion that there are people behind these fake cops who have something in mind besides 'peace on earth and goodwill to men.'"

"You've got to get rid of it."

"I'm kind of stuck," he said, shaking his head.

"No, you're not. You could give the crystal to the government and let them figure it out. You'd be done with it once and for all, and that would be that."

"There's something else I need to tell you about this thing. But hold on for a second." He went into the office and reemerged with a small, square envelope, and sat down next to her. "When my mom died, she left behind some family secrets, things she'd never shared with me before. I grew up thinking my grandparents on my dad's side had immigrated to the States from Germany before World War II in protest against what the Nazis were doing. That was the story I'd always been fed. But it was a lie."

He pulled the photos from the envelope. On the top was the picture of his grandfather standing next to Hitler in full dress uniform, wearing the medal of valor on his chest.

"That's my grandpa," he said.

She gulped.

"Now just suppose my grandpa somehow stole the crystal from Hitler. That's more likely than not, I think. If so, then Hitler must've used it to establish the Third Reich, to launch World War II, and to kill six million Jews. So, when you say, give it to the government, I can't help but imagine what might happen if it fell into the wrong hands."

"This is terrible, Clayton. The only alternative then is to destroy it."

"The chemical fire that killed my dad and grandpa was over two thousand degrees, and the chain should've melted, and the crystal should've shattered. So I have a funny feeling this thing is indestructible. And to tell you the truth, I'm not sure I'm ready to get rid of it yet."

"What?"

"We talked about researching it. Let's do that first and see where it takes us."

"What about this cabal coming after you?"

"Now that they know that I know what the crystal can do, I think they'll keep their distance, at least for the time being."

"But what about the possibility of something bad happening like what happened to Charlie?"

"I have to write a story or poem for something to happen. I've decided to put my pen down for a while. First, we research the crystal, and then we make a decision about what to do with it."

"And Derrick and his concert of death the other night?"

"The woman, Amelia, said they were picking him up when they were here. According to the press, his band members witnessed him being arrested. So he's out of the picture for now."

"Does the director have his hand on every police department?" Raven asked. "He sprung us in less than an hour."

Amelia and her team were in a second Escalade on their way to pick up the one that had been towed. Penelope was driving, Raven sat shotgun, Amelia and Tarek sat in the second row and Jake behind them.

"In a word, yes. He says there's no more than two degrees of separation between him and any office or position of power in the world," Amelia said. She looked out the window. It was raining and cold.

"Are we in trouble for what happened with Lange?" Jake asked.

"I made a miscalculation, and the director is not pleased. We should be in possession of the crystal by now. But it's on me to make it right. You did your part by picking up Derrick."

Penelope pulled the rig to the entrance of the tow yard. Raven and Tarek jumped out to retrieve their vehicle. Two hours later both SUVs pulled into the driveway of a farmhouse in upstate New York. From the outside, the place looked like an ordinary two-story home with a wraparound porch, white clapboard siding, and a pitched roof. But with independent water and energy systems, satellite communications, and enough food to feed a dozen people for six months, it was also the team's safehouse and emergency shelter. Confinement cells were underground.

This was "the farm."

After parking in a barn, they walked up to the house.

Amelia took a shower and had a cup of tea. Then she went into the basement with Jake and Raven. She pulled open the door of one of the cells. Derrick lay on his back on a cot. Jake and Raven aimed AK-47s at him.

Amelia stepped into the room. "Please sit up, Mr. Romano."

He sat and stared. "You're not FBI, are you?"

"That's irrelevant now."

"Dark state?"

"There's no such thing. Our organizational affiliations don't concern you, Mr. Romano. We have one mission, and you can help us fulfill it."

"I can't wait to hear this."

She waved to the others to lower their guns. "There's no place for you to run, Mr. Romano. So I'm going to give you a chance to act civilly and join me and my team in a more pleasant setting to continue this conversation."

He held up three fingers of his right hand. "Scout's honor."

The dining room on the first floor was between the kitchen and living room; in it was a long oak table. The team hovered around it.

Amelia sat at the table. A file folder lay in front of her. "Please have a seat across from me, Mr. Romano," she said. "Would you like something to drink?"

"A vodka martini would be great."

Penelope stood across from him next to Amelia, and he took in an eyeful of her as he sat down. "Sorry, but non-alcoholic only," she said.

"This might be why you guys are so uptight. You can see we have the makings of a party here." He eyed Penelope again. "But some water would be fine."

Penelope went to the kitchen.

"Let me premise our discussion by saying we know you possess real power to actualize your music's lyrics through dreams," Amelia said.

"You can't prove that," he said.

Penelope returned and handed him a glass of water. He slid his hand over hers as she set it down. The other team members tensed up.

"Everyone relax," Derrick said. "You know how I feel about redheads." He winked.

Penelope shook his hand away and took a step back.

Amelia ignored the remark. "Mr. Romano, you will find it interesting to know you're not the only one who has ever used this power you enjoy. Nor are you the only one who wields it now."

"Is that right?"

"Yes, it is. To make the point I want to begin by asking you to tell me what you remember about your father."

"We already had this conversation."

"Please humor me."

"He was a lawyer, and he was a bastard. He cheated on my mom and left us when I was six."

"And how did he die?"

"He had an unfortunate encounter with a school bus. Bad Dad, so sad."

Amelia flipped open the file folder and slid Derrick's crayon drawing of the bus and his dad across the table. "And you are the one who killed him."

"Where did you get this?"

"Your mother kept everything."

"You talked to her?"

"Yes."

"How is she?"

"Same as she was when you left her, but older."

"A wasted life."

"Yes. What else do you remember about your father?"

"Not much. Mom was always angry with him."

"The source of your mother's anger was her condemnation of herself for a lie she told, which metastasized in her heart like a cancer."

"What are you talking about?"

"I'm sorry to be the one to tell you this, Derrick, but Joseph Romano was not your blood father."

"What the hell?"

"The man who got your mother pregnant was her true love, but he didn't have the same aspirations she did to live in the suburbs. So she convinced Joseph Romano he was the father of her baby and to marry her. She told me she believed she would grow to love him over time. But she didn't. And she's always regretted not marrying your real father, a man who worshipped the ground she walked on."

"What kind of fucked up story is that?"

"It's the real story, Mr. Romano. We've interviewed him."

"Who is he? Is he a drug addict, too?"

"He's a novelist whose net worth is over a hundred million dollars."

"Hold on." He closed his eyes for a moment, and then he opened them wide. "Clayton Lange?"

"Yes."

"I've always felt weirdly connected to him. I love the way his stuff comes true. I've been waiting for him to do a crime novel or horror story."

"Do you know where he gets his power to make things come true, Mr. Romano?"

"I have no idea."

"Do you know why your dreams come true?"

"Nope."

"Clayton Lange possesses an ancient crystal probably first used in fourth century BC by Alexander the Great and his father, Philip II. Its purpose was to build their dynasty. However, it changed hands multiple times for millennia until your family came to possess it. We don't know why or how yet. However, Mr. Lange has the crystal, and because you are his heir, you share his power."

"I can't wait to meet him. Are you going to tell me why you kidnapped me?"

"We want you to help us acquire the crystal from your father."

Penelope pulled up his sleeve and poked him in the arm with a syringe.

"Again?" he complained.

"I want you to think about what I just told you," Amelia said. "In the meanwhile, we can't let you dream any songs, now can we?"

CHAPTER 17

13 BC – SARDINIA ISLAND, ITALY

General Agrippa enjoyed the breeze on his face as he stood on the shore of Olbia, looking out over the Black Sea. He was only a two-day journey from the Crimean Peninsula. This whole region was his home away from home. The last time he had been here, he had restructured the government. He loved the land, and he loved the people. It would be a good place to retire. That is, if he was not already wed to Rome. He was second only to Augustus and would one day be emperor.

Together, they had grown the empire, taking Spain and Gaul, Egypt and Ethiopia, Arabia and India, and subduing the tribes in the Alps and Germany. They had transformed whole bureaucracies in many places. Ten years ago they had solved the grain shortage with ease, curating the distribution of food to the masses as effectively as the famed Jew who once sat in pharaoh's court nearly 2,000 years ago. Was his god their god? Someday they would find out. And they had rebuilt Rome from the inside out, which included his pride and joy, the most beautiful project of all: the Pantheon, which he had built for the emperor's worship. Someday he would officiate his beloved partner's interment there.

A FEW MONTHS LATER – ROME

Augustus watched the sunrise paint the Pantheon gold from the balcony of his palace bedroom on Palatine Hill. He had placed the ashes of Marcus Vipsanius Agrippa there. All his men died before him. But this one was the hardest to bear; they had been closer than brothers.

The gods had given Augustus visions of many temples, porticos, and theaters. And there were the aqueducts—the glorious aqueducts! They had recreated Rome—a city once built with clay was now built with marble. His visions for the city had been as clear as the crystalline water that washed off the mountains in the springtime, visions he gave to his artists who painted them on pottery. And then he dreamed. With the dreams everything necessary to fulfill what he had originally imagined came to fruition, without fail. And Agrippa had stood by his side every step of the way as his chief engineer.

A tear fell from his eye. And he remembered: *The Pantheon was Agrippa's most beautiful building,* he reflected. *He dedicated it to me. But how could I accept such adulation and not be condemned by the people for my pride? I had to devote it to the gods.*

Besides the building projects, the two men had established the public institutions: The police and fire brigades were his favorites, and the courier service, which delivered anything to anyone from sea to sea. And the empire's standing army was unlike anything ever conceived before: It was an institution that would not end with him to be rebuilt by the next emperor—it was an institution that would continue forever. All these things were the foundation stones of his eternal kingdom.

He released a deep sigh. Ever since he had taken the crystal from Alexander's remains, he had known Tiberius would ultimately be its heir. He had hoped for Agrippa and then his grandsons. But he always knew it would be Tiberius, who was the choice of the gods. But if Tiberius was the one, Augustus must do some things to prevent him from doing anything that would undo what he had spent his whole life building.

He would make him marry his daughter, Agrippa's widow, Julia.

Granted, he was already married to Vipsania. But Tiberius knew how this worked. He would divorce Vipsania, marry Julia, and when it was his turn, the empire would enjoy an uncontested, seamless transition of leadership.

PRESENT DAY

Usually as serene and uncluttered as a Zen rock garden, Clayton's front room was now an obstacle course of stacks of books. He sat in an armchair with a book in his lap. Elowen was reading on the couch.

"After all this," he said, waving a hand over the books, "we still don't know anything more about the crystal than when we started. We've found nothing that even remotely suggests anyone anywhere ever possessed anything like it to help them rule the world."

Elowen looked up from her reading. "I'm not seeing a breadcrumb trail, either."

"All we've got is what that fake FBI agent told me: Two persons can wield the crystal's power at the same time—the one who physically possesses it and their firstborn; that the crystal's power is active only when it touches the person's skin; and that it is activated through their artistry and dreams."

Herodotus stood at the door, wiggling his tail.

"Let's go for a walk," Elowen said.

"Excellent idea."

A few minutes later they were on the street, walking toward the river. They held hands and Clayton held the dog's leash.

Elowen said, "You know, I'm thinking our search might be more efficient if we take geography and the timeline into account."

"Yeah?"

"I think we've been wasting time on paths that were impossible. Like there's no way Confucius and Buddha could've had the crystal during the same era. They lived too far apart."

Clayton looked discouraged. "And there's another thing. If my grandpa got this thing from Hitler, what does that tell us about the power behind it?"

"It makes me want to puke to think about that monster."

"Me, too." They stood on the walkway of the Hudson River and watched the water for a moment. "I think there are two possible answers. Either the crystal's amoral and it doesn't care about ethics, or it's evil. I'm ruling out the possibility that it's intrinsically good for obvious reasons."

"That sent a shiver down my back."

"Let me think out loud for a moment about what it might mean if it is evil. I'm going to hold at bay my usual skepticism that evil is actually a thing, because it helps me to articulate another very real and very personal question, which is, what is my cost for using the crystal? If it is evil, am I evil even though my mother gave it to me as a family keepsake?"

"I suppose that might be true according to someone else's formula for justice. But if there is such a thing as *divine* justice, declaring you guilty because you possessed a thing for love of your family doesn't strike me as divine or just."

"But listen: The sacred texts of the different world religions talk about how their god or gods demand remuneration for what they have done for humanity. In other words, there's no free lunch. So what's expected of me in repayment for the benefits I've received from this thing? I'm really concerned. Is my soul at stake?"

"Half the world must be hunting for me," Derrick said. He sat across from Amelia at the farmhouse dining table again. The team observed from the perimeter.

"Actually," she said, "three days after your disappearance, the commercial media machine went silent. The exception is social media, which is alive with speculation. There are several theories about what has happened to you. One theory is that your ex—her name's Tamera? —killed you on her daddy's yacht and threw your body into the ocean. Another one is that after a lifetime of struggling with mental illness, you retired from the music industry and moved to a desert oasis in Death Valley. And, of course, there's the usual chatter one hears about missing celebrities, that you've checked yourself into a high-priced rehabilitation program at a beach resort."

He *humphed*.

"You've had some time to think about my proposal?"

"To help you get the crystal from Clayton Lange in exchange for my life? What makes you think I would consider that a real offer?"

"If we acquire the crystal before you decide to play ball with us, we'll leave you in your cell until you're an old man."

"Let's cut the bullshit. This thing is priceless. It'll make whoever holds it the most powerful person in the world—they'll be virtually omnipotent. I think you must've blown your cover with Lange because if you could've gotten it from him, you would've. So now you want me to use my power to trap him and get the thing. Did you guys think this plan up together?" He looked around at them. "Give me a break."

"What do you want?"

"I want a boatload of money in an untraceable Cayman Islands bank account, I want property, and I want you all to fuck off and leave me alone."

"I'll have to get approval from my director."

"You do that," he said, and pulled up his shirt sleeve for the injection he knew was on the way.

CHAPTER 18

PRESENT DAY

Clayton groaned. Elowen rolled over and shook his shoulder. "Baby, you're having a bad dream."

Opening his eyes, he was still for a moment, and then he sat up against the headboard. "I'm sweating like crazy," he said, as he pulled off his bed shirt. The crystal stuck to his chest. "What time is it?"

"Just after three."

"I was dreaming about Derrick. I'm feeling like I'm connected to this kid."

"Do you remember the dream?"

"He was in the bottom of a dry well, clawing at its sides, trying to pull himself out. And he was dressed all in blue."

"What else?"

He closed his eyes. "There was another person. A woman. She had red hair." He looked at Elowen. "She was one of the fake FBI agents who came up here looking for the crystal. In the dream, she looked into the well, and then she and Derrick were in New York City, in Times Square." He swung his legs out of bed.

"What are you doing?"

He patted the crystal on his chest. "This thing is telling me to write. Come on."

He sat at the Underwood in the office.

Elowen sat behind him. She looked over his shoulder, while sipping chamomile tea. "He's not a good person," she said.

"I know. But Amelia and the organization she works for are worse. They abducted him, and I'm sure they're trying to use him against me."

A short while later he squeezed the release button on the typewriter and pulled a sheet of paper from the carriage. They looked it over, side by side.

"What do you think?" he asked.

"It's inspired."

"Or it's absolute gibberish. I'm not sure what it means."

Elowen read it out loud:

> Black and red
> Be whole, be led
> By the spirit who lives in you
> For freedom
>
> Black and blue
> Be whole, be true
> With the one who's come to you
> For freedom

"I'm not a poet," Clayton said.

"You're better than my five-year-old nephew."

He chuckled and set the poem on the typewriter desk. "Let's go back to bed," he said. She took his hand. "I anticipate another really weird dream."

***

She pulled the needle from his arm. "Get up," she whispered. Her red hair fell over her shoulders onto the black jumpsuit she wore.

"Huh?" Derrick mumbled. "What time is it?" He was still wearing the blue t-shirt and sweats.

"Five-thirty."

"You're Penelope, right?"

"Yeah."

"Another interview?"

"No. We're leaving these fascists behind."

"Hell, yeah."

A few minutes later they were out the door and in one of the Escalades.

"Why the change of heart?" he asked.

"Give me a sec." They drove in silence until they were on the state highway. "Have you ever had a really intense dream with poetry and rhymes?" she asked.

"All the time," he said.

"I had a dream."

"Really."

"I was singing a song I've never heard in my life." She recited the words of Clayton's poem. "I don't know why, but I knew it was about you and me. And I knew I had to set you free."

"Do you know how he escaped?" Amelia asked. She sat in the loveseat in her living room wrapped in a bathrobe, drinking her first cup of coffee, and watching the 6:00 a.m. news.

"Penelope's gone, too," Raven said. "There was an empty syringe of Ritalin on his bed. We're thinking she must've opened his cell, given him an injection to wake him up, and they left together in one of the Escalades."

"Did she show any signs that she intended to do this earlier?"

"Nothing. I'm sorry, Amelia. What do you want to do?"

"What time did they leave?"

"It was almost five-thirty when Penelope turned the security cameras off. Jake was up at six."

"Go ahead and put in a stolen vehicle report for the Escalade, though I'm sure she's dumped it by now. Close up the farm, and let's meet at my place here in the city this afternoon."

After they had disconnected, Amelia stroked the cat. "The director will not be happy. What shall we do, Gus?" His purr sounded like a small generator. "One thing we know for certain is that this little anarchist won't be able to resist holding a concert."

"Oh, Derrick, you're so delicious."

He gazed into Penelope's bright blue eyes from his position on his elbows. "The gods know redheads are my heart."

They were at a condo he kept in Midtown Manhattan. It was not far from Times Square.

"You mean *this* redhead," she scolded.

He cackled. "All right, girl. You're my one and only now and forever."

"Deeper," she moaned, and he completed the journey.

After showering, Penelope stood at a picture window with a view of the city. Derrick was still in bed. Penelope's long, thick hair flowed down her back, leading his eyes to her little butt. "It was once my fantasy to be an actor in one of those theaters on Broadway," she said with a sweep of an arm.

"What stopped you?"

"I can't act," she tittered and jumped back into the bed.

"Come on, girl, let's go," he said.

"You're amazing," she said.

An hour later, they lay quietly side by side.

"Why did you do it?" he asked.

"Free you? I feel like a different person, Derrick. Just a day ago my mission was to break you, to pull from you everything we needed to get the crystal. But now, I see things differently. You stand for something. You're freedom."

"I feel a little disoriented," Clayton said. He leaned into the kitchen island in his pajama pants. Elowen was talking to Anna, who wore a t-shirt and shorts. The clock read 10:00 a.m.

"Would you like a cup of tea?" Anna asked him.

"That would be great," he said. "I'm going to go sit on the balcony."

Elowen put her hand on his shoulder, and they walked out together. "Are you sick?"

"I don't think so."

They sat, and she put her hand on his forehead. "You don't have a fever."

"Remember how I told you I thought I was going to have a really weird dream last night after I wrote that poem?" She nodded. "I had the dream, and I'm absolutely exhausted."

Anna brought out cups of tea. "Thanks," they said together.

"Do you remember it?" Elowen asked.

"Oh, yeah." He held the steaming cup to his lips and took a sip. "The redhead? She freed Derrick from an underground cell, they got into a black SUV, and they drove into the city."

"So much detail."

"Yeah. That's the way these real dreams are. But there was something about this dream that was different from the others: The crystal seems to have taken the initiative—it woke me up, gave me the poem, and then it gave me the dream."

"That's totally *Twilight Zone*."

"It scares me."

"Me, too."

"What do you think Derrick's going to do now?"

"What he does best. He'll have a concert."

Amelia's living room walls were paneled with dark wood. Floor lamps gave the room a rich, golden ambiance. She sat in an overstuffed armchair with Gus; Tarek and Jake sat on a couch; and Raven sat in an armchair.

"Amelia, I'm not feeling like I can trust the director anymore,"

Raven said. "The crystal is more powerful than we were told. With what happened to Penelope, we now know people can be motivated and persuaded, perhaps even brainwashed to do certain things on behalf of the person who holds the crystal."

"You've seen this before," Amelia said. "Remember the man who incinerated himself at the Rose—"

"But this was Penelope, one of us," Jake said. "We thought we were insulated from anything like this, especially since we unplugged Derrick Romano. Why didn't we see this coming?"

"We're learning about this power together," Amelia said. "It does baffle me how Clayton Lange could get into Penelope's head so easily and use her to free Derrick." The cat jumped from her lap and went into the kitchen, its claws scraping across the tile floor.

"What's our next move?" Tarek asked.

"Watch and see. Derrick will want to test his powers. I suspect there's nothing that gives a young man greater pleasure at a time like this than to give his enemies the finger."

Elowen opened her eyes. The bedroom was dark but for a sliver of moonlight that crept through the curtains. Her eyes met Clayton's.

"I've been awake for an hour," he said.

"What time is it?"

"Almost four."

"Were you dreaming about Derrick Romano?"

"Yeah. I can feel him in my bones. Now that I know our souls are intertwined, I'm conscious of tracking what's going on with him emotionally. I have this sense of euphoria right now. It's like I just drank a pot of coffee, which might be what Derrick's feeling from his freedom. Or he may've just drunk a pot of coffee."

"Do you think he's able to do the same with you?"

"Probably."

CHAPTER 19

PRESENT DAY

Clayton and Elowen were still in bed.

"Look at this," she said, and she showed him her phone. "You were right: In just a week Derrick somehow organizes a concert. And it's at Notre Dame no less."

"And I bet he fills every seat."

"He's calling it the 'My Freedom Tour.'"

Clayton grunted. "He's got more than freedom on his mind. You let a starving lion out of its cage, and it's going to look to satisfy its hunger."

"Do you think there's anything we can do?"

"Maybe. But first, I need to see if we can watch the show live."

14 AD – ROME

Augustus' breathing was labored. His fever had lasted several days, and he had no color in his face. Today, Tiberius was sure his adoptive father would die. Even if it had meant the end of the dynasty, he wished Augustus had never put on that black crystal. He had used the power well, but what did that mean for the one who would follow him?

The emperor had taught him about how to succeed as a Roman general, and he had enjoyed celebrated conquests in Dalmatia, Pannonia, and Raetia. Thus his path to the throne was all but guaranteed. But how the gods must have laughed at Augustus for everything he did to ensure that the throne was filled in the way he intended after his passing.

He had insisted that Tiberius divorce his first and only love, Vipsania—so beautiful and filled with life—and marry Augustus' daughter, Julia, a slut and the most despicable creature imaginable. And for no other reason than to relieve Augustus of his paranoia that the people would not receive him, Tiberius, as his successor.

And now it was on him to carry forth the rule of the dynasty and take responsibility for that damned crystal. He felt it reaching out to him now. But he felt old—he was old! All he wanted to do was to return to the island of Rhodes. His memories of the rocky beaches, crashing waves, and his villa with its garden overlooking the harbor made him smile. He wished he would awake in the morning with the salty air in his nose.

He looked again at the emperor's colorless face. *I wish I'd never known you or this house,* he thought. He had sat beside the bed for hours until there was the hint of a sunrise on the horizon. Augustus wheezed for breath. Tiberius stood and looked into his eyes. The emperor released a final sigh, and he was dead.

"May the Fields of Elysium be forever green for you, my lord and father," Tiberius whispered as he closed Augustus' eyes. And he took the crystal from around his neck and put it on. When the stone touched his chest, his knees shook, and he grabbed the side of the bed.

PRESENT DAY

Dazzle, Rex, and TJ sat around the table in the jet's cabin, playing poker. Usually, they would be drinking and talking through the setlist for that night's concert, but Derrick and Penelope were in the back of the plane getting it on.

When Derrick finally appeared, he swaggered down the aisle zipping up his jeans with a smirk on his face.

"I got one question," TJ said.

"Yeah?"

"How do you know she ain't no spy?"

"Because she freed me from those deep state cabal motherfuckers, and they've got shit to show for all their work."

"What's next?" Dazzle asked.

"We're playing the same setlist as last time. But I've got that new song for the closing, 'My Freedom.' It's going to kick with a funky bass and guitar lead."

"Any hints about where we're going with that?" Rex asked.

"The po-po is going to have a new nickname for me."

"What's that?" TJ asked.

"Public Enemy Number One," Derrick sniggered.

Notre Dame Stadium was sold out. More than 80,000 fans chanted "Derr Me!"

Amelia watched the pre-concert show with Gus in her lap—he purred with each one of her strokes. She watched the faces of her team on another monitor.

"Aren't we going to do anything, Amelia?" Raven asked.

"Tonight, we're going to watch and see," she said. "Remember, our objective has always been to collect and disseminate data which will help the director accomplish his purpose. Presently, we simply want to know if Derrick has regained the power he used before we restrained him."

"Why let him to do any further harm?"

"Again, our role in all of this is only to fulfill the wishes of the director, which does *not* include doing anything usually reserved for law enforcement."

"But what about Penelope?" Jake asked. "She was true blue—more loyal and hardworking than any one of us. But now she's somehow become enamored with this man. She's probably been brainwashed or drugged—we don't know—and I feel like we should help her."

"We all serve at the pleasure of the director," Amelia said. "And he has not given me orders to rescue Penelope Savage. And until he does so, we will not attempt it. I told each one of you before you joined the team that if you're behind enemy lines, we don't know you, and if you turn on us, you are our enemy, and we will kill you on sight. Nothing has changed."

The chant of the tens of thousands at the stadium was a roar. Amelia watched the whole venue pulsate with the shouting and foot stomping.

Tarek rubbed his chin thoughtfully. "I understand what you're saying, Amelia. But if people die tonight, don't we have some kind of responsibility because we didn't do something?"

"None," she said. "You all need to think more carefully about what you're talking about. Besides the fact that we have no such directive, for the sake of argument, let's say we did get involved. What would we do? We wouldn't be able to arrest Derrick again. There are real police at that stadium; there are hundreds, if not thousands of them. And I'm sure Derrick's surrounded himself with bodyguards who are quite aware of what we did earlier.

"We could shoot him, I suppose. But that would cause a riot and thousands of people would be hurt or killed. We could shut down the power of the venue, but again, a riot would ensue. So, when you think about it, you can understand how we're actually quite fortunate that it is not our responsibility to interfere with Derrick Romano's mischief tonight. Our end game is simply to acquire the crystal."

Derrick knew he could sing all night and not a single person would leave. He had longed for acceptance since early in his life, and this did it for him. He could hardly wait for the grand finale—he would be a hero to a lot of people.

"What are you going to do if he tries something?" Elowen asked.

She and Clayton sat on the couch in the living room and watched the concert on the big screen TV.

Clayton pinched the chain around his neck. "Humility is one of humanity's greatest virtues."

After nearly three hours of rapping, Derrick stomped across the stage singing,

> Pick up da weapon
> And let's go
> We got nothin to lose
> We done wit da snooze
> And we pick up da gun
> And have a little fun
> And set da man on da run!

The crowd sang with him the refrain:

> Set da man on da run!
> Set da man on da run!
> Set da man on da run!

With a drum solo and ear-piercing feedback, the band finished. The whole stage went to black, and the stadium was still, silent for a complete thirty seconds. And fireworks exploded. The people waved their posters in the air and screamed, "Derr Me!"

Clayton and Elowen leaned forward on the edge of the couch.

"Here it comes," she said.

He ran a finger through his chain.

Rex, TJ, and Dazzle came back out, and the crowd's roar doubled in volume. Dazzle and TJ set down a funky rhythm, and Rex peeled off a rift for the new song. The people screamed, "Derr! Derr! Derr!"

And Derrick stepped under the spotlight. He rapped, "If there ain't no justice, we don't obey. Give me freedom!" Whirling blue lights filled the stage, the pit, and the whole stadium. He sang,

> Gangstas on da street
> Let 'em catch da beat
> Da flashin' blue light
> It never been right
>
> Now it ain't so hard
> To stomp the guard
> Cuz da warden's no more
> For he be on da floor...

"Sounds like he's trying to open the prisons and jails," Jake said.

Amelia watched him and the others—they appeared worried. They were good people; they felt a real sense of concern for the welfare of other people. But what would it matter if everyone in jail was suddenly free? In truth, half of them would be picked up within 48 hours, and most of the others would be taken in or shot dead in a month.

"This could get ugly real fast," Tarek said.

The police knew the fans were all believers in what Derrick was rapping, and they fled the stadium.

> Derrick thundered,
> Now it ain't so hard
> To stomp the guard
> Cuz da warden's no more
> For he be on da floor
>
> In a pool of blood
> A liberating flood
> And dey set 'em free
> And dey let 'em be....

"Does anyone see anything on the news channels or on the web?" Amelia said.

Tarek's face shone with the white light that came off the monitor of a second tablet. "Nothing yet."

"What do you think's going on?" Raven asked.

"I think Clayton Lange has learned how to manipulate the power of the crystal," Amelia said.

Dazzle watched the others as he played. He and TJ were in perfect sync, and Rex played as well as he ever had—his fingers feverishly ran the frets of the Stratocaster. But something was not right for Derrick. He had seen him perform thousands of times, but tonight he was different. As he sang the last verse, they made eye contact, and Derrick shook his head—he was done. Dazzle made a final cymbal crash, and the whole stage went to black.

Everyone gathered around Derrick backstage.

"What happened to you, man?" Dazzle asked. "You look like you saw a ghost."

"Get me out of here," Derrick groaned. "I don't want the roadies to see me like this."

Rex put his arm around him, and security guards formed a wedge in front of them and a wall behind them.

As they made their way to the door, Derrick yelled, "Where's Penelope?"

"I'm right here," she said over the mountain of muscle that separated them.

"Come with us, baby."

They hustled outside to a stretch and got in. Derrick and Penelope sat across from Rex, TJ, and Dazzle. The door shut, and the driver tore out of the parking lot. Derrick buried his face in his hands. "I feel like I just got kicked in the gut."

"What happened?" Penelope asked.

Derrick looked up and met her knowing eyes. "This new dad is no better than the old one," he said.

* * *

"That was dramatic," Elowen said.

Clayton clicked off the TV. It was just after 1:00 a.m. The only light was the moonlight shining through the windows. The tourmaline crystal lay in a dish on the coffee table; its edges sharp in the moonlight.

"And uneventful, it would seem," Clayton said with a smile. "There was no breaking news about prison guards being stomped to death or the incarcerated walking away from their prison cells en masse." He picked up his cellphone and clicked open a news page. "This headline just came up a minute ago: 'Does Derrick Romano Have a New Heartthrob?'" He showed Elowen the image—Derrick was reaching out from inside a limo to Penelope who was climbing in. "Look at his cow eyes."

"Is that the redhead you saw in your dream?"

"That's her."

"This is too crazy."

"It is. And something else: When I first took the crystal off I didn't feel anything. But now I'm missing it."

"Are you craving it?"

"It's a gnawing sensation."

"You know what I think would be good for you, for us?"

He winked. "Of course."

"That, too. But I'm thinking we should travel."

"Have a destination in mind?"

CHAPTER 20

38 AD – ROME

Quintus Naevius Cordus Sutorius Macro, or just Macro, sat in only his tunic on a rock in the woods, examining the hilt of the sword that had been his companion ever since he was a young boy. It was the short sword, which was what he favored in hand-to-hand combat. He had trained for his future service in the Roman legion with it.

His father and grandfather had also served in the military. It was an honorable profession—all Romans revered it. And he had risen to the top as prefect of the Praetorian Guard. He had enjoyed great power and esteem in the position for several years now. But these things came at a high cost.

The Julio-Claudian dynasty had been chosen by the gods for the propagation of the race. And how it had prospered the people! The borders of the kingdom never stopped expanding. It was the envy of the world. Tiberius had been the shining light of the empire in so many ways—he had always been his hero. As the adopted son of Caesar Augustus, he had been the assumed heir of the throne.

Unfortunately, Tiberius was tired of the political game even before he became emperor. His best years lay behind him. So he was frequently on holiday, paying little mind to what was happening in his realm. That was how Sejanus—that cruel and wicked bastard who had once held the job, he, Macro, now filled—had begun what the people called the Reign of Terror.

My gods! Macro thought. *The only thing worse than a man with a chip on his shoulder is a prefect with a chip on his shoulder!* Sejanus had purged all the public offices through his so-called courts of treason, ridding himself of men whom he hated.

Tiberius was furious when Macro told him about what Sejanus was doing, ultimately planning to make himself a dictator, and he had given Macro permission to end his career. That was how he came to order Sejanus' execution by strangulation, and the desecration of his body on the Gemonian Stairs—a very undignified but appropriate end for such a creature. The people and then the wild dogs had their way with Sejanus' corpse for three days until there was nothing left but a bone, which a doctor identified as a femur.

It was not long after Sejanus' end that Tiberius decided he had had enough of the city and retired to the island of Capri. He was over 70 years old, and his move seemed reasonable enough.

While they were enroute to the island, the emperor revealed the crystal to him. He had pulled it out from under his tunic, and the way it glistened in the sunlight had caught Macro's eye. He was mesmerized.

"This thing has been a blessing to the dynasty since Augustus," Tiberias had said, "and if something should happen to me, you must be sure my nephew, Caligula, gets it, for the gods have spoken and said he is its rightful heir."

At first, Macro felt privileged to be the personal bodyguard of the emperor and to be entrusted with such a responsibility as the transfer of the crystal. However, it was while they were on the island that he realized Tiberius was insane.

Now he regretted accepting the role, and he confessed to himself, *My gods, how I wish I could have spared my eyes and ears from what the old man did! The children he raped in his orgies! It was evil. A young boy wept and begged for mercy, and what did Tiberias do, but make me break the child's legs and throw him into the sea! And this kind of thing went on for seven years! Where did these perversions come from but that crystal?*

Macro was sorry he had seen what he saw and done the things he did. But a soldier is under the authority of his commander, and he cannot resist him short of pain of death.

In the end, it was a disease of the loins that brought the emperor down. *This must be repayment for his corruptions,* Macro thought. The priests prayed for his recovery, but to no avail, or so the people thought. Upon the announcement that the emperor had died, while he still lay in his bed, Caligula took the throne.

But Tiberius awoke, and he begged for food. Macro prayed, *My gods! Will you answer the prayers that Tiberius might live but not the cries of the children whom the same man ruined?*

Few knew Tiberius' had recovered, however, and Macro reasoned that if it were truly the will of the gods for him to live, they would have given the emperor the strength to fight against the guards whom he ordered smother him under a pile of clothes.

But Caligula was no better. He was crazier than Tiberius! He did few public works, and for everyone that he did do, he erected a half-dozen private residences which he filled with prostitutes and little boys for his own pleasure. *My gods, how I feared this would lead to the end of the empire as we knew it!*

He had heard the whisperings of the Praetorian Guard and Senate that this emperor could not stand, and he wondered, *What will become of this crystal that gives men power but also drives them insane?*

Macro gazed on the shimmering blade as he had so many times over the decades. And he smiled. It was unfortunate that the previous glory of being prefect was not enough to blot out his present humiliation of being stripped of all power by Caligula, the emperor whom he had brought to power and served faithfully. That was the cost of having risen so close to the sun.

He reversed the blade. Its tip touched his belly through the tunic, and a drop of blood appeared on the white linen. He grasped the hilt of the short sword with both hands, and drove it in, straight up under his ribcage and into his heart. Behind his eyes there was darkness. His hands were sticky wet. He was dizzy and he fell off the rock into the grass. And the last thing Macro tasted was the earth.

PRESENT DAY

The sky was clear and there was moderate traffic in Lower Manhattan.

Stepping out of the bank she worked for, Elowen took Clayton's hand. "How do you feel?" she asked.

"Each day, I feel a little better—that gnawing feeling is practically gone. And I feel less anxious with the crystal in a safe place."

"Getting out of town for a few days will be good for you. I've always wanted to go on safari."

"Tanzania is beautiful this time of the year. And it'll be fun to do something different for Christmas."

They walked down a flight of stairs to the subway. "I should be back by three or four with my bags," Elowen said.

"That'll give me plenty of time to get Herodotus to the kennel and to pack. And you're good with your employer and the band?"

"Everything's all wrapped up." The screeching sound of the oncoming subway echoed through the tunnel. "That's my car," she said.

"I'll see you this afternoon."

The two-level mansion in Malibu had an exterior of white metal and reflective glass, and it was tucked into the side of a hill facing the Pacific Ocean. Derrick and Penelope lounged in beach chairs alongside the pool. She wore a red microkini and he, trunks. They drank margaritas. The band members were on floats in the pool. The Doors' album, *Morrison Hotel,* played in the background.

"I'm so depressed," Derrick said.

"I'm sorry," Penelope said.

"From all the research you did when you were with that group, do you think Lange got rid of the crystal or what?"

"One of the things we figured out was that for the power to be used by the son, the father had to have physical contact with it."

"Do you know where it came from?"

"We were thinking Alexander the Great and his dad, Philip II, were the first to use it. And they found evidence it was later used by at least three pharaohs."

"Pharaohs, as in Egyptian pharaohs?"

"None other."

"That's sick."

"One of the issues we faced was long periods of time where the crystal's use wasn't obvious. How and when Clayton Lange came into possession of it was still a mystery when I left the team."

"I've got to get this thing from him. By the way, have you figured out what inspired you to free me?"

"Well, I've always been a huge fan. So when you became a target of the effort to get the crystal, I was in conflict. From what I know about it, I'm thinking Lange may've used it to persuade me to do what I wanted to do anyway."

"Why do you think he did it?"

"Fatherly instinct?"

"Yeah, right."

Elowen had taken Clayton's suggestion and dressed down in sweatpants and a sweatshirt. "I've never been in first class before," she said, as she pulled her legs up into the sumptuous leather seat.

"It's a lifesaver for a long flight," Clayton said.

"Twenty-six hours—that's lots of movies. But this is going to be the perfect getaway. I love nature, I adore animals, and I love to travel and take pictures."

He leaned in, and they kissed.

CHAPTER 21

41 AD – ROME

The Praetorian Guards dined in their barracks. The tables were long and filled with pitchers of wine and platters with cuts of beef, racks of lamb, pork shanks, and ribs.

Officer Cassius Chaerea stood at the head of his table and spoke: "Caligula's building projects bankrupted the empire almost as fast as his perversions corrupted its soul. The evils he committed in his orgies in the palace were matched only by his incest with his sisters and then prostituting them! And there were the games. You all remember that time when there were no more prisoners to be given to the lion for execution, and, like a spoiled child, he refused to return home so soon in the day. And what did he do but order an entire section of innocent spectators to be given to the beast!

"Some of you might argue there were things he did which were economically beneficial for the empire, such as the harbors he built in Rhegium and Sicily. Indeed, those were excellent public works with great benefits, especially for imports from Egypt. But how, I ask you, did this prosperity compare with his self-indulgence, such as the fortune he spent building that floating bridge from the resort of Baiae to the port of Puteoli? And just to ride his horse from one side to the other to contradict a soothsayer's prediction that he had no more chance of becoming emperor than of riding a horse across the Bay of Baiae? I tell you he bankrupted Rome and killed public confidence in his government. And all for nothing. Such arrogance!"

Several men raised their wine-filled chalices in agreement.

"And apparently believing his madness would best be served by more madness," Chaerea continued, "Caligula shored up the treasury by assassinating nobles and seizing their estates! But it was not just the rich he held with such contempt. The peasants loathed him for taxing the very things that brought them joy and pleasure. I'm talking about weddings and prostitutes! Such foolishness!

"But what I've told you is not why I was the first among my brothers—some of whom are here tonight—to plunge a knife into his chest. What finally convinced me that he had gone too far was his plan to move to Egypt. If he left the Eternal City for Alexandria, our world would've been cast into chaos. It would've not been unlike what happened when Alexander, who is the father of us all, left us all alone and the kingdom broke down into warring factions. It is whole now, but we owe nothing to Caligula.

"Brethren, preserving the empire as a single unified entity is the Praetorian Guard's principle duty, and that is why Emperor Caligula is now only a memory."

"What has happened to the amulet?" asked one of the Praetorian.

"It is in the great vault under the Pantheon of Agrippa," Chaerea said.

"And Claudius is emperor," said another Praetorian. "What shall we make of him?"

"He had neither the wit nor the will to use the power of the crystal when he stood to inherit it outright," Chaerea said. "He will rule, but not with the amulet, and we shall enjoy peace for a time."

PRESENT DAY

"He's hunkered down at his place in Malibu. Penelope's there with him," Jake said.

He was sitting with Amelia and the others at the table in the conference room in New York City. The recessed lighting was gradually increasing in brightness as the late afternoon sun set.

"For now, she may be more of a caretaker than a lover. I believe his spirit is probably so intertwined with the crystal he may've lost the will to sing," Amelia said. "Tarek, what's Clayton Lange's status?"

"Our connection in Tanzania said he and his girlfriend are simply being tourists on a safari. Nothing unusual has happened, as in extraordinary appearances of exotic animals or anything else that might lead us to believe he's been using the crystal."

"Because Derrick's powerless, we can assume Clayton has not been wearing the charm," said Raven.

"If he didn't take it with him," Amelia said, "where do we think it is?"

"His condo?" Jake said.

"The first thing tomorrow, you and Raven search it," Amelia said. "The doorman doesn't know you. Go as NYPD and take a search warrant."

Clayton sat on a foldout chair by the campfire, drinking coffee.

Tumo refilled his cup. He was the overseer of the camp, cooking, driving, and providing security, especially against elephants whom he chased off the grounds in the middle of the night. "As soon as the guide arrives, I'll set out breakfast and call the others," he said.

The air was crisp, and the sun shone over the acacia trees and the grasses that waved in the breeze. The fire and grill were downwind from four sleeping tents, which were arranged to create a common area in the center.

Elowen emerged from her and Clayton's tent and made her way to Clayton. Her hair was pulled back in a ponytail. She wore hip-hugging cargo pants and a white button-down shirt, the ends of which were tied up around her waist.

"Even camping, you're gorgeous," Clayton said.

"*Shush,*" she chided, and sat next to him.

A white SUV pulled into the camp, parking next to Tumo's identical rig. The driver was Jack, the guide. His clothing was different shades of olive green and brown, from his bush hat to his suede hiking shoes. "How you doing?" he greeted them. His skin was ebony black, and his accent, English, revealing an education in that system.

"I can't believe how quiet it is," Elowen said.

"Nothing but the distant sounds of foraging beasts," Jack said, smiling.

"I'm going to steal that line," Clayton said.

"I'm flattered."

Tumo rang a bell, and minutes later the other three couples who were on the safari were eating a breakfast of bread, boiled eggs, cheese, and fruit. By eight o'clock, they were loaded up into the two vehicles. Elowen had a camera bag in her lap from which she pulled a lens which she swapped for another one, on one of the two camera bodies that hung around her neck.

"You brought a lot of gear," Clayton said. "Have you worked professionally?"

"Nah. I've been a shutterbug since middle school. I shot for the yearbook and that kind of thing. Now it's just for fun."

From the truck, Elowen panned and photographed a herd of zebras racing across the plains. The guide spotted a lioness and her cubs under a cover of trees, they parked, and Elowen captured the pride with a long lens.

Later, as they ate lunch under a tree stand, a family of elephants ambled past them. "One of the smartest animals in the bush," Jack remarked.

They watched in wonder until sunset as a host of different creatures wandered across the plains in packs or alone, hunting for or gathering food.

The first night, Tumo grilled tilapia and served it with potatoes and vegetables. The routine was to stay the same for nearly two weeks: breakfast, exploring, lunch on the trail, more exploring, and a sit-down dinner in camp. As they toured the prairies, tree-fringed rivers, and rolling hills, Clayton and Elowen added leopards and monkeys, black rhinos and giraffes, wildebeests and hippos, and dozens of different species of birds to their sightings.

Finally, there was the big feast everyone had been waiting for. There was an acacia tree on the edge of the camp. It was twilight, and the tree was filled with lanterns that lit a table set for dinner. There was the mouthwatering aroma in the air of a boar roasting on a spit. Wine, sweet potato soup, roasted vegetables, and a variety of sauces covered the table.

Tumo pulled the pig off the spit, set it on a cutting block and went to work on the shoulders and legs, carving them into servable portions. He cut the pork loins and the back meat with the dexterity of a surgeon. He finished, cutting out the ribs.

Once everything was prepared, Jack stood at the head of the table and toasted. "Merry Christmas!" he said with his glass raised. "Here's to Africa, God's gift to humanity, and to you who have found a new place in your heart for this great land. Cheers."

Everyone clinked their glasses and drank.

During the feast everyone shared stories about the wonders they had seen and the experiences they would never forget. As they ate hand-churned vanilla ice cream for dessert, Clayton stood with his glass.

"My friends," he said, "I do not have words sufficient to express my joy for our days together in this timeless land. The animals and birds, the savannas, creeks, and rivers have provided me with a sense of well-being that has taken me to a place where I've rediscovered an inner peace I had forgotten existed. You've all been part of this, and I thank you. Here's to you. My hope is that we may all take with us many warm memories from our time together. Salut!"

Everyone raised their glasses and joined the toast.

"But the fondest memory I will take home with me," Clayton continued, "is how during this time I fell more deeply in love with Elowen Kensington." He set the glass on the table and pulled a ring box out of his pocket. Elowen watched him, her eyes big. He knelt before her. "On this occasion in the heart of East Africa," he said, "among our friends with whom we've wandered the grassy plains and hiked the hills of our first parents from millennia past, I, Clayton Lange, ask you, Elowen Kensington, will you marry me?"

He opened the box. The ring was a studded white gold halo with a giant diamond in its center.

With her hands on her cheeks, Elowen whispered, "I will," and she held out her hand.

He took the ring from the box and slid it onto her finger. The whole table applauded, and Clayton sat next to her with his arm around her shoulders.

CHAPTER 22

PRESENT DAY

The only sound was the hum of turbine engines at 30,000 feet, and Clayton watched Elowen snuggled up in a ball next to the window as content as a cat. The flight to Las Vegas from Tanzania had taken 40 hours, but adrenaline had carried them both. They had been like kids anticipating Christmas. But after their wedding vows, they were in zombie-land. A few days of pampering took care of that, though.

Clayton's body wanted to relax and sleep with the uniform drone of the engines, but his level of anxiety was steadily rising as they flew closer and closer to New York. There was no way he could ignore what he was feeling—pain is always a warning sign that a bad condition needs attention before it becomes a very bad condition.

The crystal was going to be a burden for as long as he possessed it.

Should I at least try to destroy it?

If it did have a mind of its own, and if it was innately evil, there would be consequences for attempting to do such a thing. *If there are spirits involved, they will avenge themselves,* he reflected, and then he realized the right side of his brain might be getting in the way of rational thinking.

On the other hand, what was rational about any of this?

I am losing my mind, he thought.

That was a possibility.

Was there someone he could talk to? A psychologist might be helpful. A spiritualist might be better. But what would they do, try to raise up Alexander the Great for some answers? That seemed like a bad idea. How about a Catholic priest? The Catholics had lots of experience with traditions outside the orthodox Christian faith. But who would know? Maybe the monks from one of the old orders?

But if they knew anything about the crystal, would they admit it? How about a geologist? But there was no reason a rock guy would know anything more about a magic crystal than he did. An historian? But he had read thousands of pages of history, and there was nothing about a black tourmaline crystal. The closest he had gotten to anything even remotely sounding like a manifestation of the crystal's power was in the folk tales of *The Arabian Nights*.

The crystal is so secret there've probably been only a couple dozen people in the world who have ever known anything about it, and most of them are dead, he thought.

There was no science that could speak to it; there was no philosophical paradigm for it; and there was no theological subset to help one understand what to do with it.

As the plane landed, Clayton opened his eyes, yawned, and stretched his arms. "Home sweet home," he said as he looked over Elowen's shoulder out the window.

"How'd you sleep?"

He looked at his watch. "I got about an hour's worth. How do you feel?"

She leaned in and they kissed. Holding up her ring finger, she said, "I can't wait to tell everyone about our new status." They kissed again.

"Anna's been trying to get me married for a long time," he said.

"I don't want to hear about it," she said as she leaned in for another kiss.

He turned on his cell phone. "Interesting," he said. "Anna's tried to call me half a dozen times since we took off."

"Maybe it's Charlie."

"I hope not." He clicked on Anna's number, and it rang once. "Hi, Anna," he said. "How're you doing?" He listened. "You're kidding me," he said. "No, don't call the police. We'll be there in a couple hours. Thanks. Bye." He looked at Elowen.

"What is it?" she said.

"Anna's at the condo. She was going to spruce things up and put some food on for us, but she said the place has been trashed."

"How's that possible?"

"That's my question, too."

It was about five in the evening when they got to the condo with their luggage. The door was open, and Anna sat on a chair in the living room with her face in her hands. The upholstery of the furniture had been slashed open. Artwork was scattered across the floor— the paper backing of the framing had all been ripped out.

Clayton, seething, snarled, "What in the hell?"

All the cupboards and drawers in the kitchen had been emptied onto the floor in a thick film of mayonnaise, olives, and broken glass.

Anna stood next to Clayton as he surveyed the mess. "I'm so sorry, Mr. Lange," she said.

He turned and wrapped his arms around her. "This has nothing to do with you, Anna. We'll bring in help to put it all back together."

Elowen had gone into his office. She stuck her head out. "Clayton, check this out."

He joined her. "Good grief," he said. "It looks like the aftermath of a tornado."

Two filing cabinets had been emptied onto the floor, along with hundreds of books, and the contents of his desk. The PC was gone, and the loveseat had been gutted. The Underwood typewriter looked like someone had taken a hammer to it.

He picked up its carriage from the floor. "Now this makes me mad," he said.

"What're you going to do?" Elowen asked.

Slapping the carriage across the palm of his hand, he turned and looked at the desk. It had been cleared of everything except for four black-and-white photos neatly lined up across the top: the pictures of Grandpa with his fellow soldiers and Adolf Hitler. The box where he had kept his mother's secrets was in a pile beside the desk, including the black jewelry box. Its contents of gold rings, watches, and bracelets all seemed to be accounted for. But the one thing that mattered the most, Grandpa's Nazi valor award, was gone.

"That damned cabal did this."

"How can you be certain?"

"Amelia Williams, or whatever the hell her name really is, sent her people here to find the crystal, which they didn't, of course. But they did find the one thing they can use against me." With the carriage in his hand, he pointed at the photos. "I knew I should've thrown it all into the Hudson."

His phone rang and he answered it: "Hi, Elliot. It was great. I highly recommend going. Hey, you won't believe— What? She did?" He paused for a long moment. "For crying out loud," he said. "Well, she sent her goons to the condo, and they trashed it from top to bottom. It'll take a couple of days to put it all back together. We'll get a room at the Ritz-Carlton. Remember those photos of my grandfather? They left those nice and neat on my desk, but they stole the medallion. Okay. We'll put our heads together. I'll see you tomorrow. Bye."

"He knew already?" Elowen guessed.

"That woman contacted him. She said she now knows that he and I were hiding information about my family's connection to Hitler and the Nazis, and that she can make this factoid front page news."

"But she's willing to forget about it if you give her the crystal?"

"That's what it sounds like."

The hotel room was quiet, and the bed was perfect. But it was a sleepless night for Clayton. He was angry and frustrated, and he couldn't turn his brain off. Not wanting to disturb Elowen with his tossing and turning, he made his way to the bar in the lobby.

Amelia had attached a ribbon to the Nazi medal and hung it on a necklace stand on her desk. It gleamed in the light from the desk lamp.

The phone rang. She did not break her gaze from the medallion as she answered the call.

"Hi, Jake," she said.

"Hi. I'm in the hotel lobby. Clayton just came down and went into the lounge."

"Good work. Keep an eye on him. If he leaves, don't lose him."

After the bar closed, Clayton retreated to the coffee shop, where, after scouring the Internet for updates on Derrick, he read several newspapers. It was 9:00 a.m., and he called Elowen: "I'm down here in the coffee shop. No, I couldn't sleep. Yeah, all night. I'm going to go see Elliot now. Talk to you later."

He came out to the curb and jumped into a cab.

Jake was in another car. "Tail them," he told the driver.

"That'll be extra, pal. And if I get a ticket, you're paying for it."

He shoved a hundred dollar bill through the hole in the Plexiglas between them. "That should get us started."

The cabbie grabbed the bill and shot out into traffic.

Twenty minutes later, Clayton got out of the cab at an office building in Midtown.

"Double-park," Jake said. "When he comes out, I want to be ready to follow him." He passed the driver another hundred.

Clayton took the elevator up to Elliot's office. The door was ajar, and he went in.

The publishing agent stood at a window looking out over the city. Elliot turned and faced him. "Your heritage has reared its ugly head. Amelia Williams seems to have sniffed you out, and now she's blackmailing the both of us. Who is she, and what was she talking about when she said you have something that belongs to her?"

Clayton shook his head. "She's the front person for a cabal whose mission is world domination."

"Of course she is."

"I'm not making this up. She came to my place a few weeks ago pretending to be FBI. She had a crew, and she was investigating what you and I've been talking about, you know, this immediate futurism."

"I see."

"In the course of our conversation, I discovered that that crystal I've worn, you've noticed it, the black one?"

"Yeah?"

"It's magical, and it has a history that goes back at least twenty-four hundred years."

"Let's sit. Would you like something to drink?"

Clayton sat across from Elliot at his desk. "I've been up all night. Some joe would be good."

Elliot called his secretary and asked her to get them both a coffee. He folded his arms and looked up at the ceiling for a moment. "Twenty-four hundred years ago," he said. "That would be the era of Alexander the Great."

"That's right."

"I knew it!"

"What?"

Elliott stood and walked across the office to a shelf filled with old, tattered paperbacks. He pulled one out and handed it to Clayton before he sat back down. Clayton read the title: "Miracles, Legends, and Myths Before Technology."

"According to that book," Elliot said, "there have been dozens of strange, supernatural manifestations for millennia, many of which were linked to supposed magical amulets and talismans."

The secretary came in with the coffees, setting them on the desk.

"Is there empirical evidence for any of it?" Clayton asked.

Elliot chuckled. "Hardly. All the stories are anecdotal. The point I'm making is that your experience is not the first time I've heard about something like this, and frankly I'm not surprised that one of these magical charms has finally shown up." He sipped his coffee.

"That makes me feel better, a little. But only a little. I've got a problem now, and I don't know what to do about it."

"It is a problem, and it's a problem we share."

"I'm sorry, Elliot."

"Can you imagine the headline? 'Jewish Literary Agent Conceals the Secrets of a Nazi War Criminal.' It wouldn't go over well at temple."

"At least you've retained your sense of humor."

"Sometimes that's all we have left, my friend. In any case, I see you're not wearing it now. What've you done with it?"

"I stowed it in a safe deposit box."

"Not a bad idea."

"As you know, yesterday Elowen and I got home from the safari, and the condo had been ransacked. They were looking for the crystal."

"And they found the pictures and medallion, instead."

"Yep. And to add to the drama of this whole thing, I've discovered I share this crazy power with another person."

"No kidding?"

"When I wear the crystal, he has equal access to its power."

"This must be about the continuous flow of power for dynastic rule," Elliot said.

"You're really into this kind of thing."

"In a literary sense, I love it."

"Same, but personally, it's a nightmare."

"What's your relationship to this other person?"

"He's my son, whom I didn't even know existed until a few weeks ago."

Elliot whistled.

"He's in Elliot Berkowitz' office," Jake said, sitting in the cab.

"Good," Amelia said. Gus purred in her lap. "That means they're working on a plan. Stay on him in case he decides to retrieve the crystal."

"Got it."

<hr>

"Have you thought about using your power against the cabal?" Elliot asked.

"Of course, but if I put it back on, my son will be re-empowered."

"That bad?"

"He's a very dark character who has it out for me."

"Pray tell."

"The rapper, Derrick Romano."

"Oy vey."

"My thoughts exactly. Did you read about his last concert?"

"No. What'd he do this time?"

"He was trying to bust open jails and prisons around the country. But I took the crystal off before he sang the song all the way through. Fortunately, nothing happened."

"So, even though there's the risk that he'll behave badly when he has this power, you can counter it."

"I'm not sure that will always be the case. I did think about destroying it. But I came to the conclusion that's probably not possible."

"Undoubtedly. When I was a kid, the books that got me into reading were sci-fi war novels and paranormal thrillers. An assumption you often find in these books is that when magic is in play, there may also be demons and angels."

"Do you believe in them?"

"For me they represent powers I can't otherwise explain."

"That makes sense."

"In any case, if you somehow did destroy it, the cabal would really come after you, and you wouldn't have any way to defend yourself."

Clayton sighed. "Are you suggesting the best thing to do is to just give the damned thing to the cabal?"

"Absolutely not! Make yourself the emperor of the world and do good. Play it out. You don't know the end of this story. In fact, it sounds like you're in charge; you're the narrator and the protagonist. And if and when your family's affiliations with the Nazis becomes public knowledge, what will it matter? You'll have the power to absolutely crush your enemies."

"Wow."

"And when you do all this, my only request is that you remember me. Make me your minister of propaganda or something." He laughed.

After his meeting with Elliot, Clayton was on the sidewalk, calling Elowen. "Hey, you," he said.

"Hey. I'm leaving just now, going out to Brooklyn for band practice. How'd your meeting go?"

"Elliot's a good man, and he's an encouragement. But the best we could come up with was that I should be king."

"That's not even funny, Clayton."

"I thought it was. Anyway, we can talk about it later. You're playing tonight?"

"Yeah, nine o'clock. Are you coming?"

"I wouldn't miss it."

After the call, Clayton hailed another cab and went back to the hotel. The fragrance of the body lotion Elowen had used still hung in the air. He lay down and sleep finally came to him.

Jake's cab trailed him.

It was seven o'clock by the time Clayton awoke. After showering and grabbing a bite to eat in the lobby, picked up a taxi. "Carlyle's in Greenwich Village," he told the driver. It was an easy ride, and ten minutes later he was at the club.

"How's Herodotus, Mr. Lange?" the hostess asked.

"He's good. Elowen and I were on vacation, and I haven't picked him up from the kennel yet."

"Would you like a table by the stage?"

"That would be great. Thanks."

Jake was on his phone. "He's at the jazz club in the Village where his girl sings," he said.

"Okay, call it a night. We'll pick this up tomorrow," Amelia said.

Elowen threw Clayton a kiss as she sang, and he threw one back to her. After the set, she sat with him.

"You sound great," he said.

"Thanks. It feels good to be back on stage. How was your day?"

"After the meeting, I went back to the hotel and slept."

"All day?"

"Yeah. I needed it."

She put an arm around him.

"So it really was Elliot's idea that I should give world domination a try. I know it sounds crazy, but he has a point. It might be the only practical solution."

"As in, the better of two evils?"

"Right."

"But you're a writer, not a politician. You'd hate the job."

"That's probably true."

"Of course it is."

"What do you think I should do?"

"Destroy it."

"We talked about that, and we're pretty sure that's impossible. In fact, it might make things worse. The crystal is more than a rock."

"This narrows your options, doesn't it? If you keep it, you use it or leave it at the bank. Or you can give it away. If you give it to the government, inevitably it'll turn up in the hands of a despot who'll take over the world. Meanwhile, Amelia will destroy you out of spite. On the other hand, if you give it to her cabal, a despot will still take over the world, but at least you'll be able go on and live your life."

"Maybe."

CHAPTER 23

PRESENT DAY

Clayton unlocked and pushed the door open for the condo.

He and Elowen and Anna stood in the doorway.

"Looks like new," he said.

Anna went into the kitchen and started opening cabinets. Clayton and Elowen ventured into the bedroom.

"You wouldn't know it had been razed," Elowen said as she ran a hand over the bedspread.

They went into the office. "It looks good, except for this," Clayton said, and he picked up the carriage of the Underwood from the desktop. "Someday, someone is going to pay for this."

"Does it have sentimental value?"

"Dr. Edward Freiwald, the head of the English Lit Department, and I were great friends in grad school. We spent hours reading pages of our work to each other or talking about writing. That was his typewriter, the only thing he had brought from Michigan with him to New York City besides the shirt on his back when he began his writing career. I'd told him that anyone who could actually type on that monster and turn out a book deserved any and all praise they got. He died ten years ago and as it turned out he had willed the darn thing to me. He left a card that said, "Clayton, may every word you type on this monster be blessed with praise."

"I'm sorry."

"Me, too." He sniffled as he set the carriage down.

Anna joined them. "Everything is in order, Mr. Lange?"

"The refrigerator?"

"They restocked it just as I asked them to."

"Who does this kind of work?" Elowen asked.

"It's a cleanup outfit I learned about from some research I did for an espionage novel I wrote a few years ago. They're very expensive, but very thorough."

"And let me guess, they can even make dead bodies disappear."

"Well, that's what I wrote in my book. But I don't really know."

"I remember."

Anna shook her head. "Would you two like lunch now?"

"That'd be great, Anna. Thanks," Clayton said.

After they had eaten, they went for a walk. "I think I'm ready to call it a day with this crystal and to give it up to the cabal," Clayton said.

"But we need some kind of guarantee that we'll be safe," Elowen said.

"You're right. Any ideas?"

"I do. I'm thinking that the cabal has to have some skin in the game...."

It was several hours later when they returned to the condo. Anna was leaving, and she gave them instructions for dinner that was ready to be served.

They ate in the dining room. "Whether it's Italian or French or Americana, Anna does it well," Elowen said.

"She's remarkable," Clayton said with another bite from a slice of the ketchup-lathered meatloaf.

After dinner, they sat on the couch in the front room and enjoyed cherry spumoni and espresso. Clayton asked, "Shall we give Ms. Williams a call?"

Elowen nodded as she licked the back of her spoon.

He picked up his cell and clicked on the number, setting the receiver to speakerphone.

"Hello, Mr. Lange. How are you?" Amelia answered.

"Just lovely, after putting my home back together."

"I apologize for your inconvenience, Mr. Lange."

"Really?"

"Surely. Now, to what good fortune do I owe your call?"

He smiled. "What is the crystal worth to you?"

"I am so glad to hear that you've come around. In the end—"

"Please cut the crap and answer the question."

She cleared her throat. "The director's prepared to offer you twenty-five million dollars, using whatever means you prefer."

"I don't need your money. What else have you got?"

"We have prime real estate in several locations in Manhattan, Los Angeles, the Florida Keys—"

"I don't need your property. What else have you got?"

"What do you want?"

"Glad you asked. I'll give you the item in question on three conditions."

"Okay."

"First, you're going to pay the bill for the wreckage your crew did to my home. Like I said, I don't need your money, but it's a matter of principle."

"Consider it done."

"Second, you're going to reveal your identity to me. I want your driver's license, Social Security number, and other pieces of information which will make you vulnerable to me."

She jeered at him, "Not in a million—"

"Okay. Please send my regrets to your boss that we couldn't come to an agreement. I'm sure he'll understand. Goodbye."

"Hold on," she said. The line was quiet for a long time. And then she continued, "Okay. I'll do it. What else?"

"Third, you're going to guarantee the safety of myself and everyone to whom I'm related or associated, including but not limited to my wife, Elowen, her parents and grandparents, and our aunts, uncles, and cousins, plus Anna and Charlie Kravets, and Elliot and Sarah Berkowitz.”

“Mr. Lange, this is not possible.”

“My grandmother always used to say, ‘Where there’s a will there’s a way.’”

“That must be thirty or forty people.”

“Probably closer to a hundred.”

“I can’t take responsibility for that many lives. Accidents happen every day.”

“Not to these people, not if you value your anonymity.”

With that, he let his offer hang in the air. They could hear her breathing.

“Okay, it’s a deal,” she said.

“Tomorrow morning you’ll receive a text on your cellphone with instructions,” Clayton said, and he disconnected.

It was just after 9:00 a.m. the following day, Amelia was on the subway to Lower Manhattan, and she was on a call. “Did you make the wire transfer to Lange for his repair bill?” she asked.

“That’s done,” Tarek said.

“I’m going to guess he’s sent me on a treasure hunt,” she said.

The subway squealed to a halt.

“The tracking device is working fine,” Tarek said. “We can see you’ll be at your first stop in about a minute.”

“I’ll call you when I know where I’m going next.”

Amelia deboarded at Bowling Green and took the escalator to street level. A Starbucks was on the corner. She went in, looked around, and waited. A barista held up a to-go cup and called out, “One upside-down venti caramel macchiato double-blended with heavy cream, one shot of honey blend, and a banana for Westin from Midtown.”

She went to the counter and took the cup. “Thanks,” she said, rolling her eyes. A black coffee would have suited her. Outside, she took a sip of the drink, scrunched up her nose, and dropped the cup in a trashcan on the corner. As she went back underground, she took her phone from her purse.

Tarek picked up the call. "Where next?"

"I'm going to the Westin Hotel in Midtown."

"Be careful."

"Always," she said.

She boarded the next subway. Every minute or two it stopped: The doors slid open, people got off, people got on, the doors slid shut, and the car shot down the tracks again.

They probably got the idea of a treasure hunt from a movie, she thought. *But it doesn't really work anymore because of GPS and our ability to set a team on the ground in seconds.* Her lips twitched with a grin.

She got off at 59th Street and walked up the stairs to the sidewalk. The tracking device on her phone showed that an MD 520N helicopter—the quietest aircraft of its kind—was not far away. It would descend with a moment's notice to an altitude where a team of four men could repel to the ground when she finally sighted Clayton, and they would take him to the farm.

A young man with black trousers and a red jacket in front of the Westin Hotel opened the door for Amelia. "Welcome, ma'am," he said.

She muttered a thank you and went in. To her right was a podium with a brass nameplate marked "Concierge."

A gray-haired man in suit and tie standing behind it asked her, "Are you Madam Amelia Williams?"

She raised an eyebrow. "Yes."

He handed her a piece of paper. She unfolded it and read it to herself: *Meet us at Tony's Restaurant in Little Italy.* She turned on her heel and returned to the street. She knew where Tony's was. Every New Yorker did. When she had been at the Starbucks, she was only a couple blocks away from it. She had sent lots of people on treasure hunts before, but she had never been on the other end. And she was angry. She could not wait to bring hell down on Clayton Lange.

Back on the subway, she looked around at the faces of her fellow passengers. *It was very clever making me backtrack.* She got off at the next stop—she could play this game—and she waited for another train to see if anyone had followed her. There was no one, and she reboarded.

At Spring Street, she got off, went to the surface, and began her walk to the restaurant. It was less than a quarter mile away. Her phone dinged.

"We see you," Tarek had texted. "I'm meeting them at Tony's," Amelia texted back.

She saw the façade of the restaurant. Little Italy had retained a lot of its charm over the years with its eateries, markets, and grocers. Many of them were still owned by the Sicilian families who had made their fortunes here generations earlier. Tony's was one of them—it was a neighborhood treasure.

Amelia stepped into the restaurant's foyer. It was all black with silver molding and dimly lit. Supple leather benches lined the walls. There was the hint of garlic in the air. A man with slicked back hair and dressed in a black suit and tie invited her to follow him. It was after lunch and there was only one table still being served—four men, all of whom could have been soldiers for a mafia family. Amelia followed the host through the main dining hall and into another room, one that might be suitable for a reception.

There was a woman seated at a small table typing on a tablet. She wore her gray hair on top of her head in a bun, and she sported a beige pencil skirt and white blouse with a bow at the neck. Eyeglasses sat low on her nose.

Amelia saw a service entrance to the room. In the mafia movies, that would have been the escape route for her assassin.

"Madam, please be seated," said the host as he pulled a chair out from the table across from the woman working on the tablet. She sat. "Would you like something to drink?" he asked.

"Mineral water, please."

He left them, and Amelia watched the woman. She said, "What's the meaning of—"

Without looking up, the woman said, "Just a moment, please."

A waiter dressed in all black appeared with a bottle of mineral water and a glass. He served her and left the room.

Without looking up, the woman asked, "What's your Social Security number?" Amelia recited it. "May I see your driver's license, please?" Amelia produced it, and the woman took it, scanned it with her cellphone, and handed it back.

"Are we done?" Amelia asked.

The woman looked up over the top of her glasses and met Amelia's stare. "Ma'am, I don't know who you are or why the person who hired me has gone to the expense of verifying your identity, but I do not have the power to give you further instruction until I have finished what I am doing." She looked back down at the screen of the tablet and typed.

Amelia folded her arms and closed her eyes in frustration.

Five minutes later, the woman said, "The address on your driver's license has changed since it was issued. What is it now?" Amelia told her. "Thank you. I confirm that," the woman said.

"May I ask what system you're using?" Amelia asked.

"I'm sorry, but it's proprietary," she said, and she typed some more. Thirty minutes passed before she looked up again from the screen. "Amelia K. Irons, alias Amelia Williams, is this information correct?" she asked as she spun the tablet around.

Everything in Amelia's life had been reduced to numbers, names, and places on a map. It was all there. She clenched her teeth. It showed that she had just turned 70 years old and that she had never married. As she scrolled down the pages, she saw they had a list of her schools with links to her transcripts, every location where she had ever lived with photographs, her complete employment record with dates and salaries, names and locations of her family members—living and deceased—her travels—*This woman obviously has a tie-in with Customs, the IRS, and the FBI,* she thought—her bank accounts with balances, and just to rub in the thoroughness of the investigation, an analysis of her credit card purchases by category for the past ten years.

I've spent a fortune on dining, she mused.

"Is this all correct, ma'am?" the woman asked again.

"Yes."

"Thank you. Your confirmation has been added to this document as an audio signature giving the collector of said information the power to sue you if they should discover anything in this report is fraudulent and/or you intentionally meant to mislead them."

Amelia stared at the gray-haired woman.

"Would you like to retract anything which is in this report because it is inaccurate, Ms. Irons?"

"No."

She typed some more. "I have submitted your data to the other party. Here is their response." She turned the screen around again. It read: "Go to the post office on Houston Street and 6th Avenue. Ask for a package with your alias name on it. After you have received it, open it for further instructions."

Amelia looked at the woman hard. She returned the stare without expression. "Please press 'Enter,' Ms. Irons," she said, "and the message will delete itself. This is for security purposes."

Amelia released her breath and pressed the key. "Now may I leave?"

"Yes, you may. Have a nice day."

Sitting at his desk, having reviewed Amelia's background information, Clayton said, "This was a great idea, my love. And we couldn't have done this without your connection at the bank."

"Gladys is hardcore," Elowen said.

"Her nickname suits her."

"'The Hammer'? Absolutely."

"And Tony's was the perfect setting."

"It was, wasn't it? My band loves playing there. When I told the management what we were doing, they said I'm family, and that they still have enough Sicilian treachery in their blood to stick it to the enemy from time to time."

Amelia paid the cabbie, went into the post office, and asked for her mail. The postal worker retrieved a small manila envelope. Amelia ripped it open inside the building. Inside there was a key with a note. It read, "For a safe deposit box at Washington Federal Bank on Canal Street."

Out on the sidewalk, she looked down the street in both directions. *Very clever, Clayton,* she thought. *I'm no closer to bringing you in than I was before. I'd hire you if I didn't want to kill you.* But maybe he would show up just to mock her. She could not touch him, and he knew it. The helicopter was still close by; she would not send it home quite yet.

When she got to the bank, she found a manager who escorted her to the safe deposit box vault. Inside, there was a long, metal table with a couple of padded chairs. Three of the four walls were filled with secured crypts. Amelia followed the manager to a box in the middle of the far wall. He invited her to insert her key into its lock. She did so and he did the same with the bank's key. He opened it and slid a metal box out, which he placed on the table.

"Please take your time, ma'am," he said.

"Thank you," she said, and she sat down with the box.

After he was gone, she opened the box's lid. There was a black plastic jewelry box. She took it out, sat it in front of her, and opened it. The overhead fluorescent light made the black crystal shimmer.

And she remembered: *When I was a little girl, my family had nothing. My father was a drunk, and my mother's three jobs were hardly enough to keep a roof over our heads and food on the table. I slept together with my two sisters in a double bed. I was number three, and I wore their hand-me-downs until I graduated from high school. I remember when I bought my first new skirt at J.C. Penny's, and I swore I'd never fall into poverty again. Never.*

The crystal held her stare, and her thoughts continued: *I have done well. I completed law school at Yale, and I fast-tracked at one of the best firms in New York City. And here I am now, sitting with the single greatest source of power known to humanity. If I took this crystal for myself, I could rule the world.*

There was a voice. The bank manager's. It was distant: "Ma'am, it's been thirty minutes." She was riveted to the black crystal. "Ma'am, are you okay? Do you need more time?"

With every ounce of her strength, she pulled her eyes from the crystal and redirected her gaze to the man. He stood at the entrance to the vault. "I'm done," she said.

Without looking at the crystal again, she snapped the lid box lid shut and put it in her purse.

Out on the sidewalk she texted Tarek: "Call off the helicopter. We're not bringing Clayton Lange in today."

PART TWO

CHAPTER 24

PRESENT DAY

Victor Penlick's penthouse office suite had a bird's-eye view of the cityscape of downtown Dallas. The space was a chilly 64 degrees year around; it kept one alert. He was in his 60s, but his hair was still thick and dark. He had held the gray at bay, as his stylist liked to rhyme. His eyes were big and steel-blue and his jaw firm. He was clean-shaven, and he projected strength and confidence. His suits were tailored Italian. One floor below the office was his private gym.

Ever since he was a young man, he had been Vic to friends and family, except to his estranged son, Dakota, who called him Victor. That hurt his feelings—he did wish he called him Dad. He had not seen Dakota for ten years, but he had kept up on his progress—the kid had fulfilled his dream of becoming an engineer. His field was oil, and he was working in Kuwait.

Victor's golfing buddies called him by his last name, Penlick. It was all the same to him, though he did enjoy the blushing frustration of those who struggled over what to call him when they realized how much power he wielded. He was fluent in seven languages, including Spanish, Vietnamese, and German. This was helpful in his law practice, among other things.

Right outside Victor's glass-encased office sat his secretary,

Madison Jewel. She tapped away on her computer. There was a long black conference table in the middle of the suite and a 70" screen monitor on an inside wall.

Victor sat at the conference table with Amelia Irons at his side. They faced the monitor. The black jewelry box with the crystal was on the table in front of her.

The faces of the six men who were in Victor's gentlemen's club were on the big screen. They all lived in the US, but some were teleconferencing from other parts of the world. Ben Greenbaugh was on retreat with his board of directors and transmitting from the Bahamas. Adam Stone was signing a deal with a Chinese billionaire in Taipei. And General Hammerman was taking a break from a NATO meeting in Paris.

"I know we all want to cut to the chase concerning the amulet," Victor said. "But first I want to address some old business."

The heads on the screen nodded.

"The oil pipeline debate has finally ended with a five to four decision in our favor," Victor continued. "Thank you, Justice Orden for pulling the trigger and pushing the Indians back to the reservation."

"My thoughts exactly," Roger Skarlyle said—his granddad had dug the first well on the property, and he would have been proud. "I'll add my own metaphor to the conversation: The operation was surgical. Our business is the heart of America, and oil is our blood. All the valves are clear now, and we're planning for a beautiful future."

"And, Senator Cockler," Victor said, "thanks to Oliver Tanneman's withdrawal, you'll certainly win your primary."

"It is a shame that his wife, a fifty-year old woman, can't walk across a shopping mall parking lot without the threat of rape," the gray-haired legislator said.

"And finally, Ben, I believe you have some good news for us," Victor said.

"Yeah," Benjamin Greenbaugh agreed. "We got a big break on that antitrust suit. We're all happy, and so is the A.G., who realized there are times when even the best among us can use a leg up."

"Poor guy. Thirty years ago a frat boy getting a high school girl pregnant was called courtship." General Hammerman chuckled. "But today it's called rape. *Tsk, tsk.* It was a story that should've been quashed a long time ago."

"Now, about the object of our mutual interest," Victor said, "that which has been the source of power for emperors, kings, and—as it turns out—an author and a musician: First, I want to thank Amelia for all the work she's done to bring it to us."

Everyone smiled broadly, except for Amelia.

"The box you see in front of her contains the black tourmaline crystal, which was not an easy acquisition. It cost Amelia dearly. A part of her deal with Clayton Lange was that she give him critical information concerning her identity."

Amelia turned and stared at Victor with contempt. He stared back at her.

"Ms. Irons, the men have the right to know everything which might impact their own security."

Breaking the stare, Amelia turned her gaze back to the jewelry box. She was going to regret not keeping the crystal for herself.

"My friends," Victor said, "what I propose now is that before we do anything with the crystal, we study it. It would be to our benefit to understand as much about it as possible before we put it to use."

"For example?" Senator Cockler asked, broadcasting from his office in DC.

"We have friends in the professions whom I would like to bring in," Victor said. "For example, Wyett Wolfson is an optical engineer. Adam, you introduced him to us two years ago when we capitalized his lens-making business."

"He is the best," Adam said.

"And I'm also thinking about an electrical engineer and a geologist. They could conduct tests which would be invaluable. Myself, I'm a history buff, and I want to dive into the crystal's historical background. We know a little about its origin, and we know a lot about Clayton Lange and Derrick Romano, but it would be immensely helpful to know more about how it was used during the time in between."

Justice Orden asked, "In the meanwhile, how are we going to keep this thing from falling into the wrong hands?" He was probably more wary of people's intentions than any of the others. Suspicion was second-nature to him after 30 years on the bench. "In fact, how can we be sure you won't take it for yourself?"

"The stone is being stored in this office in the safe," Victor said, glancing over his shoulder at a vault that was mounted in the wall behind him. "Anyone who examines the crystal, including myself, will do so here, under the supervision of armed security. In addition, there's twenty-four-hour visual security on the safe, which you all have access to. Whenever the safe is opened, you will be alerted. And of course, our agreement still stands concerning the secrecy of our special relationship and each man's ability to unravel it. How's that sound?"

"You answered my question, Victor," the judge said.

Clayton and Elowen stopped at the edge of the lake in Central Park and gazed across the water. It was February and just a little above freezing.

Elowen knelt and scratched Herodotus under the chin. "I love his sweater and boots."

"Frenchies don't do well in the cold," Clayton said. "By the way, is everything set for the dinner tonight? Do we need to pick up anything on the way home?"

"Anna said we're good to go. How're you doing?"

"I feel like I'm ready to start writing again."

"That's your wellness meter, isn't it?"

"I like to compare it to what you've said about how singing transforms your heart."

She smiled and took his hand.

That evening, everyone mingled over sparkling cider. There was a German chocolate cake with candles on a service table in the condo's dining room, a Happy Birthday! banner had been strung overhead, and there were purple balloons and streamers. Classical music played in the background.

Sarah, Elliot's wife—her naturally curly gray hair falling to her shoulders—eyes bright and inquisitive—engaged Anna, discovering they both loved bridge.

Elliot talked to Charlie about how he might work with a ghost-writer to tell his story.

"This is a celebration for everyone, including you and Charlie," Elowen said to Anna, as she joined her in the kitchen. "Let me help you serve," she said. It took some coaxing, but Anna finally relented, and together they filled the table with platters of pot roast and lamb and side dishes of vegetables, potatoes, and Caesar salad.

As they ate, Clayton raised his glass of cider. "I want to toast Elliot, the world's best publishing agent. Without you, I would still be at the coffee shops reading bad poetry. Happy birthday, my friend!" he said. Everyone clinked glasses, and they drank. "Secondly," Clayton continued, "I want to congratulate Charlie for how he's taken hold of his rehabilitation with so much vim and vigor." Again they clinked and drank.

"Thank you, Mr. Lange," Charlie said. "You've been an inspiration. The prosthetics you bought have made me into the Six Million Dollar Man. I'll always be in your debt." He raised his glass to Clayton.

Everyone toasted Clayton, whose face was turning bright red.

Elowen said, "Clayton and I have a couple of announcements to make. You'll notice the purple balloons: We're having a baby in October!"

Everyone clapped.

"Secondly," Clayton said, "we're moving to Queens."

"Where?" Sarah asked.

"Flushing," Elowen said.

Elliot chuckled and, looking at Clayton, said, "You've finally come to your senses."

"It only took a baby," Clayton said.

CHAPTER 25

PRESENT DAY

Curled up on the couch with a cup of tea, Elowen watched the winter rain fall on the balcony.

Clayton sat in an armchair. "It's coming down in buckets."

"It's relaxing. After we move, I'm going to miss the view."

"How're you feeling?"

"Still nauseous. But the doctor said the first trimester is always the hardest, and I should be over it in a week or two."

He spotted a book on the end table near her head. "What've you been reading?"

"It's about the Roman Empire. Have you ever thought that after Alexander and the pharaohs, the crystal could've made its way to Augustus?"

"Who used it to lay the foundation for an empire that would last five hundred years?"

"That's what I'm thinking. And later there was Constantine. He founded the Christian church, didn't he?"

"Christians will tell you Jesus founded it, St. Paul wrote its dogma, and Constantine opened the door for it to grow through a series of public policies."

"Augustus and Constantine were in power for so long and did so much, if anyone in that kingdom had the crystal, I'd bet they did."

312 AD – ROME, ITALY

"When we meet Constantine and his misfit army in the field beyond the river, they will run like girls or they will fall like fools," Maxentius declared. "I propose we put this before the men that they might wager among themselves."

His servants chuckled as they assisted him into his armor and weaponry in the palace armory.

Members of the Praetorian Guard looked on, but they did not laugh.

"Emperor, may I speak?" Lucius Clarus asked, already arrayed for battle with breastplate, helmet, and broadsword.

"Speak, Prefect," Maxentius said.

"Rome has twice been under siege, and twice its great walls have proved reliable with little loss of life. We anticipated that Constantine would lay siege to the city, too, and we have stores of food and water which will last for months. Why do we challenge the gods?"

"The soothsayers have said that the enemy of the Romans will perish today, and I intend to fulfill that prophesy," Maxentius said.

His servants cinched up the straps of his breastplate while others attached metal shin guards.

"I will ride to your glory, Emperor. But may I speak again?" Lucius asked.

"Yes, but be brief!"

"It is dangerous to underestimate an enemy. If I may be so bold? Constantine's army is not misfit. He and his troops crossed the Alps and marched on Segusium, which they took easily. And then they descended on Taurinorum and Milan. We were crushed in Verona, and Prefect Pompeianus was killed. Nothing stopped Constantine between Aquileia and Mutina. And now he taunts us from across the river to meet him in battle. Emperor, I beg you to reconsider our options."

"How did *you* ever rise to the exalted position of prefect? Clearly, it was an oversight. Have you not listened to your own scouts that our troops outnumber Constantine's two to one?" He stared at Lucius with disdain, and he met the eyes of each one of the guardsmen who stood with him. "Have you all become eunuchs?" With his armor complete, his servants stepped back from him. He brandished his sword. "This day," he declared, "I will immerse my blade in the blood of Constantine!"

The Pantheon in Rome had been built by Agrippa for his friend and emperor Augustus in 27 BC. But after the turn of the millennium, it burned to the ground. It was rebuilt, but it burned again. However, the underground vault was never touched by flames. In 126 AD, Hadrian rebuilt the monument on a scale even grander than its original magnificence. And the vault guarded the black tourmaline crystal just as it had since it was last seen by Caligula's Praetorian Guard in 41 AD.

Constantine and General Aelius sat on their horses just north of Rome, surveying the hundred thousand troops that gathered on the other side of the Tiber River.

"Emperor," Aelius said, "I have never questioned your command, and I do not question it now. But I ache to know what your spirit says to you as you watch this army gather?"

"I have always been filled with this strange confidence, my friend. I do not understand it myself," Constantine said. "But my spirit has served me well. And the vision I had two days ago while we marched multiplied this confidence a thousandfold. In the sun I saw the words, 'THOU SHALT CONQUER.' They were seared into my mind like an iron burns a mark into the flesh of an animal. Aelius, I feel drawn to the Eternal City by a power greater than anything I have ever known. It has gripped me."

"We all believe you are guided by the gods," Aelius said.

"Or perhaps by my mother's one god."

"I meant no offense, Emperor. Of course, your mother's god, Christos."

"It is an interesting proposition, Aelius, and worthy of consideration, is it not? The followers of this god came to Rome, and they have been a benefit to all people, even to those who have persecuted them. They have been model citizens, showing charity to the poor and sick and obeying all the Roman ordinances. Well, except for one."

"They will not burn incense to your worship?"

"And I take no issue with that."

"But it will bankrupt the incense makers," Aelius jested.

"Indeed. But I'm sure the charity of the followers of Christos will sustain even them." As they spoke, Maxentius' cavalry began to cross the river on the Milvian Bridge. "Mother told me these people pray for me and that their god guides me. I was skeptical of her claim, that it was wishful thinking. However, the vision of light which I described to you persuaded me to believe Christos is going to use me to deliver the Roman people from this despot emperor."

The stone bridge groaned under the weight of the tens of thousands of troops and their thousands of horses. As they lined up before them, Constantine rode the length of his cavalry and infantry with his sword raised over his head. "We shall conquer!" he shouted repeatedly. A thunderous hoorah followed him down the line. He came back around, and front and center, he cried, "Victory for Christos!"

As his men had done so many times before, on his signal they charged the enemy and broke through their line like a hot iron through lard. The infantry followed the charge, pushing hundreds of Maxentius' troops into the river. Enveloped by a thousand praetorians, Maxentius held his ground. When he saw his remaining soldiers retreating to the city, however, he followed them. But it was too late. When he was in the middle of the bridge, it collapsed into the river, and he drowned.

That night, the people from the city came to Constantine's camp to celebrate the victory, shouting, "The tyrant is dead! Long live Constantine!" They came with roasted pig and goat, fish and cheese, and bread and wine. There was music and dancing, and the party continued until the early morning hours.

After the people had returned to their homes, stars filled the night sky, and Constantine traced the constellations with a finger as he lay in a pile of wolf furs. Fires burned around the perimeter of the camp, and he could hear his men sing. They would revel in their victory until morning. They would be remembered forever as the greatest army that had ever fought for the empire.

It gave Constantine pleasure to rise before the sun and go on long walks, drinking in the sights, sounds, and smells of nature, whether it be from the plains or rolling hills, a forest or a river, a garden or a desert.

He walked the ruins of the Milvian Bridge and envisioned the battle from the day before. He knew it would always be remembered as the beginning of his eternal residence in the hearts of the Roman people.

Late in the morning, priests and senators emerged from the city with the masses following them. Constantine was resplendent mounted on a horse, robed in a purple toga banded with gold. His generals wore white togas, and together they rode to meet the Romans with their troops in tow.

When the peasants saw Constantine, they hailed, "The emperor is divine! May he live forever!"

Aelius rode next to Constantine. "They are happy to see you."

Constantine glanced over his shoulder at the horseman who rode behind them with Maxentius' head on a pike. "Perhaps even happier to see what has come of him."

The city was filled with streamers and banners flapping in the wind. Jubilant cries from the citizens and festive music filled the air. All the people—the rich and the poor, shoemakers and farmers, midwives and artists, shop owners, musicians, and servants—lined the streets, applauding and cheering. As Constantine and his men passed by, the people fell in after them, creating a mile-long train which wove through the streets.

The parade ended at the entrance to Circus Maximus, which filled to capacity with over 200,000 spectators. As Constantine rode into the Circus with his entourage, the people stamped their feet, and chanted, "Victory belongs to Constantine!"

There was a throne in the first row of seating, filled with cushions embellished with semi-precious stones. A eunuch guided Constantine to his seat. Aelius and the other generals sat behind him.

Robed with an ornate ceremonial cloak, the prefect of the city came into the center of the Circus. Upon welcoming the people, he directed his attention to the emperor and declared, "Emperor Constantine, you have liberated the Eternal City from tyranny! Our hearts are filled with love for you! Your appointment is divine, and we can only fall to our knees with gratitude! I am just one of the tens of thousands of this city, and yet with confidence I say for us all that we are honored and proud to stand with you today as a new and prosperous era is born!"

The prefect stepped aside, and the priest of the Temple of Jupiter came forward. He wore a red chasuble over a white cloak. With his arms raised to the sky, he blessed Constantine, his army, and the athletes. He closed with a benediction and declared, "Let the games begin!"

The people lost themselves in the celebration—their merriment was without comparison, eating and drinking with abandon as innumerable tournaments of strength and daring took place in the Circus. On the second day, amid the people's jollity, Constantine and his generals walked the winding streets of the city to the Senate House. Hundreds of people followed them.

Aelius was perturbed when he noticed many citizens found opportunity to brush against the emperor. "The people touch you intentionally. Shall we increase security?"

"No, Aelius. That is not necessary."

"They will claim power came forth from you, and that they were healed of some malady or delivered of a demon."

"No, but they ache to be counted."

A hundred men wearing white togas banded with purple were seated in three rows in the Senate House. Some remained seated and spoke in whispered tones to one another, while others stared straight ahead expressionless, and still others stood when Constantine entered.

"What do you think?" Aelius asked.

"Some hope for pardon," Constantine said. "Others believe I will exile or execute them." He let his eyes settle on each man. "And yet they have all come to welcome me."

"They know it is pointless to hide."

"But do you see the resolve in their eyes? They are not afraid to die for their city."

Constantine took his place in the center of the senate and raised his right hand with the palm up. The room fell silent. "Venerable and esteemed senators of Rome, thank you for your gracious welcome. It is a great privilege and honor to be among you as your emperor now for two days. I have found the experience most gratifying, and I will be happy to continue for at least another two days."

A few of the senators managed a chuckle.

"The first thing I would like you to know is I hold no ill feelings against any one of you who supported Maxentius. Whether you did it for personal gain or to promote his politics, if you swear to support the cause of the Eternal City under my crown, it is my desire that your legislative powers be fully restored to what they were before Diocletian stripped them away twenty years ago." The senators began to applaud, but Constantine again raised his hand, and there was silence. "And, furthermore, I desire your assistance in reforming what is left of the Roman government."

A senator shouted, "The great Augustus!" And another one shouted the same. And then every man stood, and they chanted in unison, "The great Augustus!"

Constantine turned and left the building with his entourage.

Just outside the door of the senate stood the high priest of the Temple of Jupiter who had blessed Constantine at the games, still wearing a cloak and bright red chasuble. "Holy Emperor," he addressed Constantine, "I am Petronius Armianus, a Praetorian and the high priest. It is for the preservation of the whole kingdom that the gods have given me the responsibility to open a door to a power whose limits are only in your imagination."

"Is this a riddle?"

"No, but it is an enigma. Please come with me."

They walked side by side to the center of the city. Constantine's generals followed. With each step, Constantine felt the familiar tug on his spirit grow. It had an affirming quality to it, like the feeling one might have if he was on his way to a party in his honor.

Shortly, they stood before a monumental building with a frieze with the inscription: "Marcus Agrippa, son of Lucius, three times consul, made this."

"It is here," the priest said.

"The Pantheon?" Constantine asked. "I feel it."

"We shall enter the temple in a moment. But first, I must tell you something: In antiquity, the Praetorian Guard monitored the welfare of the state. And to the point, if an emperor lost his mind, the guard would remove him from office and replace him. Caligula was such an emperor, and he was assassinated more than two hundred seventy years ago by the guard."

"Yes, I know the story."

"What you do not know, however, is the guard had an unusual problem with Caligula. He possessed a strange power which they believed he might use to dismantle and destroy the empire. They had discovered he intended to declare himself a god and retire to Egypt. He had already begun the process to accomplish this, and they had no reason to believe he would not continue. So they killed him, and the prefect removed from his person the thing that had given him his strength."

Constantine looked at the priest with amazement. "I have heard of this device, but I thought it only a legend for the peasants, a story to help them understand an emperor's power."

"Many of the things which have been said about it are fictions, such as giving its bearer the ability to fly or to call fire out of heaven. But the object of which I speak is real, and it is a source of great power, indeed. It rests in the underground vault here at the Pantheon, and now I will reveal it to you."

The priest led Constantine and the generals around the rows of columns on the porch of the Pantheon and through its great doors. Inside, the space was cavernous—the apex of the dome was seven stories high.

"Emperor," the priest said, "I can take only you underground to the vault. Your men must remain here."

"And if I were to command you to do otherwise as the final authority of all things mortal and immortal?"

"I would take my life, and this object of which I speak would be lost forever."

Constantine saw the priest held a blade to his own gut, and he waved over Aelius. "Do you share with me my confidence that my mother's god brought us here?" he asked.

"I do."

"Then share with me the confidence that that same god is with me as I go alone with this priest into the vault to retrieve the device which has been preserved for me."

"But—"

Constantine held up a hand. "My mother's god."

Aelius nodded and kept his peace.

The temple's interior was circular, and Constantine and the priest walked on the diagonal from the entrance to the incense altar. There was a recessed space with a metal door on the righthand side along the wall before the altar. The priest pulled a ring of keys from underneath the sleeve of his toga and unlocked the door. He took a torch from the wall, pushed the door open, and invited Constantine to step onto the landing. He followed, shutting the door behind them.

"There is only one set of keys. It has been passed down from generation to generation, from high priest to high priest, under the watchful eye of the guard." He began to descend the stairs.

There was another metal door at a second landing, which the priest unlocked. Inside, there was a large open space, in the center of which was a single long wooden table with chairs. Locked chambers filled the walls. A ladder leaned against one of them.

"What do these safes hold?" Constantine asked.

"The relics and treasures of great men who have preceded us," the priest answered.

He handed Constantine the torch and walked across the room to the ladder, which he took up and set in a corner of the room. He climbed to the top, unlocked one of the safes, and pulled from it a silver tray. He came down and set the tray on the table. The two men sat side by side and stared at the object in the tray. Constantine's torch flickered, and light danced over the object: a black tourmaline crystal on a white gold rope chain.

The priest explained what he had been taught about how the crystal was used in tandem with art and dreams to bring to fruition whatever the one who wore it desired. "And when you don this crystal," the priest said, "you and your first born will possess this power equally for the sake of the kingdom."

"Where did it come from?"

"Tradition holds that it was created by the Oracle of Hades, who is our god, Pluto, for Philip II of Macedonia and his son, Alexander. After Alexander's death, the kingdom was divided up among Alexander's generals, one of whom took a second name: He was known in Egypt as Pharaoh Ptolemy I Soter. He's the one who took the crystal, and there it remained in Egypt until Caesar Augustus attained it."

Constantine handed the torch to the priest and picked up the crystal by its chain. He dangled it before his eyes; its facets glimmered in the light. And he placed it around his neck. The crystal touched his flesh, and he slammed the palms of his hands flat on the table. "I saw an explosion of light," he exclaimed with a gasp.

CHAPTER 26

PRESENT DAY

With spring, the leaves of the elm trees were full, and they cast shade from one end of the avenue to the other. Clayton and Elowen's new home in Flushing, Queens, had two stories with a pitched roof and dormers, and even had an enclosed porch. Forest-green shutters accented the white siding. Rose bushes distinguished the property line.

Clayton came up into the kitchen from the basement. The appliances were all stainless steel, the counters were granite, and the floor was travertine. Anna was unpacking dishes.

"Is everything in one piece?" he asked her.

"Yes, everything's fine, Mr. Lange."

"How's Charlie?"

"He's in the cottage taking a nap. We're so happy you invited us to come live with you."

"We can't live without you, Anna, especially with the baby on the way. And Charlie is a great addition to the household. I didn't need a handyman in the condo. But now I can't say how invaluable he's been." Clayton looked out the window to the backyard. Herodotus chased a squirrel. "It feels like a great place to raise a family, doesn't it?"

"It does, Mr. Lange."

Clayton's sneakers squeaked across the hardwood floor as he made his way from the dining room to the front room. There was a room on the right separated from the rest by an opening with crown molding. His desk and boxes of books already crowded it. Furniture was still wrapped in plastic in the front room.

He surveyed the yard from the front porch and watched Elowen trim the roses. He joined her. "You look like you know what you're doing."

"I haven't had a garden since I lived at home. But I love it so much," she said, clipping another stem.

"You look good."

"I feel good."

"Anna and Charlie seem happy."

"They're a blessing."

He followed her as she worked her way from bush to bush. "After I get the furniture unwrapped, I'm going to start writing again," he said.

"I'm excited for you."

"I want to get your opinion on something I've been thinking about."

She stopped and looked him in the eye. "About the crystal?"

"Yeah. It's been on my mind a lot. I've been thinking that if Hitler used this thing to start a war and kill millions of innocent people, maybe I've placed my own peace of mind above my responsibility to serve the common good. Maybe I made a mistake giving it to the cabal."

She put a hand on her belly. "You did the right thing for yourself and for us. And, besides, there's nothing you can do about it now."

320 AD – NORTHERN BOUNDARY, ROMAN EMPIRE

The forest was thick up to the edge of a grassy clearing which overlooked the banks of the Rhine River. As the soldiers celebrated another victory, their laughter carried over the surface of the water.

Caesar Crispus had led them in their conquest of the Franks and the Alamanni. It was not the first time—the Germanic tribes were slow learners.

The men's triumph was reason enough for drinking, but they also drank to Crispus, who had been made Commander of Gaul, a declaration his father, Emperor Constantine, had just announced. The river flowed lazily from the Swiss Alps to the North Sea as the soldiers drank and sang.

Crispus and Constantine reclined on their tunics on couches in the grass. With goblets full of wine, they watched the river.

"It is a glorious day, Father."

"It is," Constantine said. "Again you have demonstrated that you are truly my son. Your victory was spectacular." He raised his cup. "I salute you."

"Thank you."

Constantine ran a finger through the chain around his neck. "How did you use your power this time?"

"Do you remember how, when all this began, I wrote music with the minstrels and made merry before I dreamed and went into battle?"

"Yes, of course. You were as I was when I was your age."

"However, as you've given me more responsibility and the challenges have become greater, I've found that simply drawing in the dirt with a staff what I see in my imagination is enough."

"You are shrewd."

They again toasted their success.

"Where will you go now?" Crispus asked.

"I will return to Sirmium. There is much work to do with the fleets on the Danube River. And I will inspect the garrisons throughout the region. Our greatest struggle will always be with the tribal people who are antireligious and uncivil."

"When you speak of religion, Father, I am reminded of Grandmother Helena's convictions. I am sometimes bewildered by them."

"I understand. But listen: Like you, I am a man who leads other men in war on behalf of the state: I build cities and harbors, write treaties, make pacts, and I declare judgments. I make a thousand decisions every day on behalf of these people, a people who made me their emperor. Indeed, I live for Rome, and I will die for Rome.

"As you know, over the years the spirit of the nation has ceded to this deity from Palestine, who is called Christos. He is a humble god, and the people love him. Indeed, your grandmother loves him very much.

"As a nation we stand to benefit from these people whom we have seen in their most dire circumstances. Their response to persecution has been more than admirable. Despite being imprisoned, tortured with fire, impaled, and fed to the lions, their only response has been charity and kindness. Many ask, how is this possible? The followers of Christos claim they imitate their god, who came in the flesh and suffered for their sins.

"You see how your men drink and sing now?" Constantine nodded at the troops.

Crispus grinned for his men's gaiety.

"This would not be possible if it were not for these people who call themselves Christians, who do not drink and who volunteered for guard duty without additional compensation."

"I think I understand what you are saying, Father, that they are a virtuous people who have served the empire."

"So let us not speak evil of this movement. We will befriend it that the whole empire may enjoy peace and prosperity."

"You do not believe?"

"I believe in the state, my son. But your grandmother believes in this god, and her heart is pure. She is very passionate. Daily, she presses me to be baptized into this faith. Perhaps one day I will do so. But not yet."

CHAPTER 27

Clayton closed the book and gazed out the window of his office. The trees and garden had a calming effect; he would go for a walk in the afternoon.

He had never anticipated getting as wrapped up in Constantine as he had. But after Elowen had made her point about the emperor, he started reading his history, and the more he read, the more he was persuaded that if ever a Roman emperor held the crystal after Augustus' dynasty, Constantine was the one.

324 AD – THESSALONIKI, GREECE

Constantine, his generals, and Crispus were hunched over a table in the palace war room, examining maps of the waterways of Eastern Europe and Asia Minor. The harbor was in view from the balcony.

"Licinius is no longer accommodating the followers of Christos in the east," Constantine stated. "And you know how I value the support of that movement."

The generals nodded in agreement.

"Thus you wish to remove Licinius once and for all from his throne, Father?"

"Yes, I do. We have brought him to his knees many times and each time he has promised to work with us. But he speaks out of both sides of his mouth: One moment he says he favors the followers of Christos, but with the next breath he kowtows to the pagans and imprisons them. He cannot be trusted.

"I have decided we shall put the whole empire under one banner. This is what the people want, this is what I want, and we shall proceed accordingly."

He turned and waved to a man who wore a tunic and an apron splattered with paint. Two others dressed as he was presented a giant painting on wood, measuring three meters wide and half that length tall.

The painting was of a sea battle with ships coming at each other and colliding. A face easily recognizable in the lead ship on the left was that of Crispus, who chuckled when he saw his image. The uniform of the man at the front of the vessel that floundered before Crispus' ship, was that of an admiral. His sailors floundered in the sea or gripped the sides of the ship, fighting for their lives.

"Father, do you envision my navy taking down Licinius' fleet? I recognize the admiral. He is Abantus. Perhaps we will meet in Hellespont, and I will chase him down the Bosphorus Strait?"

"It is as you see it, my son," Constantine said. He said to the artist, "Bring the second painting."

The painter gestured and two other assistants appeared with another work of the same dimensions as the first. It was of a city under siege.

"Behold, Byzantium," Constantine said.

The painting showed a portion of the city's wall in ruins. A warrior—recognizably Constantine—was on horseback at the front of a legion of troops entering the city through the breech.

"Crispus, you will take our enemy on the water, and I will subdue him in the city. We will launch our attacks at the same time, and Licinius will be overwhelmed. He will flee the region with his cavalry.

But he will have nowhere to go, and he will surrender his crown to save his life."

"And what will become of Byzantium?" one of the generals asked.

"The people despise Licinius, thus they will gladly accept my rule. We shall establish a new Rome in the city. The old city has not aged well; it is a mausoleum. Byzantium is the better location with the addition of the east to our rule."

"And what will you call it?" another general asked.

"Constantinople."

PRESENT DAY

With chiseled face and thick black mane, women often told Wyett Wolfson he was handsome. But he had never been much interested. They were a distraction. Studying the eye and optics had been his first love ever since he had been introduced to it in a fifth grade science class.

He had set up a lab in Penlick's office suite. Tented, there was little dust to contend with. The station included a microscope, magnifiers, and lasers mounted on radial arms which he used to measure the crystal's reflective properties, internal angularity, and electromagnetism. He wore gloves, and there was always a guard present.

At first, Wyett had thought Victor's security protocol was over the top. He had a stellar reputation, and he could not care less for the man's crystal. *I'm glad I don't work for him; he would be a miserable boss,* he remembered thinking. But as he worked with the crystal, he felt that it pulled on his soul. He was not a religious man, but "soul" was the only word he had for whatever inside of him was being lured to put the thing around his neck.

If I were alone, I would put it on, he had thought. *Victor Penlick may be a control freak, but he knows what he's dealing with.*

But the results of his tests showed that it was ordinary. It was from the Schorl species, which was very common. Probably it was harvested in South Asia. It was almost eight centimeters in length and nine millimeters in thickness with six faces which were lightly polished. It was opaque, and its refraction of light, minimal. It had a high iron content, which was normal, and it had the usual magnetic susceptibilities. He concluded that the crystal was worth about ten bucks.

The security guard watched him carefully as he returned the crystal to the safe.

324 AD – 326 AD FROM CONSTANTINOPLE TO ROME

Constantine and Crispus warred against Licinius just as they had envisioned and dreamed, working in harmony. And they were victorious, chasing Licinius to Chrysopolis and then to Nicomedia, where he finally surrendered, throwing himself on the emperor's mercy, which the emperor granted.

Nonetheless, it was not a year after his defeat that Licinius secretly attempted to build a coalition with the Goths. But Constantine easily saw through Licinius' false loyalties, and he beat down his rebellion, again capturing him, but this time he hung him for treason.

With a single unified empire, Constantine's efforts to build it went unhindered. Commerce exploded with success, the public works of sewers, aqueducts, and roads enjoyed heavy investment, the arts flourished, the institutions of science and medicine celebrated new breakthroughs. And the Christian church grew with the establishment of a single unifying creed after nearly 300 years of discord. As Byzantium was reborn Constantinople, a new age was ushered in.

Crispus stood at his father's side on a terrace of the palace in the new capital. They looked out over the grounds below. Everything he had learned and experienced prepared him for the throne. "Father, our success in building the empire has provided a moment of relief from what once seemed to be a never ending series of wars."

"Let us enjoy it while it lasts, for the barbarians will come again," Constantine said.

"Indeed. During this time of peace, I would like to return to Rome to be with my wife and son whom I have hardly seen in three years."

"It is well that you do so. I will follow you in a few weeks, and together we will celebrate with the people my twentieth anniversary as emperor and your place as my heir."

Days later, with his caravan prepared to depart for Rome, Crispus embraced his father, who encouraged him to consider the faith of his grandmother, Helena, during his travels. "This faith will be invaluable to you, your family, and the kingdom in the future," Constantine remarked.

The young Caesar took his time passing through Asia Minor and Greece with his army, enjoying the fruits of his imperial status, especially the affections of the young maidens.

Rufrius was Crispus' valet and his closest confidante. They were riding side by side the morning after Crispus and his army had scandalized the virgins of an entire village the night before.

Rufrius said to Crispus, "What we have done since we left your father may precede us and fall on your grandmother's ears. She will not be pleased."

"It is naught for worry," Crispus said. "Her god will forgive me, and so will she." In silence, they continued to ride, until he added, "That is, when I am ready to be forgiven."

When he arrived on the shoreline of Greece, Crispus ferried with his army to Southern Italy. They deboarded and continued their ride north, up the coast, celebrating his fame all along the way.

CHAPTER 28

Victor and Amelia sat side by side at the conference table.

Senator Cockler complained via the video call, "I don't like it," he said. "There's no such thing as magic."

Victor watched the senator's eyes shift—he was watching the faces of the other men on his monitor just as he and Amelia were.

"It's demonic; it's from the devil," the senator continued. "And I don't like messing with him, or anything associated with him."

"You're a politician and a lawyer, Pierce," Victor said. "For the sake of this discussion, could you please put aside the superstitious vagaries of your Catholicism?"

The senator folded his arms across his chest and stuck out his chin.

Victor sighed. "Okay, let me entertain what you're saying for a moment: If there was a devil, don't you think he'd be more engaged with humanity than he presently seems to be? Wouldn't he be celebrating the illicit behavior of your constituents you're always complaining about?"

"And who's to say he isn't?" the senator asked.

"I agree," Justice Orden said. "This is an issue, Victor. I know you're not a believer, but that doesn't negate anyone else's faith. And the fact of the matter is is that there's no rational explanation for what the crystal can do."

General Hammerman rolled his shoulders. "Everyone who examined the crystal—the optical engineer, the geologist, and the electrician—said they felt it tug on their soul. Didn't you feel it, Victor?"

"My friends, please relax," Victor said, his palms raised defensively. "I'm not attempting to invalidate anyone's faith. What I'm trying to say is let's not jump to conclusions, as in, 'It's the devil, and thus sayeth the Lord.' Let's be open-minded as we explore this thing."

"For how much longer are we going to sit on it?" Amelia asked.

"Just a few more weeks. I want to be absolutely certain we've done everything in our powers to understand it," Victor said.

326 AD – ROME, ITALY

The army rode behind Crispus and Rufrius. They were only one day out from Rome. Crispus swayed in his saddle.

"Caesar?" Rufrius asked. "Are you not well?" He saw that his master's eyes were glassy. "What is wrong?"

"I have seen a vision," Crispus said. He blinked several times. "It was at once beautiful and disturbing. Let us rest for a moment." He held up a hand, and the army halted behind them.

Crispus dismounted, as did Rufrius

"Give me your staff," Crispus demanded.

Rufrius did so, and Crispus drew in the dirt a rough outline of a person. Its large breasts revealed it was a woman. And he drew another figure which faced the woman. It had a giant penis. He drew a circle around the two figures.

"Master, whom do you desire?" Rufrius asked.

"No one shall know this but you and I." Rufrius nodded. "My father's wife, Fausta. The vision I was given was that I shall bed her before my father returns home."

"But why?" Rufrius cried. "This will be an abomination to your father, indeed, to every Roman."

"I don't know why. But I do know that it is my destiny."

The next day Crispus and his regiment wore full battle gear with helmets and swords as they rode through the gates of the city. The people lined the great avenue, cheering.

Fausta was on the balcony when they passed by the royal palace. Every man drew his sword, held it before his face, and shouted, "To the empire, to the empress!"

Her dark tresses fell over her shoulders, shiny in the sunlight. Her eyes were outlined with broad swaths of eyeliner. Around her neck and on her ears were brilliant green emeralds. A sheer purple scarf lay across her shoulders, but it hid nothing as her white tunic was tight and lowcut, showing off her full breasts and hips. She wore solid gold snake bracelets around both arms. They had fallen out of style with the advent of Christianity as the religion of the empire. But not today, not for Fausta.

As Crispus' eyes consumed what they saw, he felt his heart pound hard. "Rufrius," he said.

"Yes, my sovereign?"

"I will see her tonight after dinner."

Rufrius held his breath for a moment. And then he sighed. "Yes, Master, I will make the necessary arrangements."

The tryst was secret—no one knew about it but Fausta and her servant girl, and Crispus and Rufrius.

They met in Fausta's bedchamber, and without a word, like animals, they tore one another's clothes off. They pushed and prodded, touched and tasted for hours until they lay in one another's arms fast asleep.

The next morning as the sun streamed through the windows, Crispus awoke. The woman lay across his chest. "What have I done?" he groaned. And he freed himself from her and got out of bed.

As he let his tunic fall over his head, he watched her pull a blanket over a shoulder. Slipping on his sandals and cloak, he left the room.

As promised, sixteen weeks later Constantine came to Rome with his men for the twenty year celebration of his inauguration as emperor. The citizens welcomed him with great fanfare. The troops hailed Fausta as she stood on the balcony of the palace. But what they saw was much different from what Crispus had seen when he came into the city: Her hair was in a bun, and she wore a white *palla*—a wrap she had worn continuously for the past month; her figure was indefinable. She wore a silver crucifix around her neck.

Within the hour, Constantine came to Fausta in her room. "My love!" she cried, and she ran up to him weeping. They embraced.

But Constantine pushed her back. "What is this?" he asked as he tore the wrap off her body, revealing her protruding belly.

"Your son raped me, my lord, and I am pregnant!"

"I felt this evil thing in my soul when it happened," he cried. "And as I approached the city, my spirit raged!"

She fell to his feet. "What will you do?" she sobbed.

He placed his hands on her head, and snarled, "Nothing, until after the festival."

The Christian Church celebrated Constantine's anniversary with a week of homilies at the Colosseum. It was not difficult for the people to see their God's hand in the emperor's work and how he must have earned many crowns in heaven. Speaking numerous times throughout the event, Constantine repeatedly thanked the people for how they had drawn together and pledged themselves to fight the godless barbarians on their borders.

It was on a Sunday, the official day of rest which the emperor had instituted years earlier, when Petronium Armianus officiated at the closing ceremonies in the church. He had been the priest of Jupiter, but he was now the priest of Christ. The church had been the Temple of Jupiter—it was a magnificent building with a portico, grand entrance, and vaulted ceilings. But now it was the cathedral of the episcopal see of the western church.

Constantine and his family sat below the pulpit of the priest, who was dressed in a fashion reminiscent of his years of service to the pagan deity, with full chasuble and stole.

Petronium declared before the congregation, "The family is the most sacred of institutions, for it is the very root system of society. And so I commend to you, Augustus Flavius Valerius Constantinus, his wife, Fausta, their six children, especially the celebrated Caesar Crispus, his wife and son, and the emperor's mother, Helena, as our model for family unity and love...." He continued with a homily about the importance of the family and God's promises to bless it.

After the sermon, the people professed their faith, reciting the creed which had been written in Asia Minor, in the city of Nicaea, just the previous year at Constantine's order. They then prayed the prayer Jesus had taught his disciples. Petronium proceeded with the words, "On the night he was betrayed, Kurios Christos took bread...."

Jupiter had never instituted the use of food in worship, but this god gave his flesh and his blood in bread and wine for the nourishment of the people.

What a great god these people have! Petronium reflected.

Following the worship ceremony, the celebration of Constantine's anniversary was done, and the peasants, shop owners, soldiers—all the people—returned to their homes with a sense of dignity and purpose in their hearts.

But that feeling was lost on the royal family. Fausta's pregnancy had been kept secret from ordinary people, hiding it under her garments, as she did. But the courts of the palace buzzed with talk. As the gates for the palace grounds closed behind Constantine and the others, the emperor invited Crispus to follow him into the garden. It was under a thick cluster of trees, hidden from the prying eyes of the servants, where Constantine turned on him.

"What have you done?" he demanded of his son.

"Father?"

"The most treacherous thing one man might do to another man, you have done to your own blood!"

"I do not know—"

Constantine slapped Crispus across the face with an open hand. "You raped my wife!"

"But Father, I did not—"

He slapped him again, and this time Crispus' eyes lit up with anger.

"Will you return the blow?" Constantine called for guards to take Crispus into custody.

Within days, Crispus was transported to Milan where he was tried for treason and sentenced to death by suicide.

But the servants talked, and their whispers made it to Constantine's ears: There was the stinging gossip that Fausta had seduced Crispus, that when the prince had entered the city she had presented herself to him whorishly.

Constantine was out of his mind with anger for the betrayal. It was the night before Fausta would have her unborn child aborted by the palace doctor, when he went into her bedchamber and gazed on her as she slept. She was in the same bed where they had conceived five children. He watched her for a long time. Tomorrow, the physician would apply special oils to her body, she would drink a potion made of cherry juice and magnesium, and the spawn of evil would be expelled from her body in her private bath. But now that he knew the truth, that would not be enough.

The doctor lived in a room on the ground floor of the palace, not far from the kitchen. His name was Alfenius. He was an elderly man who was a master of potions and treatments for ailments and diseases. Constantine woke him.

"Emperor?" the doctor asked, startled, as he struggled to pull himself up from his cot.

Looking him in the eye, Constantine said, "I am sorry, my friend, that I have come to you at this late hour. But our meeting must remain secret for the sake of the empire."

"Of course, Emperor."

Constantine's words were few, but his message was clear, and the conversation was over in just a couple of minutes.

The next day, Fausta was in the palace bath, which included a sauna, a swimming pool, and submerged tubs of heated water. White tiles covered the concrete walls of the bath. The empress lay in cotton sheets on a bed as Alfenius massaged into her legs and extended belly a concoction of oils and herbs. He wore a toga with bands of blue around the hem.

"My flesh tingles," she said.

"Good. The treatment is working."

What he did was not his responsibility but that of his emperor, who held the keys of life and death for everyone who lived in his realm.

He finished the massage and extended his hand. "Let me help you into the tub."

Her legs wobbled as she stood. She chuckled. "That was very relaxing. I can hardly walk."

He led her to one of the tubs. As she stepped into the water, she said it seemed hotter than usual.

"Yes, it is. For this treatment to be effective, the water must be very hot." After she was submerged up to her neck, he stooped down and gave her a glass of cherry juice. Chilled, it was a refreshing antidote for the heat, he told her.

"Will this take long?" she asked.

"No, Empress. It will not take long at all," he said, and he excused himself.

"When you return, please bring me more juice," she said.

"Of course," he said, and he turned to leave.

"Doctor?"

"Yes, Empress?"

"Is it normal for my legs to feel so lifeless?"

"Yes, it is. The water, the oils, and the juice create a relaxing sensation. This will all be over very soon."

"Thank you, Doctor. It will be good to have my life back." She tipped her head back on the edge of the tub and closed her eyes.

On his way to the door, Alfenius went to the furnace room. He looked in and nodded to the servant boy, and he left the bath. The servant stoked the furnace until it would not hold another chock of wood, and he also left, shutting the door behind him.

As the temperature of the water rose, Fausta tried to get out of the tub, but her whole body was in paralysis—she could not move. She screamed. But her voice could not be heard outside the walls of the bath. When her flesh began to fall away, she went into shock, and she drowned.

Later, Alfenius returned to the bath. Upon pulling open the door, a cloud of pink steam rolled out over him. He left the bath and departed the grounds.

Constantine held court weekly in the great room of the palace. Helena, his pious mother, sat in the audience with her attendees observing her son's judgments upon his subjects. And she prayed. Many compared her to Anna, the widow who in her old age prayed unceasingly in the temple in Jerusalem for a savior, who was rewarded with the revelation of the Christ in her lifetime.

The emperor had ordered Crispus' name stricken from all government records and histories and from every marble in the city and that it not be said in his presence. It was after Fausta's death the herald of the court came before the emperor and declared, "Rufrius Apollo, the former aide of the one whose name is unmentionable, beseeches thee."

Constantine gazed vacantly into the distance from the throne. But he did not give a thumbs down, and the herald gestured to Rufrius to make his petition known.

As Crispus' valet stood before the emperor, his knees knocked in terror. "Great and mighty emperor, I have yearned to come before you for many days, but it has not been easy to gain entrance to your holy throne. Nonetheless, it is with great regret and fear that I stand before you now. Please do not be angry with me. I come in humility, risking my very life, to share with you the truth of the souls which now surely writhe in the fires of hell."

Constantine nodded for him to continue.

"The one whose name shall not be uttered, on the night before we entered the gates of the Eternal City, suffered a vision of such magnitude that he nearly fell from his horse. I rode beside him, Emperor, and I swear in the name of Christos that what I tell you now is true. When I asked him what ailed him, he halted our march and dismounted. He then took my staff, and he drew in the dirt. It was an unspeakable image, dear Emperor, but it was the thing which precipitated the tragic and terrible incident which followed." He looked at the floor.

"Describe the image," Constantine said.

Rufrius shuddered. "I will Emperor, but I fear I will lose my life for doing so. But if I do not do so, I fear that God will judge me ever so severely." He paused for a long moment. Without blinking, Constantine stared at him. Rufrius returned the gaze and said, "The image which was drawn by the one with the unspeakable name was of a woman with great breasts and of a man with a prodigious penis. He drew a circle around the two figures. And then he told me the woman was his father's wife." He broke Constantine's stare and looked again at the floor.

"Continue."

"Emperor, please—"

"Continue!"

"Yes, Emperor," he said, again locking eyes with Constantine. "The one with the unspeakable name said, 'I have been given a vision that I shall bed her before her husband returns home.'"

Constantine released a cry that filled the great room—it was so terrible the servants spoke of it for many years thereafter. And he pulled the crystal and chain from around his neck.

Helena ran to the foot of the throne. "My son, what have you done?"

"This stone, it is evil, and I have used it wickedly. I am ruined!"

"Give it to me, and I will use it to glorify Christos."

"Mother, how? This thing is of the devil!"

"Did not God use the devil to demonstrate his wisdom in the life of Job? Did not Christos use the devil to persuade one of his own disciples and the governor of the land to condemn him that he might bring salvation to the world? My son, do not despair! The Lord will provide for you a successor from among your own sons, and you will know the affections of other women. But give me the crystal that I might seek out the treasures of Christos in Palestine."

Constantine's hand trembled as he placed the black tourmaline crystal in his mother's palm.

When the crystal touched her flesh, her eyes rolled back, and she fell into him on the throne.

He caressed her brow. "When you gave me the crystal, I saw a fantastic light," she said.

"Mother, you shall go to Palestine."

She held the crystal in her left hand around which she wrapped the chain. That was the way she would hold on to it until she reached her final destination.

CHAPTER 29

Clayton and Elowen sat in their enclosed porch and watched the rain come down.

"I said I would miss the view of the Manhattan skyline on a rainy day when we were still in the condo, but I'm loving this view just as much," she said.

"Me, too," he agreed. "By the way, I wanted to tell you I really enjoyed hearing you sing again last night. I don't know if it's you or me, but I think you sound better." He put his arm around her.

"It might be a little of both. My therapist said she thought I was feeling more comfortable in my own skin. That's probably a part of it." The rain pattered on the sidewalk. "Have you been thinking about the crystal?"

"I can't stop thinking about it. Why?"

"I'm not surprised. You wore it for forty years. Well, I've been thinking about Constantine. I've been wondering who may've had it after him."

"Good question. There was only a handful of people who would have known about it."

She held up her hand and put up a finger as she named each one:

"His firstborn son, Crispus, his first wife, Fausta, the high priest, and the general of his army." She looked up at the ceiling. "But," she began, and she took her phone off the coffee table and tapped something into it. After a moment she held it up for him to see. "His mom," she said. Her cell showed a webpage that was dedicated to St. Helena.

"She might actually be the one."

She read the webpage silently for a few moments. "Did you know Crispus and Fausta both died the same year Helena went on her pilgrimage to the Holy Land?"

326 AD – 328 AD THE HOLY LAND

Helena had been a follower of Christ for more than two decades, but with the crystal she had a spiritual keenness which caused her faith to explode with a fervor greater than she had ever experienced before. How she longed to know the land where her Lord had performed his miracles and preached his message of redemption! Constantine had sent her on her way to the Holy Land with a company of soldiers and an entourage that numbered over a hundred, with servants, cooks, and physicians.

His last words to her were, "Mother, when you arrive at Calvary, pray for me that my soul may be redeemed from the fires of hell."

Reaching the shores of Israel, Helena began her journey inland. As she clung to the crystal, she found inspiration in music. Nearly every day she would compose a new song, and when she would sleep, she would dream the song. In those dreams she saw with a vividness her Lord conduct his ministry throughout the land.

Helena's inspiration came in different ways. On one occasion it was as she traveled east through a valley with her consort, from Jerusalem to Jericho. The cloud cover was thick, the sky was gray, and it rained. But the rain stopped for a time, and when it did the sun peeked through a slit in the clouds—it was a single stream of light which fell on a place of lodging, the only place of its kind as far as the eye could see in any direction.

Immediately, Helena knew the inn's significance, and she stopped the caravan and jumped from her carriage. Sloshing through the mud to the lodge, she fell to her knees on the steps of the place and wept.

The innkeeper was there, and he knelt beside her. "Mother of the Emperor, what is it that moves you with such emotion?"

"I dreamed of this place last night," Helena said through her tears. "It is the inn where the Good Samaritan brought the man he had found beaten and half dead on the side of the road."

The man told her he had heard the stories. Now with Helena's blessing, that site was certified as Ihe inn of the Good Samaritan.

Helena stayed at a hostel in Bethlehem during Christmas time. The Christmas Eve celebration was a grand affair preceded by a feast and followed by many worship services, consummated with the midnight vigil. There, Helena sang a song she had written. It began,

> Shepherds,
> favored by God
> touched by angels
> Beheld this night
> The Messiah swathed in cloth
> A babe wrapped in glory....

As Helena slept that night, she dreamed her song. "So much light —the angels!" she gasped, wide awake after the dream. She leaped out of bed, threw on her clothes, and ran out the door. She raced across a cart path and into a field. She lifted her hands up high and shouted in the middle of the field, "This field is where the shepherds received the song of the angels on the first Christmas!"

Later, Helena went into the northern region of Israel, to Galilee where her Lord was born and raised and began his ministry. One morning, as she looked out over grassy plains from the Sea of Galilee, she recognized it as the place she had sung about and seen in another dream: It was where Christ and his disciples had fed thousands of people with five loaves of bread and two fishes.

There were only ruins in Jesus' hometown of Nazareth. After he had been crucified, disease, earthquakes, crop infestations, and violence plagued the region. The people thought it had been cursed and they abandoned it. Now, it was nothing but a watering hole for herds of sheep and goats. As Helena toured it, she hummed a melody for a new song, the words of which fell from her lips spontaneously.

That night she dreamed her song, and when she woke, she remembered a particular shanty she had seen the day before, which was inhabited by goats. "That is the place where Joseph and Jesus worked with wood," she said to those who traveled with her.

It was in Jerusalem on Easter when Helena made her greatest discovery. She had written a hymn for the Saturday Vigil, which she sang during the communal celebration of Jesus' resurrection. That night she dreamed the song, and it was so dramatic, so disturbing, she awoke trembling and crying out. It was Easter morning, but still dark. Her attendants came with lamps and helped her up. She walked into the heart of the Holy City, holding the amulet in her hand, until she came to the foot of a hill, where she looked up into a thick forest of columns. She gripped the crystal so tightly her hand filled with blood. A monumental structure on top of the hill was a forest of carved statues of the bare-breasted goddess, Venus.

In her dream, Helena had seen the same temple. But jutting up from its center were three roughhewn crosses, which reached to the sky. Their crossbeams stretched from horizon to horizon. And the history of the site became clear to her: The temple to Venus had been built by Emperor Hadrian 200 years earlier over the place where her savior had been crucified for her sins! The Roman goddess of sex and fertility was worshipped on the hill that was Calvary!

Over the following weeks Helena worked with city officials and Father Macarius, the bishop of the Jerusalem church, to bring on engineers and laborers to destroy the Temple of Venus and to rededicate the site.

The workers crushed the statues of the goddess into gravel from the pediment to the columns to the foundation, taking the temple apart stone by stone. When the excavation was complete, there was nothing left on the hill but a slab of shale rock that lay across its top.

Helena ascended the hill on her knees, reciting the "Our Father" with each step. When she reached the top, she found the shale slab. It was about ten meters long and five meters wide, and she drew her hands across the entire surface. Three square holes had been chiseled into it, roughly equidistant from each other.

"This center hole is where they planted the cross of my savior!" she declared.

A cistern had been discovered during the course of the excavation. Helena stood with Macarius and the foreman of the work, peering into the great hole, in the bottom of which lay three crosses.

The foreman pointed a finger into the hole. "There's something else. Is that a plaque?"

They all then saw what looked like a piece of wood with writing on it.

"Quickly," Helena said, "send someone down there to get it."

A worker scrambled into the cistern and retrieved the plaque. Emerging from the pit, he gave it to Helena, who examined it with the bishop. They discussed it for a few moments until Macarius declared to everyone, "There is a single phrase on this sign which is written in Aramaic, Latin, and Greek. Mother Helena, please do us the honor of translating these words."

Helena smiled broadly as she said with a loud voice, "The plaque reads, 'Jesus the Nazarene, King of the Jews.'" Lifting up her hands, she said, "Let us pray!" And she continued: "My God, for the triumph of the Christian empire and for my pious son and emperor, and for his sons, reveal to us today how we might glorify your name for this gift to your church!"

"And the crosses, what do you think?" Macarius asked Helena.

"The Lord was crucified on one of them," she said.

The crosses all appeared to be identical, so the bishop asked his assistant to bring to them a certain noble woman whom he knew was deathly ill.

A short while later, thousands of people watched as the bishop and the woman were lowered into the cistern on a plank with ropes and pulleys. The woman was so weak she was unable to stand, and so Macarius carried her in his arms to each cross, thinking she would be healed if she touched the cross of the Lord.

The noble woman touched the first cross. But nothing happened.

It was the same for the second cross. With what seemed like her last bit of strength, the woman extended her hand to the third cross, and, as the people watched from above, when she touched it her eyes opened wide, and she cried out, "He is risen!" And she leaped from the bishop's arms and kissed the cross. "I am healed!" she rejoiced. And she clapped her hands and sang, "Holy, holy, holy, Lord God Almighty!"

Helena gifted the bishop with resources to prosper the whole church of Palestine and to build a great basilica on Calvary. She told him, "You shall name that place Church of the Holy Sepulchre, for here Kurios Christos was crucified, died, and was buried. This will be the greatest monument of Christendom—it will be filled with the relics of Christos and the saints, that the blessings of the Almighty may flow to all believers who make pilgrimage to this holy place."

Helena scoured Palestine for two years for relics and the sites of her Lord's earthly ministry. With her songs and dreams she identified many places important to her faith, including the grotto in Bethlehem where Christ had been born, and Mt. Olives where he had ascended into heaven after his resurrection.

On the last night of her pilgrimage, after all the goodbyes had been said and everything had been prepared for an early morning departure to Rome, in the depths of the night, Helena left the bishop's palace alone, filled with a sense of anticipation. It would be her last act of devotion on the hill of her Lord. She dressed in the skirt, blouse, and sandals of a maid, and she made her way from her room through the rear service door of the palace kitchen to an alleyway.

Scurrying from doorway to doorway by the light of the moon and street lanterns, Helena came to the hill that was Calvary. There were guards around its perimeter who had orders to protect its sanctity. However, in her explorations of the area she had found a cave under a heavy cover of shrubs. She was thankful she had kept the discovery a secret.

With a street lantern, she scrambled through bushes into the mouth of the cave. It may have been a place young people came to during the day to spend their time. But it was deserted now.

The cave was deep, and in its rear there was a crevice that opened to a passageway. The lantern lit a long descent which ultimately leveled out and ascended again until it came into a second cave. She was now inside the guarded fence of the hill.

She left the lantern in the cave and climbed up the hill until she stood on a black slab of shale. She went to the center hole that had been bored into the rock. Kneeling, she kissed it and prayed, "Almighty God, merciful Father in Heaven, I come to you at this hallowed site on behalf of my dear son, Constantine. Evil has befallen his home, and he fears for his soul. Has he used this crystal which I hold in my hand for his own glory? Has he been unjust in any way? No, dear Father in Heaven, he has not. But he has been your faithful servant. Lord, please, I beg you, deliver him from any sins, envelope him in your love, and fill him with the confidence of eternal life!

"My God, you see how I have used this amulet to glorify your holy name, bringing your children together to celebrate your glorious work on earth and to worship you. This device is not evil, but it is the tool you have given me to bless your people.

"Father God, I am returning home now, and when I arrive I will declare to the people the great things you have done. And when I speak to them, they will rejoice! With this crystal we will build up your church until the whole earth is your living sanctuary. Dear God, make me the empress of your kingdom that we may conquer all your enemies and bless your holy name."

It had begun to rain as Helena prayed. She looked up into the heavens, and said, "Thank you, dear God, for this refreshment, this reminder of my baptism into Christos. I am yours, and you are mine."

She stood and with her arms extended and continued her prayer. The moonlight glittered on the wet crystal in the palm of her hand. The shale underneath her feet was slick, and when she had finished praying, she stepped back from the hole, and she slipped and fell. Breathless, she lay motionless for a long moment. She tried her feet and hands, her legs and arms. Nothing was broken. But she had dropped the crystal and chain. Scrambling to her knees, she crawled across the length and breadth of the slab. But the amulet was gone.

She returned on her knees to the hole where the cross of Christ had been planted, and there in the bottom of it was a smaller hole for drainage. That was the only explanation: The crystal and chain had fallen into the hole and down the drain when they had slipped from her hand with her fall. The rain came down harder.

She looked into the sky, and prayed, "My God and Savior, not my will, but thine be done. Amen."

The crystal was gone and so too were Helena's visions.

CHAPTER 30

PRESENT DAY

Clayton sat in the armchair in the front room, reading, and Elowen lay on the couch, napping.

"This is really interesting," he said.

She opened her eyes. "What is it?"

"I'm reading a history of Islam." He held up the book and showed her the cover. "I've been looking for someone who may've had an interest in Jerusalem after Helena was there."

"Any clues?"

"I'm intrigued by Caliph al-Hakim."

"Never heard of him."

"But if you were a Muslim, especially a Shi'a Muslim from Egypt, you would be very familiar with him. He was a ruler with a caliphate that extended from North Africa up through the Levant for twenty-five years at the beginning of the second millennium. At one point, he sent his army to destroy all Christian churches, including those in Jerusalem."

"But what would that have to do with the crystal?"

"That is the question."

1009 AD – CAIRO, EGYPT and BEYOND

The sofa on which al-Hakim reclined was covered with purple silk. The sun that soaked the side of the palace streamed through a window onto the caliph's white turban and robe, which made them glow.

"General al-Washa, if you will not go, I will find someone who will go," he had said.

Al-Washa remembered that meeting with al-Hakim like it was yesterday. Himself, he had worn a dark brown cloak. His beard was full, and he had shown no emotion with his steady, black eyes.

Bowing deeply, he had said, "Of course, Caliph al-Hakim. I will honor your request. But as you know, what you are ordering me to do is contrary to the tradition that we allow People of the Book to preserve their places of worship."

The caliph's blue eyes were flecked with gold, and the general had felt them sear straight through him. "I've lived with these so-called People of the Book long enough!" he said. "Their behavior is insolent, and their speech, condescending. Since they will not accept Allah peacefully, I will tear their idols away from them.

"You and your men shall topple every stone and burn every timber of their synagogues and churches, from Chinguetti to Alexandria to Jerusalem, cleansing my kingdom of their filth!"

"Yes, Caliph, I will do this," he had said, bowing again.

The first thing al-Washa did was send a messenger to his mother. She was a Christian, and he warned her about the coming purge. He did not want to do it, but he had no choice. He recruited troops from his cavalry to go east and west to level the holy places. He would accompany those who rode east, to Israel.

As al-Washa and his men went from town to town, he was surprised by the people's response. The parish priest and the rabbi would call their people together in front of their respective places of worship, they would join hands, and they would pray. The soldiers looked on stoically. When the people had finished their prayers many of them returned to their homes. However, there were always a few who remained and gave water and food to the soldiers. That was how al-Washa came to understand his mother's humble faith.

But Jerusalem was different, for it was the center of Christendom and filled with historical monuments, many of which had been commissioned by Helena, whom the people revered as a saint. Thus they protested in great numbers and sometimes with violence. Al-Washa had his orders, however, and he was forced to increase the size of his forces, ensuring his success. For weeks the cobblestone streets of the Holy City were awash with blood.

Al-Washa's memory was clear, too clear. Even now at home in Cairo, the smell of burning firewood reminded him of the Church of the Holy Sepulchre aflame. Dozens of dead priests lay amid its destruction.

When he had toured the ruins of the church, al-Washa directed his attention to the slab of black shale which rested on the mound where Christians believed their messiah had been crucified between two thieves. There were three holes chiseled into the rock where the three crosses were supposedly planted.

"Bust up this stone!" he hollered. "Otherwise, after we have gone, the Christians will return and worship this place."

A half-dozen men set to work with wedges and hammers. It was not much later when one of them found a trough that ran underneath the three holes.

For rain runoff, he thought.

Intrigued, he smashed through the brittle rock. He discovered that the trough ran for several meters until it ended at a clay pipe, which emptied into a cistern. Something caught one worker's eye, and he called to al-Washa. The general came and knelt to the ground, where he saw what appeared to be a strand of silver sticking up out of the pipe. He pinched it between his fingers and pulled it out. It was a necklace with a black tourmaline crystal.

PRESENT DAY

"Let's say al-Hakim somehow got the crystal. Why didn't he create an empire like the others did?" Elowen asked.

"I didn't build an empire, either," Clayton said. "He was a mystic.

He was so eccentric some called him the Mad Caliph. And he was very erratic. A case in point: Just three years after he leveled all the churches and synagogues in his realm, he let the people rebuild."

"Including the Church of the Holy Sepulchre?"

"That was the exception. That wasn't rebuilt for another thirty-plus years."

"What do you think happened to al-Hakim?"

"Sunni Muslims declared jihad on him because of his unorthodox spirituality."

"His mysticism?"

"I don't think it was that. In one thousand eight AD, at the beginning of the second half of his reign, a new religion was born. It was called Druze—"

"I've heard of it. It's a unitarian faith, right?"

"Yep. And the founder declared that al-Hakim was God incarnate. The Sunnis may've thought the caliph enjoyed that title a little too much."

1021 AD – CAIRO, EGYPT

"Ever since my father's eunuch placed on my head the turban of the caliph and kissed the ground on which my feet stood, I've been enveloped by the divine," al-Hakim said. He reclined on a divan on the palace portico, wearing a white turban and cloak, his customary attire.

"Yes, my lord, I believe," his aide said. He waited on the caliph, serving him tea.

"And after I liberated the Holy Land and, indeed, the whole caliphate from the pride of the Christians, Jews, and our wrong-headed Muslim brothers, my place as the heir of the Prophet has become incontrovertible in the eyes of the people."

"Yes, my lord."

"As I deliberate the future of our kingdom, I will go on retreat tomorrow to fast and pray."

"Will you go to the Mokattam Hills?"

"Yes, to the cave that looks out over the necropolis. There, I have met the spirits of many of our ancestors, who have never declined my petitions for revelation and wisdom."

"I will accompany you, Master, for as you know—"

"Will you provoke he who has promised to shield me from all danger? Nothing can hurt me. God's hand is on me."

"But there are so many who have threatened to harm you, Master."

"I will go alone with only a donkey and what is on my mind and heart and the clothes on my back." He patted his chest. "And of course, my special jewel. This is all I need."

PRESENT DAY

"So whoever got the crystal after al-Hakim may not have known what it was," Elowen said. She faced Clayton on the couch, her legs folded. "It could've ended up in his killer's pocket as a trophy or for sale in a market as a memento of the Mad Caliph."

He put his hand on her knee. "And yet, for some reason, it came to me."

"Maybe that's it: It came to you. Somehow, someway it objectively chose you. And if it chose you, it chose Adolf Hitler."

"That's what it's beginning to sound like, doesn't it? But I don't get it. It's been used for the ultimate evil, but it's also been used for good, like the things I've written about in my books, such as a cure for cancer."

"Maybe that's a ploy to get you to trust it. Someone once said the greatest trick the devil ever pulled was convincing the world he didn't exist."

"Do you believe in the devil?"

"I've seen some pretty bad things in the music business. I don't know if it's the devil, but I'm sure there's something out there that's more terrible than any human has ever been able to create in his own heart."

"I guess I believe that, too. It would follow that if there's an ultimate evil, there's an ultimate good. The former is the devil, and the latter is God, at least in the monotheistic religions. Clearly, the power in this thing isn't of God—"

"Who is love."

Clayton sat back in the couch and put a hand to his chin. "Therefore, the crystal's power must come from the devil or some other force that is malevolent."

"Which means?"

"Even though we don't have it now, I still feel a responsibility to make it go away once and for all."

CHAPTER 31

12th c. AD – BOSRA, SYRIA

"Allah be praised!" Sindbad shouted over the waves of the sea.

He looked like any other man on the wharf of the port of Basra, wearing a white turban and a beige jalabiya, which hung down to his ankles. But his spirit was filled with an unusual sense of joy as he remembered his most recent voyage. The caliph—the Prince of the Faithful in Bagdad—had commanded him, "Go to the island of Sri Lanka with my letter and gifts for their king."

All his voyages of late had been filled with adventure and good fortune, and he did not doubt for a minute that this one would be anything less. And he had been right!

In the story he shared with the public, he spoke in detail about the magnificence of the caliph's gifts to the king. And he described with thankfulness the hospitality the king had shown him while he stayed in his palace. His highness had withheld nothing from him, and he was truly grateful. Nonetheless, the king's kindnesses were all but lost when, after Sindbad had departed to return home to Basra, the king had given chase, captured him, and then sold him into slavery! He was absolutely mad!

Sindbad clutched the black crystal that hung around his neck. Who knows how many times he could have been murdered, lost at sea, or eaten by a great sea monster if not for this magic rock? The king of Sri Lanka had sold him to a businessman, whom he had envisioned and written a song about in the king's dungeon. His new master turned out to be a good man, a kind man, just as he had dreamed. However, he had not given consideration to his trade. Initially, this was to his shame. Nonetheless, it would be for his deliverance in the end: His master killed elephants and sold their tusks for profit. In his new role, Sindbad was to hunt the mighty beasts and harvest their ivory. His father had been a sailor, but his grandfather had been a hunter, and neither man spared him when it came to teaching him his trade. Thus, Sindbad was one of those rare men with a dual vocation.

Despite his initial reluctance to hunt elephants, he resolved to fulfill his master's bidding, for the crystal had given him what he had wished for. He found a tree which lay on a path that elephants regularly tromped on, and in that tree he built a blind where he stored food and water and kept a bow and a quiver full of arrows.

In the morning, on the day of a hunt, Sindbad would draw with an arrow a circle around the base of the tree. Across from the tree he would draw an elephant. It was a very simple drawing—it was a round four-footed beast with tusks and a trunk. Then he would draw the path of an arrow he would shoot from the tree at the elephant to that point where he imagined the arrow would pierce the creature's skin and impale its heart. Finished with his drawing, he would climb into the blind and lay his head down. Upon falling asleep, he would dream, but for a very short time. For he would awaken with a start to the rumble and roar-scream of an elephant who would be standing across the path from his tree. In silence, he would rise to his knees, string the bow, and kill the beast with a single arrow.

Such a strategy he used night after night, and his master was very pleased with his success, for his rapid acquisition of elephant tusks made him richer than he had ever been before.

One afternoon as Sindbad filled his quiver with arrows, he had an idea: If he could persuade an elephant to take him to the place where elephants died—that place which all elephants knew but no man had ever yet found—he would find hundreds of tusks, which his master would rejoice to possess. They would make him so wealthy, perhaps he would set him free.

The next time Sindbad drew a circle around the base of his tree he also drew a circle in the middle of the path in which he drew a bunch of elephants. However, these creatures were all lying on their backs with their legs in the air. Then he connected the two circles with a line in the dirt.

He took his place in the blind and promptly fell asleep. And there was a rumble and a roar/scream. It was louder than anything he had ever heard before! At the foot of the tree there was a herd of bull elephants! And there was their king, a great elephant whom he called Khalid.

The mighty elephant took hold of his tree with its trunk, and he shook it violently, so much so Sindbad fell onto the animal's back. And the elephant ran. In fear, Sindbad clutched the thick hide of Khalid's neck, and he held on for his life.

Khalid led the other elephants, trampling through the forest. They ran for miles. It was such a great distance, Sindbad thought his strength would fail him, and he would fall under the feet of the beasts and die. But just as he was about to lose his grip, they came into a clearing where they stopped. For a long moment the only sound was the wind in the trees, which were so tall and thick the light from the full moon was dim. Nonetheless, as the elephants mournfully wagged their heads and trunks and slowly moved through the clearing, Sindbad could see the dry bones and tusks of the elephants' predecessors.

PRESENT DAY

The sun was bright and there was a light breeze as Clayton and Elowen drank iced tea at the patio table. He rested a hand on the cover of a book. Herodotus chased the squirrel, who was a regular now.

"I think that squirrel actually taunts the dog for his own amusement," Clayton said.

"Of course he does," Elowen said.

He held up the book. On the cover there was a cartoon drawing of a turbaned man flying on a carpet in a nighttime sky. The title was, *The Arabian Nights: Tales of 1001 Nights.* "I'm thinking the stories in this book might include allusions to the crystal." He set it back down.

"Whatever gave you that idea?"

"They were written during a time which includes the period following the disappearance of al-Hakim. And the geography and culture works, encompassing the regions of Turkey, Persia, North Africa, and Arabia."

"But they're just children's stories."

"Only as they were rewritten and animated by Disney and company. Originally, they were metanarratives. Things like the magic lantern and genie were only symbols for communicating a deeper meaning."

"Such as?"

"Like other metanarratives, they included moralistic teachings. But I also think they may've been used to whitewash the sudden accumulation of wealth and power by people who used the crystal."

"You're saying they were used to redirect outside scrutiny of a certain person's unexplainable good fortune?"

"Maybe." He tapped the cover of the book with his finger. "I like the story of *Sindbad the Sailor,* and also *"Ali Baba and the Forty Thieves."*

"I love that one."

"Do you remember Ali Baba's co-star?"

"Of course: the servant girl, Morgiana. She was my hero. She saved Ali Baba. I remember she was one of the few female heroes who was not a princess when I was growing up."

"So you'll also remember that Ali Baba acquired his riches from a cave, which was where a band of thieves kept their loot. He had overheard them use a secret spell to open the cave, and he used it himself to break in and steal their loot."

"*Open sesame.*"

"What?"

"That was the incantation they used to open secret passage to the cave."

"Exactly. So the bandits caught up with Ali Baba, and they nearly killed him. And this is where your heroine, Morgiana, saved him, and by the end of the story he was rich again."

"And your alternative version with the crystal?"

"I believe Morgiana was even more remarkable than you thought. Here's my theory: She acquired the amulet in the market, maybe thinking it was a good luck charm. But she quickly discovered it was more than that. A genius, she taught herself how to use it, but because of the social constraints of her culture she was compelled to bring Ali Baba on board and reveal to him the source of her recent good luck. Together, they went on to use the crystal to build a business which was incredibly successful, and they became very wealthy. This is where the story about the forty thieves came into play—it was designed to camouflage the truth about the crystal and Ali Baba and Morgiana's sudden prosperity."

"Where's this fit on the timeline?"

"Pre-Ottoman Empire. The setting is somewhere in North Africa along the Mediterranean."

"What about the Ottomans? Do you think any of the stories help us to understand it?"

"I like *Aladdin*," Clayton said.

"But wasn't that story set in China?"

"It includes mention of 'Cathay,' which was Northern China, a region that was controlled by the Mongol Empire. But there's also the inclusion of the 'land of the Moors in Africa,' which was North Africa, and—this is important—the Moors were Sunni Muslims as were the Ottomans. In the story there are also several cultural signs of Islam with references to Allah, the Prophet, and daily prayers. There's the 'hammam,' which was a Muslim public bath, and there're the offices which were common in Muslim countries, such as that of the sultan and the grand vizier. And there's a woman's use of the title, 'uncle,' to refer to a man who was not her husband or son but with whom she was permitted to have a private conversation, a designation used by Muslims.

"In the thirteenth and fourteenth centuries the Mongol Empire peaked in its power under the Khans, as in Genghis Khan and Kublai

Khan, and the Ottoman Empire was just beginning. The Aladdin story may be about how the Ottoman's came into possession of the crystal after the Khans."

16*th* c. AD – ISTANBUL, TURKEY

Fatma, wearing a deep-blue silk gown, reclined on a sofa which rested on the roof of the palace. There was a spectacular view of the estate with its imperial buildings, a private mosque, and gardens. Outside the walls of the property, there was the city, which was carved up by meandering roads and alleys where her brother the sultan's subjects drove their animals and carts.

The roof was her favorite place to escape to. She drank red wine from a giant mug, and she was plenty drunk. The Prophet would not have approved, but Allah understood. It was not easy being the sister of the sultan, the most powerful man in the world. There were so many expectations of her from so many different directions.

"Thank you, Allah, for your wisdom, for making him our leader," she prayed.

But the fact was that if it had not been for the magic crystal her brother had inherited from generations past, she might not be any better off than the servant girl who massaged her feet at that moment. "Now, my legs," she instructed her. Gently, the girl worked her fingers up and over her ankles, and she caressed the muscles in her calves. The girl's features were delicate, and her eyes were bright. She was very beautiful. And she had strong hands—she would make an excellent wife when she came of age.

Having just completed another tale of fantasy, Fatma was content. The story was about a lazy young man who got lucky when he came into great riches through his discovery of a magic lamp. She called him Aladdin. Inside the lamp lived a demon who served whoever possessed it. She giggled to herself. "How the imam will squirm when he reads this story!" But she had included in the story a warning about trafficking with devils so that no one would think that she promoted such naughty behavior.

She had read the story to the servant girl, who was delighted with it. Her smile revealed beautiful teeth, which was quite unusual for one who was so poor. Perhaps she would write a story about a girl who, like the servant girl, was poor but was also beautiful with a lovely figure, a fine complexion, and the most peaceable disposition. She would be discovered by a young, handsome prince, who would make her his princess, for he loved her, and he would give her all the jewels and dresses and palace comforts one could ever possibly imagine. What a lovely story that would be.

Hardly anyone knew about the magic crystal, and it was supposed to remain that way. What a scandal it would be if it became public knowledge that the sultan possessed such a device, one that gave him so much power over other people and kingdoms! But the issue was not so much the power itself. What would be important to the Muslim people would be the source of that power. Some held that it came from the devil, which of course would be entirely unacceptable in a kingdom built in the name of the one and only God!

Fatma believed the crystal's power was neutral, that it could be used for good or evil. Consider the music and literature, the architecture and art, and the wealth—so much wealth—that had been created for generations by Ottoman emperors. There was the matter of the tradition of the assassination of a new emperor's siblings when he took power, which she found troubling. But was the crystal itself evil?

For her, the tale of Aladdin had been inspired by the unexpected good fortune of Osman I nearly 300 years ago. He had claimed to have had a dream which explained everything. In that dream, he had seen himself and Sheikh Edebali, his spiritual mentor, asleep in the same room. A full moon had risen out of Edebali's chest and had settled into his own, from which grew a tree. It was a great tree, and its shade touched every corner of the world. The next morning, Osman shared the dream with Edebali, who told him it meant God had blessed him and his descendants with a great kingdom, and thus he would give him his daughter, Malhun, in marriage. Arranged marriages were not always a success, but this one was a great blessing for both parties as well as the country which they led. Because she was a hopeless romantic, Fatma alluded to the marriage in the final chapter of her story when Aladdin married his sweetheart, Jasmine.

In truth, everything Osman did to build the empire began with the black crystal. What Fatma had learned was that it had been acquired from an Egyptian mercenary for a not so small fortune. Had the mercenary been commissioned to make the acquisition? No one seemed to know. However, what was known was that he had traveled a great distance into north China in pursuit of a man whose wealth and fame were linked to his wife, who was reportedly brilliant in all matters concerning business.

During his quest, the mercenary had discovered that the wealthy man's father had recently died. What a boon! When he finally found the man, he presented himself as a distant cousin. Upon hearing about the man's loss, he wept with him.

As they spoke, the mercenary revealed his heritage, which included a marriage long ago of a great uncle to a Mongolian woman. "It's a miracle I have found you," he said. "I do not have another person in the world whom I can call family." The rich man said the same, and he invited the mercenary to stay with him and his wife, "For we only have each other now. My sons were killed in battle, and now I have only my wife."

After several weeks together, during a large meal with much wine, the rich man revealed the source of his affluence: his wife had once been a nanny for the emperor of the Khan dynasty, and she had stolen a magic crystal from him. When the rich man showed the crystal to the mercenary, the latter killed the couple. Not long thereafter, Osman came into possession of it. He invented the dream about himself and Edebali, and he married Malhun. That was the foundation of what would become the Ottoman Empire.

In her story, Fatma was not explicit about who her characters represented or where their good luck came from. She could not be too careful in how she wrote about her family's secret. But the essence of it was there. And it accomplished its purpose, which, besides amusing the reader, provided a backdrop for poor people to believe that some-times a person—even the father of her nation—just gets lucky and acquires wealth and power the way another person might catch a cold.

PRESENT DAY

Anna served lunch while Clayton and Elowen talked at the kitchen table. "Grilled cheese on rye with tomato soup and feta," Anna said.

"Smells delicious," Elowen said. She took a bite of the sandwich and licked her fingers. "So how long do you think the Ottomans had the crystal?"

"From their beginnings in the late thirteenth century through the reign of Suleiman the Magnificent, who died in fifteen sixty-six," Clayton said.

"That's a big chunk of time with a lot of emperors. Many were mediocre at best, and there were others who were complete duds."

"You never cease to amaze me."

"I went on a Mediterranean cruise a couple years ago. We had a stop in Istanbul, and I went to the museum. I just told you everything I remember about the Ottomans."

"Well, you make a good point. I think their religion was the culprit. I'm going to guess there were rulers who refused to use the crystal because it seemed contrary to their faith. And so they may've stored it in a vault where it was forgotten. But then a new emperor who was more interested in power than orthodoxy would somehow learn about it, and he would put it to use. But because it didn't come with a user's manual, he had to learn how to use it by trial and error. Sometimes he'd get it right, but sometimes he'd blow it. But in the end the net results were that the empire blossomed."

"So what happened after Suleiman died?"

"There was a battle called the Siege of Szigetvar, which was the Ottomans versus the Holy Roman Empire, which at the time was controlled by the Habsburgs, the ruling Hungarian dynasty. I know, too much information. In any case, historians say that even before the siege began, Suleiman was weak, nearly blind, and his memory was shot. Nonetheless, because a sultan always accompanied his soldiers on campaigns, he was there. It was a hell of a situation. He died in his sleep as the battle raged. But because his inner circle feared the men would lose their will to fight if they knew he was dead, they kept it a secret until they returned home.

"During the siege, the Ottomans slaughtered the Hungarians, but not without great losses of their own. They outnumbered their enemy by more than thirty to one. But for every dead Hungarian, there were ten dead Ottomans. Among the dead—and this is the really interesting part for us—there were seven Hungarian survivors."

"Seven?"

"And one of them kept a journal. His name was Peter Karlovic."

"You're going to tell me his journal is online, and you read it."

"It is, and I did. Peter wrote that while he fought, he was hit on the head with a broadsword. Lucky for him he fell unconscious, and he was left for dead. Eventually, he regained consciousness, and when nighttime came he crawled out from under a mass of corpses. Wandering the camp, he found six other soldiers who had also survived.

"As they searched the area for things of value, they came upon a large tent with a *tughra*, the calligraphic monogram of the emperor, Suleiman the Magnificent.

"Peter wrote that he and his fellow soldiers were God-fearing men, and none of them wanted to go into the tent of an emperor whom they believed was anointed by God, enemy or not. On the other hand, it was their duty as soldiers to search it. So they drew straws, and Peter drew the short one.

"Carrying a torch, he entered the tent. There was nothing but a few cushions. However, on one side along a fold in the tent he spotted something glittery. It was a crystal attached to a chain. He wrote that the thing seemed 'strangely foreign.' Again, a religious man and probably superstitious, he didn't want to touch it. He grabbed his tobacco pouch, scooped the crystal into it, cinched up its straps, and hung it on his belt. He wrote that he said nothing to anyone else about the thing except Emperor Maximilian II, to whom he gave it."

CHAPTER 32

PRESENT DAY

A brilliant stream of light shined through French doors on one end of Victor Penlick's home office, which danced across a Persian carpet that ran the length of the room, past a fireplace and recessed bookcases. The light fell on a dark hardwood desk where he sat. There were stacks of books on top of and beside the desk, a sampling of the 130,000 volumes that had been published over the years about Hitler and the Third Reich, each one attempting to add something new to the world's understanding about the man and his institution which would forever be synonymous with evil.

Written countless times in the books was the age-old question concerning Hitler's character: Was it the result of nurture or nature? He may have been the product of an abusive father. Or he may have been born a sociopath. Perhaps he did what he did to make up for his insecurities and a fear of abandonment—his mother died when he was very young. Maybe he was an antisocial opportunist who took advantage of the internal weaknesses of Germany's political order to catapult himself to fame and fortune.

Victor waded through the psychobabble patiently as he searched for even a hint that Hitler had possessed the crystal.

Even he had begun to doubt that any such evidence existed after reviewing hundreds of books. It seemed like the best he might be able to do was draw a connection by way of inference from what he had learned about the Holy Roman Empire. He was certain some of those who held the throne had used the crystal. Maximilian II had acquired it, but he had put it away as a memento from the Siege of Szigetvar in 1566. However, Rudolf II had certainly used it. The man was crazy and his son, certifiable, had ultimately died on the street a schizophrenic. The emperor drove the kingdom into the Thirty Years' War, but his patronage of the arts and especially education planted the seeds for what later would be called the Scientific Revolution. After his reign, it appeared the stone was stored in Rudolf II's cabinet of curiosities for several generations until Leopold Ignaz Joseph Balthasar Felician, or Leopold I, who ruled from 1658 to 1705, somehow discovered it.

The most obvious clue that Leopold had used the crystal was Romeyn de Hooghe's etching, "Tribute of Hungarians and Tyranny of Turks and Tartars." The emperor had commissioned it just six weeks before the battle that saved Vienna from the Ottomans.

The work showed the Hungarians surveying the battlefield, smugly gazing over the defeated Turks who paid homage to them. Victor knew when the purchase happened because payment for the work had been preserved in the emperor's accounting records, which were in the HRE archives. However, the aftermath of the battle victory was lackluster, for it involved only a peace treaty with the Ottoman sultan.

A biographer wrote, "Emperor Leopold II was not an industrious builder like many of his predecessors and successors. His contemporaries complained that he was sickly, self-absorbed, intensely pious, and phlegmatic. Perhaps his health and character help to explain his mediocre performance."

It was easy to imagine Leopold using the crystal just once and putting it back where he had found it. That told Victor the crystal's power was limited by the imagination and the strength of will of its user.

His doorbell rang, and a few moments later his butler, Clive

Marquette, came to him with a package. The return address was for "WW2 Memorabilia and More."

"Ahh, this might be it," Victor said. "Thank you, Clive."

Victor tore the package open. Inside was a slim book, about 150 pages. It was written in German, printed in Argentina, and titled, *Mein Fuehrer, Mein Erloeser.* He translated the title to himself, "My Leader, My Redeemer."

In the book's forward the author gushed with admiration for the fuehrer, that he had lived a victorious life, that despite the abuse he had experienced at the hands of his father throughout his childhood, the death of his mother at an early age, and his failure as an artist, he had cast a vision which animated an entire nation, a people who had suffered a humiliating wartime defeat twenty years earlier and was in the middle of the greatest economic depression the world had ever known.

After detailing Adolf's birth as the fourth child of Alois and Klara Hitler—he was the first one who would live more than two years after birth—the author wrote about Hitler's early success in school: He had begun reading when he was very young, an interest he took with him into adulthood. And he relished the arts, which the author illustrated by describing a field trip Hitler had taken to a museum in Vienna when he was ten years old. The focal point of the tour was a new exhibit featuring the art collection and crown jewels of the Habsburg dynasty, the family that had ruled the Holy Roman Empire for nearly 400 years.

When Victor finished the story, he leaned back in his chair and closed his eyes. *This is the missing link in the fuehrer's story that I've been looking for,* he reflected.

9 OCTOBER 1900 – AUSTRIA

The train rumbled down the tracks from Linz to Vienna. It had hardly been an hour, and already Adolf missed his mother. He was her darling, and she, his. But the sacrifice would be worth the experience he would have at the new museum, not to mention the two-day escape from his usually drunk and always violent father.

Nowadays every Austrian school sent their fifth class to tour the Kunsthistorisches Museum. The adults thought he and his classmates were ignorant of their designs to indoctrinate them. But he enjoyed it. Austria was a great country, a famous country for many reasons, including all manner of the arts. The opera—Mozart, Strauss, and especially Wagner—spoke to his spirit. And he was mesmerized by the ballet. But today he would focus on the exhibit of the Habsburg dynasty, a family that had been one of intrigue, power, and great fortune, having held the Holy Roman Empire in its grip for hundreds of years. The collection of art its members had amassed surpassed that of any other family on earth. He dreamed that someday he would be an artist. It was his passion.

The train arrived at the station, which was not far from the museum. The instructor led the students on a walking tour of the great city on their way to their destination.

At the entrance to the grounds of the museum, Adolf's eyes were wide with wonder as he took in the sprawling garden and sculpted hedges.

"Magnificent!" was the first word that fell from his lips.

"Let's move along, children," the teacher said.

None of his classmates appreciated art as deeply as he did. He could not wait for their next class period when the teacher would ask them questions about what they had seen. He would remember everything. But these dolts? He would be surprised if they remembered the name of the family after whom the exhibit was erected.

The Habsburg collection included the paintings of van Eyck, Durer, Raphael, and many others. But there were also display cases filled with the physical artifacts of the emperors, such as the helmets they had worn in battle and the goblets from which they had drunk. There were the swords the great warriors had held in their hands. Hitler could almost feel the power emanating from the things which were once possessed by these men of renown.

One case showed off the Austrian Crown Jewels, including scepters, orbs, swords, rings, crowns, and holy relics.

Adolf pointed to a necklace. "What is the significance of that?" he asked the guide.

"My young historian, you are looking at one of the great enigmas of this exhibit," he said. "That is a tourmaline crystal on a white gold chain. Some claim the crystal is magical. Others say it is only a worthless good luck charm on a very expensive chain. Reportedly, Emperor Charles VI wore it until his death in seventeen forty. Since then, the amulet has been in storage or on display."

The rest of the tour was a blur to Adolf. The image of the black crystal gleaming under the display lamp was seared into his mind. Thereafter, he would draw it, and dream about it.

PRESENT DAY

I get it, Victor thought. On the surface, the Habsburgs' rise to power seemed so unlikely, so arbitrary. But with the crystal, anything was possible. He did a search for "Habsburgs" and "crystal," online and the result was an article in *The New York Times* archive dated Monday, 5 January 1925. It was titled, "Habsburg Crystal Stolen From Museum."

His breath quickened. The piece reported that a gold chain with a crystal had been stolen from a famous museum in Vienna over the New Year holiday. The museum curator explained the exhibit was filled with hundreds of priceless treasures, but the only thing missing was that. Why? Perhaps it was the chain. However, it would be hard to fence because of its unique design—but a private collector might pay a high price for it as it was very beautiful, and it had belonged to the Habsburgs. On the other hand, the crystal was only of value to collectors as it was very common and not worth more than a couple of marks on the open market.

Victor remembered from his readings that Hitler was jailed in Landsberg Prison for a riot he stirred up in Munich in 1924. His nine months there he later called his baptism by fire for he had empathized with the heart of the German people, which was filled with so much grief. He concluded that all their problems were rooted in the treacherous designs of the enemies of Nazism.

That was when he wrote *Mein Kampf.* Germany was the birthplace of the uber-race, the Aryans, and it was his duty to do whatever was necessary to catapult it to its rightful place as the ruling class of Germany and, ultimately, the world. Doing so would demand that he destroy all the vermin who believed otherwise.

There was no way it was a coincidence that Hitler had been released from prison just two weeks before the crystal was stolen.

This little black stone made the Third Reich possible, Victor reflected. *But how did he acquire it?* A question not answered in any biography.

1 JANUARY 1925 – AUSTRIA

The train's cabin was quiet—there was only a handful of passengers. It seemed as though the whole continent was still asleep after a long night of revelry, celebrating the New Year. But Adolf had never let alcohol touch his tongue. In a few hours he would be at the Kunsthistorisches Museum sober and filled with anticipation.

The tug he felt on his spirit was familiar, though he had not experienced it since he was in grammar school, that time when he saw the crystal of the Habsburgs at the museum in Vienna more than two decades before. He had forgotten about it, until now. And the voice of his mentor, the late Dietrich Eckart, was in his head as it had been so many times over the years.

They had talked for hours about the German messiah and the Nazi Movement, which would usher in an age of prosperity. Eckart had said the messiah would use a talisman to cleanse the land of everything that soiled the spirit of what was once so great a people, and that this charm had been possessed by all the great dynasties of yesteryear, such as the Julio-Claudians, the Ottomans, and the Habsburgs.

Adolf felt the heart of the German people as if it were his own, and it was being crushed against the mortar of the status quo by the pestle which demanded a purging of the lies and perversions of the communists, the Jews, and the homosexuals. He was sure the crystal in the museum he had seen as a child was the amulet Eckart had talked about. With it he would save the Fatherland.

The train arrived in the city, and as he suspected, the streets of Vienna were virtually deserted. Though the sky was clear, the temperature was freezing, and his walk to the museum was brisk.

The museum garden was breathtaking even in January. A handful of people milled about, but the exhibits were closed. Adolf met two guards at the museum door. They recognized him and appeared to be enthralled by his presence.

"I would like to take a private tour," Hitler said to the guards.

Hans, who had blond hair and blue eyes, blushed. "Sir," he said, "as you can see, the museum is closed, and we cannot permit it."

"My friends, you know how I love our country's history. But you can only imagine how much of a disturbance it is for the ordinary people to enjoy the museum's treasures when I visit during the usual hours."

Josef was the other guard. His hair was dark. "Perhaps we should let him in. It is an honor to do a favor for a man of such great stature."

Hans wrinkled his nose, but then he agreed with a shrug of his shoulders.

After explaining where he would like to go, Hitler was ushered into the Habsburgs' Imperial Collections. The guards left him alone, shutting the door behind him. It was very much like what he remembered from his visit as a young man, though there were many more artifacts. However, the crystal appeared just as he had seen it originally, in a glass display case, hanging on a necklace stand.

He had tucked a ball-peen hammer in his belt, which he gripped in his right hand. Shattering the glass case with a single blow, he snatched up the crystal by its chain and shoved it into his coat pocket. He avoided the guards by leaving the museum by a rear exit. "The poor schmucks will have to deal with the mess on their own," he sniggered to himself.

Back home in Munich, Hitler stood nude before a full-length mirror in his bedroom. He admired the crystal as it dangled on the chain from his fingers. Then he put it around his neck. When the crystal touched his chest, his knees buckled, and he fell to the floor.

"The light! I'm dying!" he gasped.

He struggled to regain his footing only to double over, gasping for breath. He gripped the back of a chair as his imagination surged with images of the Fatherland in the years to come.

"What am I seeing?" he yelled.

Words and images flooded his mind: *There are boys in uniform standing in formation like a giant swastika in a stadium, and they salute me. The Reichstag burns, and Chancellor Hindenburg gasps in horror as he watches it. And there are swastika flags and banners on the streets of Berlin, and thousands of troops march down the streets with so much pride!*

Hitler's heart beat hard. He saw the words, "*Arbeit Macht Frei*" hanging over an arch under which marched an endless stream of men and women, each one wearing a yellow patch with the Star of David sewn onto their sleeve.

"Mein Kampf," he muttered as he fell to his knees again. And he saw the face of a bespectacled young man. He had met him at a Nazi rally before his imprisonment. His name was Heinrich Himmler. *You and I will manifest this vision*, he thought. He gripped the black crystal that hung around his neck and looked at it for a long time. "This is the key to our future."

PRESENT DAY

With a copy of the *Times* article sitting beside the anonymous biography, Victor made a list of everything the dictator and his colleagues had done after the crystal had been stolen from the museum.

There was the Hitler Youth—a massive reorganization of the League of German Worker Youth, an innocuous organization for young men and women. Hitler linked the organization to his national indoctrination campaign, which multiplied its membership tenfold. Then he militarized it, training the boys in weapons, hand-to-hand combat, and fomenting disorder, which they practiced in their church youth groups. This became the root system for the *Schutzstaffel,* or simply, the SS.

The SS had once been only a presidential bodyguard unit of eight men. In less than ten years, however, it numbered over 200,000 troops. The organization infiltrated every law enforcement agency and military command in the country and established concentration camps for the termination of enemies of state, which, in the end, was more than 20 million men, women, and children, including six million Jews.

Next on the list was the Reichstag fire. If one event made Hitler what he was, that was it.

It makes so much sense now, Victor thought.

Hitler somehow coordinated the fire, which gave the illusion that the German government was under attack—and then he persuaded President Paul von Hindenburg to accept the Enabling Act, that piece of legislation that gave Adolf almost authoritarian control over the whole government.

Union leaders and communists were the first to be arrested and shipped to the concentration camps—another telling sign. And there was Hitler's influence on the cabinet of the president to abolish the presidential office upon the death of Hindenburg the following year and to vest him with all the powers of the state once and for all as chancellor. This was the work of a remarkable conman, or a man with a magic amulet.

CHAPTER 33

Victor spread out Clayton's Nazi grandfather's black-and-white photos on the desk in his home office. Karl Lange had loved his country, Germany—he wore the biggest grin on his face as he stood next to Adolf Hitler and his fellow troops.

The quirky little biography about Hitler had a handful of clues concerning the crystal, like the story about the party where the fuehrer said he was the heir apparent of Alexander the Great, Augustus, Suleiman the Magnificent, and Charles VI. Since those men never had any physical or political connection, if he was referring to a literal inheritance when he said he was their heir apparent, he must have been referring to the crystal.

Another thing the biographer wrote about was how no one who really knew Hitler believed he had committed suicide. Hardly a day before his death, he had married Eva Braun, whom he loved deeply. He had also promised his generals he had an "exquisite plan" which would reverse their fortunes. And, finally, there was the physical evidence: the gunshot was into the left side of Hitler's head, an almost impossible angle for a right-handed person. The biographer wrote, "In my opinion, the fuehrer's personal aide killed him and his wife."

Victor looked again at the photo of Karl Lange proudly wearing his medal of valor standing next to Hitler. Had he been his aide? It was entirely conceivable that Adolf would have wanted such a highly decorated man by his side. This may very well have been the crystal's path from Europe to the States and ultimately into the hands of Clayton Lange and now the cabal.

30 APRIL 1945 – BERLIN, GERMANY

"Fraulein, you know how I love you," Adolf said.

"Yes I do, *mein liebe*. And you made me so happy when you took my hand," Eva said.

They lay on a cot, their limbs intertwined. The room was small, but it was enough. They were safe. The concrete bunker in the heart of Berlin was their home away from home.

"You are my spirit and soul," she said.

He pulled her tight and they kissed. The cot rocked, and she was breathless.

"I love only you," she said, and he said the same.

When they had finished, she asked if she could have a cigarette.

"*Meine liebe*, you may."

She sat on the edge of the cot, and after she had taken a deep drag, she said, "Do you suppose they will hang us as they did Mussolini?"

"I know our situation seems dire, but I still have the power to save us."

"*Liebe*, are you saying that just to protect my heart? You don't have to. I can take the truth."

He sat up next to her. The crystal dangled from his neck. He put his hand under her chin. "No, *fraulein*," he said. "This is the truth. Soon, the world will know I am the master of our destiny, of Germany's, of Europe's, and, indeed, the destiny of the whole world. Do not worry. This will all work out for the best."

Her eyes pleaded for further explanation.

"Let me share with you my secret: I possess a special power. It is the same power the great emperors of the past have used, and let's just say that by force of will and a little luck I am their heir."

"I don't understand," she complained.

"But I must confess I made an error in judgment—"

"No, *mein fuehrer*. Please do not talk like that."

"In the beginning, my appointment of Himmler was well imagined. Without him we would not have accomplished half of what we did with the SS and the camps. So, I trusted him. But it was an unmeasured trust. Distracted by other things, I permitted him to become commander of the whole army. But he became proud, and he ran our forces into the ground. Even so, what happened will only be remembered in the history books as a minor setback. Despite our two enemies breathing down our necks, in only a couple of days they will castrate one another's armies and we will regain our place as the foremost power of the world, in fact, the only power. This is what I've seen in my painting and in my dreams: the Allies and Russians will fail, and we will be victorious."

"Paintings? Dreams?"

"And we will have a son, *fraulein*, and he will be my heir."

"*Liebling*, you will give me a baby?" She began to cry. "But how?"

He took the crystal between his index finger and thumb. "It is all in this charm. It made the emperors of the past what they were, from the Greeks to the Ottomans to the Holy Roman Emperors, and now me."

"That is a laugh." It was the voice of a man.

Startled, Adolf and Eva whipped around on the cot, looking for the source of the mocking words. A figure emerged from the shadows. He was dressed in an SS uniform, and he held a Luger in a gloved hand, which he pointed at the dictator's head.

In horror, Eva pressed a hand over her mouth. Hitler scowled at the man. "Lieutenant Colonel Lange," he said, and he began to stand. "I think—"

Lange took two long strides, and he slapped Hitler across the face with the barrel of the gun. "Sit down!"

The sight on the pistol had ripped open the dictator's cheek, and blood poured from the gash. Eva cried.

Adolf sneered as he held his face. "Have I been betrayed by a man whom I created?"

"If you created me, how did you not anticipate my rejection of your tyranny?"

"Come, come now, Karl. You know this is all only politics. Indeed, your path to glory will always be on my shoulders."

"Path to glory? More like the path to death and hell."

"Lange, you are a sorry specimen of a soldier; you are a dog. But you are a result of Himmler's scheme, which went awry. For that reason, I will overlook your indiscretion. But first you must put down that gun."

"Have you missed my Aryan attributes, the blue eyes and blond hair? If I am a dog, what are you but the feces of a dog?" He snatched the crystal from around Hitler's neck and pulled it over his head.

Rage lit up the dictator's eyes, and he lunged into Lange. In one another's arms, they crashed onto the floor. Adolf was on top of Karl, and he grabbed for the gun. It went off. Karl gasped for breath as the fuehrer's naked body collapsed onto him.

Lange pushed Hitler off and scrambled to his knees, putting the amulet in a pocket and the gun in his belt. Eva sat on the bed in shock, and he pounced on her. Pushing her onto her back, he straddled her as he dug a pill out of his trousers' pocket. He pinched open her jaw, dropped the tablet into her mouth, and spit into her throat. She gagged, she coughed, and she swallowed the lethal dose of cyanide. Within seconds she convulsed, foaming at the mouth.

There was pounding on the door. "Fuehrer! Do you need help?" someone yelled.

Karl picked up Hitler and laid him next to Eva. He put the gun in the dictator's hand.

The soldiers were yelling and beating on the other side of the door. He unlocked it, and throwing it open, he hollered, "Medic! The fuehrer has shot himself!"

As half a dozen men pushed into the room, Lange ran to the stairs and climbed to street level where he shouted at the two guards, "The fuehrer needs your help!" The men ran down the stairs and into the bunker.

CHAPTER 34

1955 AD – QUEENS, NYC

Hitler's obsession with the occult, amulets, and relics had given Karl Lange reason to wonder if the dictator had not actually found something that had given him an edge over his opponents. There was the time when they were in Berlin, and he had called him into his office to discuss a topic he intended to present at a dinner meeting he was hosting that evening. While they talked, the fuehrer changed clothes, and Karl saw around his neck a rope chain, which was no great surprise as many soldiers wore chains with the Iron Cross or swastika. But he wore neither of those icons.

Karl could not see exactly what it was, as it was beneath his undershirt, but it appeared to be a stone of some sort. He had many times seen him place the palm of his hand in the middle of his chest, and he had thought that might be a practice he had acquired from his Catholic upbringing. Now he was certain the dictator had been pressing the stone against his flesh.

The conversation he had overheard him have with Eva in the bunker and his attribution of his power and that of emperors who had preceded him to the crystal was the final piece of evidence which proved his theory that Hitler had somehow acquired a magic charm.

Outside the bunker, at the top of the stairs, Karl put the chain and crystal around his neck. When the cold stone touched his skin, there was a flash of light and he gulped for breath. *Am I having a stroke?* he remembered asking himself. His imagination then exploded with a journey into the future. He saw many things: There was the New York City harbor and the Statue of Liberty; a two-story house surrounded by trees; and a chemical plant—the pipes, scaffolding, silos, and a distillation column gave it away.

The vision seemed to last a long time, but when he heard his name called from the bunker, he knew it had only been a few seconds. And he bolted, running down the street, never turning back. It was all just a blur now, but somehow he got to the airport where he boarded an emergency flight with an elite corps of Nazi officers and their families to Spain and then to Argentina.

Two years later, after immigrating to the US, Karl had bought a house in the Bronx with his wife, whom he met in Argentina. Her name was Greta. She gave him a son. They named him Henrick, but they called him Henry. With an unsecured loan of $50,000 from a savings and loan, Karl had started a business. Chemical engineering was his education and trade, and he had dreamed of building a plant for years. By the end of his first full year, he was reporting a net income. Everything he had imagined when he had first put on the crystal had come true.

Much of what the crystal could do had taken Karl by surprise, not the least of which was its empowerment of his son. It was at breakfast on Henry's sixth birthday when the boy told him and Greta that the night before he dreamed he had gotten a pony for his birthday. He showed them a drawing he had made on a piece of paper with crayons. It was all white with brown spots.

Karl remembered getting goose bumps up and down his arms as he looked at it. He, too, after hearing Hitler talk about his dreams and artwork, had been doodling and dreaming his wishes into reality, from his immigration, to his home, to his business.

When the boy stepped out the front door to go to school half an hour later, they heard his delighted squeal. They ran to the porch and saw him petting a Shetland pony in the front yard—it was all white with brown spots. Greta looked at Karl with a knowing expression, of course thinking he had bought the horse without consulting her. Words of denial were on his lips, but, thankfully, he realized it would be better to tell a white lie than to reveal the crystal.

That was how the story of Lange's plant managers pitching in to buy a pony for the boy was invented. It satisfied Greta, and he had learned a relatively painless lesson about one aspect of the crystal's power: His son had it, too. From that moment on until he was able to entrust Henry with the power without fear that he would do something foolish or unwitting with it, he only used it when he had an important decision to make.

1985 AD – QUEENS, NYC

Henrik had many fond memories of business meetings with his dad. From his earliest years, that is what they had called them. Their regular meeting would go for an hour or two. Sometimes Mom would sit in, and Dad would teach them something about money or budgeting or about the chemical business.

But that was just the warmup for the real meeting, the secret meeting, something Mom never knew anything about. That meeting always included things Dad had learned about the crystal from his experiments. For example, he had once run a test using a Saudi prince with whom he was doing business. Dad wanted to find out how far he could push a person to do something that was outside their field of self-interest.

Karl had scribbled a drawing of the prince and himself. They were only distinguishable by their names he had printed in block lettering over their heads and the very bad drawing of a headdress for the prince. Dad was handing the prince an invoice with the name of a product he had sold him. And the prince was handing Dad a check with the amount he was paying for the product written on it, which was ten times more than what the prince could have purchased the same product for from any other manufacturer. Karl told Henry about how he had dreamed the exchange, and that it happened a month later just as he had envisioned it.

But perhaps the most meaningful business meeting they ever had was after the sixth game of the World Series. The Detroit Tigers had tied it up with the St. Louis Cardinals. It was also Henry's eighteenth birthday. Mom had gone to bed, and Karl turned off the TV.

"I hereby call to order our secret meeting for all things concerning the magic crystal," he said. He sat on the couch, and Henry was in an armchair.

"Sounds good, Dad."

"I think you're now ready to use it."

"Really?" he said, surprised.

"You're an adult."

"But aren't you afraid I'll make a mistake or do something dumb?"

"You're a smart young man, son, and I trust you completely."

"Thanks. What do you think I should do with it?"

"Give it a test drive. Do something small, something that won't draw too much attention to us. But be sure it's quirky enough so that you know for sure that you were responsible for it."

Henry closed his eyes for a moment and then opened them with a smile. "Okay, I've got an idea. Do you want to hear it?"

"No, surprise me," Karl said, and he took the crystal from his shirt pocket and put it around his neck.

The next day Karl, Greta, and Henry sat in the living room watching game seven of the World Series on TV. It was being played in St. Louis. It was the top of the seventh, the score was 0-0, and the Tigers were up to bat with two outs. Norm Cash hit a single. Willie Horton was the next up, and he knocked one into left field also for a single. In the stands, the crowd's screaming was deafening. Jim Northrup was up next, and he smashed the ball to deep center. A winner of multiple Golden Glove awards, Curt Flood, would have caught the ball easily if he had not misjudged the hit, and had started in. When he realized he had gone the wrong way, he turned, but he slipped in the grass and nearly fell. He caught himself, but he was too late. Cash and Horton both scored runs.

After the game Henry showed the drawing he had made to his dad: It was a baseball diamond with players in front of all three bases, a ball in the air in centerfield, and the centerfielder was facing home plate. The scoreboard at the back of the field showed that it was the seventh inning, and the score was Home: 0, Visitors: 3.

"Well done, son," Karl said.

"Thanks, Dad."

Through his college years, and over the following decade, Henry and Karl worked together to create one of the most profitable chemical companies in the industry. Henry married his college sweetheart, Linda Dieter, an English literature major. Clayton was their only child, born two years after they exchanged vows.

Now, Henry was apprehensive about a meeting with his dad. Karl wanted to talk about plans to take the business public, something Henry fiercely opposed. He pulled into the plant's parking lot.

"This is such a dumb idea," he muttered to himself as he dragged himself to the meeting.

Henry sat across from Karl at his desk in the office. "What's going on, Dad?"

"I've made my decision," Karl said. What was left of his hair was all white; there were only tufts of it over his ears and a few wisps across the top. But his eyes were still bright with a frenetic energy, absorbing the details of everything they saw. "We're going public."

"But we'll lose control if we do that." He looked a lot like his dad thirty years earlier with blond hair, blue eyes, a high forehead, and a Roman nose.

"No, we won't. We'll hold on to a controlling interest and continue to do as we've always done. For me, the real issue is capital."

"Why not secure a bank loan?"

"There's not enough of that kind of money laying around to do what I want to do."

"Dad, we've been growing steadily on our own. With the magic crystal, we don't need anyone else's money. Honestly, I'm afraid if we go public, we'll grow too fast and burn the whole thing down." He was doodling on his legal pad as he spoke.

"Damn it, Henry, that kind of language is not funny in this business. And for the record, I'm using the magic crystal to get complete buy-in on Wall Street so we can set our initial public offering at a premium. Now, my decision is final. I'm going to meet with the attorneys and accountants in an hour. If you attend the meeting, I expect you to keep your views to yourself."

That evening, Henry ate dinner with Linda and Clayton, who was only six. The phone rang in the kitchen. "It's probably Dad," Henry said, and he got up and answered it. "Hi, Dad. That's what I figured. Okay. Talk to you later." He hung up and came back into the dining room. His face was red.

"He went through with it?"

"Yep."

"And you're angry?"

"I have really good instincts for things like this, and I thought he trusted me."

"What are you going to do?"

"I don't know. I'm too upset to make a decision now."

That night, they were sound asleep when Henry jolted awake. He gasped, "The drawing."

"What?" murmured Linda.

He reached over the nightstand, grabbed the receiver of the telephone, and tapped in a number. "I'm calling Dad," he said. On the sixth ring, it picked up: "Hi, Mom. Sorry to wake you. Is Dad there? Okay. I love you, too."

"What's going on?" Linda asked.

He got out of bed and started getting dressed. "Dad went back to the plant after dinner."

"He does that all the time."

"I know." He pulled on his boots. "But this time when we argued I said some things and I drew some things—I can't explain it right now. I've got to go find him." He kissed her. "I'll be back in a little bit."

Hours later, Linda sat in her bathrobe next to her mother-in-law and her son on the couch in her front room. A police officer sat across from them.

"Firefighters are trying to control the fire after several explosions," he said. "I'm sorry, but it's unlikely there are any survivors."

PART THREE

CHAPTER 35

PRESENT DAY

Lying in bed on his side, Derrick looked over Penelope at the clock: 4:00 a.m. He felt it in his soul—something dramatic was about to happen. He looked out the window. The moon was full, and the surf beat hard against the Malibu beach—water sprayed 20 feet into the air.

The band was usually in high gear by this time, practicing hard, preparing for the summer touring season. But he had been feeling blah. Not depressed. Not discouraged. Just blah. He wanted to sing— he loved to sing—but the power he had used to ignite his fans was gone. It was like taking a girl out but knowing nothing was going to happen because you were impotent. He turned onto his back and sighed.

I am impotent, he reflected. *And something is going on with that damned crystal. I can feel it.*

It was 7:00 a.m. Eastern Time, and Clayton was reading a novel in bed. He suddenly shivered hard. *Where'd that come from?* he wondered. A sense of anxiety had just fallen on his chest like a box of books.

He set the novel in his lap and adjusted the pillow. Elowen had performed the previous night at Carlyle's and had gone out with her band afterward. She was still asleep.

Clayton had committed himself to write 10 pages a day come hell or high water. It had been hell. *The crystal is a writing aphrodisiac,* he thought. He wondered what the cabal was planning to do with it. The secret organization could turn the world into one giant labor camp for themselves or they could make subtle adjustments in the markets behind the scenes while pouring their newfound wealth into offshore accounts, positioning themselves to dominate politicians, generals, academics, celebrities, and other influencers to fulfill their objectives, whatever those might be.

Have they begun?

It was 6:00 a.m. in Dallas, and Victor Penlick was in his home office alone, standing behind his desk. It was still dark, and only the desk lamp lit up a small area.

Despite what he had told the men in the cabal, he was ready. He had collected as much information about the crystal as he would ever find, it was his birthday, and he was going to gift himself with the crystal.

The black jewelry box was open on the desk and the crystal glittered in the light. It had never been in the office vault. When Amelia had sent him a photo of the box, he had easily found one like it, and he bought a crystal and rope chain to put in it. He had switched it for the real thing when Amelia had come to the office for their meeting with the cabal—she had foolishly left the jewelry box on the conference table when she had gone to the ladies' room. He had to laugh at how the men they had hired to examine the crystal had all claimed that the crystal tugged on their spirits. As specialists, they were the best. But their smarts stopped where their superstitious fantasies began.

He plucked the crystal out of the box by its chain and gazed at it as he hummed the Happy Birthday tune to himself. He put it around his neck and with a gasp he slapped his hands over his eyes.

"What was that?" he muttered as he fell back into his chair. He doubled over. "Am I dying?"

People's faces flooded his mind. And there was Dakota, his son. He had not thought about him as part of the equation, but he realized now that he would share this power with him.

What will he do?

Dakota had just finished three days on an oilrig and was driving back to the hotel. He had made a fortune as a drilling engineer at home, but working offshore in Kuwait multiplied his salary 10-fold, not including his suite at a five-star hotel with unlimited food and drink. It was a pretty sweet arrangement. Hot girls roamed the premises at all hours. He enjoyed it.

He had just had the funniest idea, and he pulled over to the side of the road. It was Victor's birthday—he would never call that bastard "Dad." He didn't deserve it. What he had done to his mom was disgusting—he was a pig. It had all happened 20 years ago. But fuck him. Everyone said he looked just like that piece of shit—tall and fit with the strong jaw and piercing blue eyes, so he could never deny their relationship, but DNA didn't mean jack to him.

He got on his phone and opened an app for a flower store in the States. Black roses, two dozen of them—easy peasy. And a card. He snickered. He was not much of a poet, but he tapped in his ditty anyway.

For years, Amelia had gone after every lead, gathered thousands of clues, and had ultimately drawn a treasure map which got her to the crystal. She was faithful, and she was passionate in her work. But she had begun to falter.

Victor had seen the same thing happen with other leaders who had been perfect. Everything they did was flawless day after day, year after year, until that fateful moment when their humanity reared its ugly head. In an ordinary setting, that was okay. All can be forgiven and forgotten. But in a high stakes game with life or death consequences, perfection was not optional.

Amelia had underestimated Clayton Lange, and everything was put at risk when she was arrested with her team. And she had lost Penelope and Derrick. Clayton had outsmarted her team using the crystal. She should have seen that as a possibility and made the necessary adjustments in her plans. Pride—it so often got in the way. But these things were excusable since the cabal had finally acquired the crystal. But there was that one thing Amelia had done that was not forgivable: She had given up her identity to Lange. That was not something he could let stand.

Victor had the perfect solution for testing the power of the crystal and for resolving his issue with Amelia.

In her office in downtown Dallas, Harriet looked at the computer monitor, examining the flower orders that had come in during the night. They were the usual—anniversaries, birthdays, and what she guessed were one-night stands. She adjusted a daisy over her ear. Among the purchases there was one very dark order: two dozen black roses with the message,

> Victor—
> Roses are black,
> Poppies are red,
> I hope you die
> With a bullet in your head.
> Happy Birthday
> —Dakota

The store's policy was to refuse delivery of threatening messages from anonymous sources. However, this one, while threatening, was not anonymous. Obviously, it was a joke. The address was 437 Berry Lane in Bailey Pond, North Dallas. She could expect a nice tip in that neighborhood. She would deliver it herself.

Victor watched from his front door as the florist pulled out of his driveway. He never tipped such creatures because he knew they expected it in his neighborhood. But it was a gift from his son, and he could not help himself, so he sprung and gave her two bucks.

They were black roses—strange, but it was a start. He went to the office and set them on the mantle across from his desk. He sat and looked at them for a moment. They were pretty in their own way. Dakota had never sent him anything before. It was something.

He admired a piece of work on the computer monitor an artist had sent him. He had hired him to draw a cartoon series based on a short story he had written. There were several images drawn in cartoon blocks. There were two characters. The main colors were black and red. Lots of red for lots of blood. It was just as Victor had imagined it, including a clock and a calendar in the first frame. It was perfect. If everything went according to plan, Raven would replace Amelia by noon tomorrow.

CHAPTER 36

Elowen sat next to Clayton in the kitchen nook for a lunch of hot pastrami sandwiches and minestrone soup.

He held his arm out over the table. "I've got the chills," he said.

"But we're having a heatwave," she said.

"I know. Do you remember how I told you I thought the crystal's power might be lingering over me?"

She raised an eyebrow.

"I don't think it's anything to be concerned about, at least not yet. But it's like the thing's reminding me of the relationship we once had."

"Like an ex texting you when she goes out on a date with her new boyfriend."

"Do people do that?"

"Gen Z."

"Of course they do." He rubbed his arm and looked at the goosebumps again.

"This is really scaring me, Clayton. If it is seeking you out, I can't even imagine the kinds of bad things that might happen to us if you get it again." She rubbed her stomach.

"But why me? If it is controlled by a malevolent force, I'm hardly the dark lord it's looking for."

"Maybe it thinks you're easier to manipulate than its present handlers."

"That's more likely true than not. I have been blind to its power over my life for decades." He shuddered.

Wearing leggings, a tee, and sneakers, Amelia had just finished an in-home video workout. She had taken her days off midweek for years. Most of her peers worked at least six and often seven days a week. They paid mortgages on gorgeous estates, but did they ever take the time to enjoy them? She was sure their live-in help took more pleasure in their homes than they ever did.

Wistfully, she surveyed her lunch: a salad of spinach and greens with feta cheese, cherry tomatoes, and thin slices of Persian cucumber topped with a splash of olive oil and balsamic vinegar. She glanced at the clock. It was twelve noon.

The doorbell rang. *A delivery,* she thought.

Raven had been thinking about her future ever since she had joined the black ops crew. One of the first women in history to become a Navy Seal, she had served her country for more than 20 years. But she had always known that would not be her last or most significant achievement. It was in her heart to excel in whatever she did. She strove to rise to the top in any job, any position she held. Her teammates on the black ops team did not have that kind of vision. Their aspirations were very shallow and shortsighted. They were happy with what they were, with what they had. But that was not her.

She parked her white Lexus north of the city, in the Bronx, in front of Amelia's house. It was colonial style: Two stories with a hipped roof and columns and a porch. It was all white except for the frames of double hung windows and shutters, which were gray. Raven rang the doorbell; it gonged so loudly it could be heard halfway to the sidewalk.

The door opened, and Amelia looked at her sideways. No one on her team knew where she lived.

Raven knew that was what she thought.

"Raven, what—"

The black woman's shoulders filled the door frame. Stepping in, she simultaneously placed her left hand on Amelia's throat and with her right hand drew a five-inch blade from her belt. Amelia was falling backward as she grabbed Raven's hand on her neck. Raven kicked the door shut behind them as she fell into Amelia. They hit the floor. Amelia gasped for breath under Raven's weight, but she was unable to say a word as the other woman plunged the knife into her.

Raven stabbed her passionately, and hard, and fast. When she was done there was nothing left but a glistening pool of blood in an open cavity that had once been the woman's chest. Amelia's dead eyes were filled with horror. A snarl pulled on Raven's lips as she straddled the dead woman and pulled the ring with the giant emerald off her finger and slid it onto her own.

Again, Clayton rubbed his arm. He blinked. "It's gone," he said. "The feeling's gone."

"Just like that?" Elowen said.

"Yeah."

"I wonder what happened."

The phone rang, and Victor picked it up: "Hi, Raven." He listened for a moment. "Good. Tonight the group will meet. Catch a flight to Dallas so you can join us."

Behind his desk, he again admired the cartoon he had commissioned. It had come true just as he had imagined and dreamed.

Dakota had often thought of returning home to Dallas. There was a girl there who loved him. But the money in Kuwait was so good he had decided to stay on a while longer. Presently, he was sleeping off a four-day binge, his body rebuilding itself in preparation for three long days on the rig. He had hardly twitched a muscle as he slept except for the last 20 minutes when he had dreamed a dream that ended violently. He hollered so loudly, he woke himself and the girl who slept with him, whose name he had forgotten two days ago. He chuckled as he watched her throw on her clothes and flee the room.

Slowly, he remembered the dream.

Raven carried a firearm. Victor knew that, and he had always been okay with it. He was a Texas boy; that was how he was raised. But she was black. So what? Why should that make any difference? That was something a racist would say. And, besides, she was a vet decorated for valor. Today, she had conducted the mission he had dreamed without even knowing she had been manipulated. But he was nervous. He thought he heard gunshots ringing in his head.

Is this a premonition? he wondered.

He looked at Madison. She didn't pack. She was harmless. But the senator had shown up and he definitely did pack. *He'll keep his peace.... Or will he?*

The others joined them by video.

Victor had turned up all the lights—there were no shadows. He knew it gave him a false sense of security, but it did calm his nerves.

He called the meeting to order: "Thank you all for coming, especially Raven, who flew in on a moment's notice." He looked into each person's eyes. They were content. Even Raven looked well. *Where does she keep her gun?*

"As you know," he said, "Amelia Irons has been terminated. I propose we replace her with Raven. Over the years, she's demonstrated that she has the knowledge, the skills, and the temperament necessary to take on this role, and she has told me she's ready to do so immediately. I would hope you all would accept my recommendation to make her the head of the black ops team." Hammerman gave a thumbs up, and Skarlyle, the oilman, said, "She would be invaluable in that role." The others also affirmed Raven. Victor thanked her for accepting the position. "Your leadership will take us to the next level," he said.

"It's been a very full day," she said. "And I'm feeling a little overwhelmed. Even so, I'm very thankful to you all for entrusting me with this position. I look forward to working with you."

After reviewing Raven's compensation agreement, Victor closed the meeting. Everyone congratulated and thanked Raven, and they signed out.

The senator, the secretary, and Raven left the building, and only Victor and Blade, his bodyguard, were left. Victor was feeling a rising sense of anxiety. *Blade has a gun,* he thought. Blade's dad had been his bodyguard before he took a bullet in the gut for him five years ago. He had always thought Blade's loyalty was in his DNA. But was it really?

"Let's go home, Blade," he said.

Together, they walked to the door and into the elevator. Underground, they stepped out into the parking garage. A silver Porsche Cayenne waited for them. Malik was the driver's name. Victor went around to the passenger side. As he got in, he peered over the seat at Malik for a long moment. *He has a gun, too.* Victor had known him for 15 years.

"Yes, Mr. Penlick?" Malik asked.

"It's nothing. Let's go."

"This is what I was feeling," Clayton said.

He and Elowen watched the late night news on TV. The chief of the Bronx police department was talking:

I can't give a lot of details because the case is under investigation. However, I can tell you the victim was Amelia K. Irons, a longtime resident of the borough. She was found by a colleague...

A photo of Raven appeared in a block in the upper right corner of the TV screen.

Presently, we do not have a motive or a suspect. I would like to encourage your viewers to call us if they know anything about this tragic event....

"Do you think the cabal killed Amelia?" Elowen asked.

"I know it did, and I'll bet that woman, her colleague, the one who found her, is the one who made the hit."

When Eddie Brooks had come home from Vietnam, he was all screwed up with PTSD. Drop a can of soda or pop a balloon, and he would be on his belly looking for Charlie through an imaginary rifle scope. And there were the nightmares. But his issues were not all in his head: His lungs were wasted because of Agent Orange. And drugs and alcohol had wrecked his body; there was hardly anything left but a skeleton. But there was the hardware—it gave him a sense of belonging; it was a vote of confidence, so to speak.

Eddie used to dream of a life in the suburbs: There was the den with a pool table, a pinball machine, and a juke box. There was a big screen TV with surround sound in the living room. There were two German shepherds in the yard. And he and his wife had filled up the house with a whole bunch of kids.

But sometimes what is going on in one's heart will not permit what seems to make sense in one's mind. His third divorce confirmed that. But it had all turned out for the best. If he had been doing what everyone else was doing, he would not have been chosen for this mission. The level of risk was just too great for a married man.

He used to resent the hardware, the chip the military had planted in his brain right before he was discharged. And he had especially been angry about the officer who had been chosen to be in his head every day. For some reason Colonel Brent MacKenzie had been assigned to him. When he had been a mere lieutenant, Brent had nearly gotten him killed when they were in Nam. He chuckled to himself. Since that time they had talked for hundreds of hours and had become friends.

Eddie had been sleeping on a bedroll against the cinderblock wall of a strip mall in South Dallas when he got the call to duty. The chip made the familiar click, and Colonel MacKenzie hollered in his head, "Up and at 'em, Eddie! You have a mission, soldier. These orders come from on high. Command says you're perfect for the call because of your location, marksmanship, and selfless sense of duty."

Stumbling to his feet, Eddit stood at attention the best he could manage—his hair was askew and his clothing in tatters. But his voice was loud and crisp as shouted back, "Sir, yes, sir," with a salute to the air.

There were two dumpsters behind the mall. Colonel MacKenzie shouted, "Seek and ye shall find!"

"Sir, yes, sir," Eddie shouted. Light from the streetlights created stark shadows and made the desolate parking lot appear even more bleak. Eddie crawled into the first dumpster and rooted around. There was a bag of fortune cookies from a Chinese restaurant in the mall. He broke open one of the cookies for the fortune. It read, "Your life will be richer when you reach out." That was something he had always believed was true. He took a bite of the cookie. It was stale. The restaurant never threw away the good stuff. But that was okay, and he finished the cookie. Pulling himself up and over the lip of the container, he swung his legs to the other side and landed on the ground.

Colonel MacKenzie shouted again, "Seek and ye shall find!"

Eddie threw open the giant plastic lid of the second dumpster and looked in. He squinted, saw a barely visible wallet mostly covered by trash. He clambered into the container singing, "I believe in miracles," the lyrics from a favorite '70s song. Pushing the bag aside, he grabbed the wallet. There was ID but no money. Light from the lamps over- head shimmered on something metallic. He poked at it: It was a chrome-plated handgun. He picked it up and released the magazine. There were seven rounds left. He smelled the barrel. It had been fired recently. Reinserting the magazine, he put the gun in his belt.

Victor's first run with the crystal had been seamless—he had used it to eliminate his program director by manipulating one of her agents. All the cops found was Raven covered in blood weeping over her dead mentor. Despite the fact that they were looking straight into the eyes of the murderer and that the knife she had used to kill Amelia was in her hand, they were baffled, and they left the bloody scene scratching their heads. It was just as Victor had had his artist draw the last frame of his story. It was almost too easy.

Reclining in an armchair, his feet on an ottoman, Victor took a sip of brandy and a drag on a Cuban cigar. Flames licked the flue of the fireplace. He still felt that creeping sense of anxiety that had been gnawing at him all day. *This must be the cross I bear for wearing the crystal,* he thought.

The cabbie parked on the curb in front of the gate at 437 Berry Lane. "That'll be thirty-eight dollars," he said.

"I'm a government agent," Eddie said. "Your employer will be contacted with your compensation."

"What the—?"

Eddie pointed the gun at him. "I'm *dead* serious."

As the taxi sped away, Eddie stood on the sidewalk and surveyed the neighborhood. He had not been to Bailey Pond since he was a little boy. It was still as he remembered it—palatial estates with circular driveways and eight-foot wrought-iron gates. There were great oak trees down the median, which created a natural awning along the street. Mom and Dad used to drive him and his sisters through the neighborhood to see the houses and talk about how someday they would live in one of them when Dad became a manager at the refinery. Unfortunately, Dad died on the job before that promotion ever came.

Seek and ye shall find, the colonel whispered, and Eddie climbed over the gate.

Clive had been Victor Penlick's butler his entire adult life. They had grown up together, as his parents had been servants to Victor's parents at the same estate. It was just the two of them in the house now. Victor had fallen asleep in the armchair in the den. Clive stoked the fire and unfurled a light blanket over him. A cigar smoldered in an ashtray, and he put it out. "Interesting," he muttered to himself, noticing a rope chain necklace around his boss's neck. He had encyclopedic knowledge of everything the man possessed—this was new. He scrunched up his nose. Victor had never worn jewelry except for a class ring from Dartmouth and a black steel Cartier wristwatch.

***

The colonel directed Eddie to the back of the property. There was a stone walkway covered with dew. It was slippery, but he negotiated it without any trouble. He came around to a patio and pool, just as the colonel had said he would. There were French doors into the house. He peered in through a window in one of the doors. Flames in a fireplace revealed a man sleeping in a chair. Eddie tried the door, and it fell open.

***

Clayton sat up in bed. Elowen rolled over. "What's wrong?"

"I have to go to Dallas," he said.

"What? Why? It's three in the morning."

"It's the crystal."

"But, Clayton, what about our discussion?"

"I know, I know. But I had a dream, or a premonition, or something. I saw unimaginable poverty in the streets of a city, public buildings were in flames, and dead bodies lay on the shore for miles. It was horrific. And over it all hung the crystal. It was like a giant pendulum swinging back and forth over the mayhem I watched unfold."

"I don't get it. Are you supposed to stop this from happening?"

"I don't know."

"Is the devil manipulating you like we talked about?"

He groaned. "I just don't know. Maybe it's the angels of God—they've decided it's time to put the brakes on this thing's deadly program before it's too late." He swung his legs out of the bed onto the floor. "I'm sorry. I have to go."

In Nam, Eddie had never questioned his CO's orders, and he was not questioning them now. Orders were orders. If an officer had to justify every order he gave to the grunts under him, he would never fulfill his mission, which he had been given by his commander, and the entire enterprise of war would be a lost cause. Orders were orders.

As he stepped over the threshold into the firelit den, he pulled the handgun from his waistband. He was 12 feet away from the man, and he felt a sense of peace that he had not known since active duty. He knelt, aimed the gun, and pulled the trigger. The man was dead before his ears could inform his brain that a bullet had been fired. After the initial discharge, Eddie released six more shots because Colonel MacKenzie told him to do so.

As the gunshots exploded in Victor Penlick's study, Clive rolled out of bed onto the floor. His room was on the second floor above the den. But the shots sounded as though they were just outside his door. He got on his knees and grabbed his cell phone.

The shots not only woke up Clive but the 5,000 residents of Bailey Pond. They also activated a dozen car alarms and agitated everyone's dogs, who set to barking and howling with abandon. The exclusive neighborhood was the pride of Dallas, and it was only minutes before the flashing blue and red lights of squad cars filled the streets. The police found the residents already waiting for them in their bathrobes and flannel PJs, bearing pistols and long guns locked and loaded.

Eddie looked at the man whose head he had nearly blown off. He did not know who he was. He felt strange, like what had just happened was a dream. But the colonel was saying he had fulfilled his mission and that he would get a commendation.

Outside, the lights from the cars in the driveway and street bounced off the trees and across the water of the swimming pool. The doorbell rang. Eddie looked to the front of the house and then back at the patio. The bell rang again. The back yard was deep and dark. He dropped the gun, and ran from the study, around the pool, and through the grass.

CHAPTER 37

The flight lifted off the LaGuardia tarmac at 5:50 a.m. Clayton would be in Dallas by about nine. He did not know if he would find the crystal there or discover something else. If he was lucky, it would turn out to be a big nothing-burger, and he would be home in time for dinner. He closed his eyes as the aircraft climbed into the sky.

"Victor's dead"—the words rang in Raven's ears. It was 7:00 a.m., and she was on the phone with Victor's secretary. "I'm still in Dallas. I'm at the airport hotel. Yes, I can be back at the office at nine."

The secretary blubbered through the whole call as she tried to explain: A known homeless man from the southside, a vet, somehow got into Victor's house and blew his brains out.

Raven asked the waitress for another cup of coffee and a bagel. It was going to be an interesting day.

Clayton had been to Dallas several times before, but always for an explicit purpose. This time his visit was based only on a gut feeling.

As the plane taxied to the terminal, he turned on his smartphone.

The banner of a news app read, "Breaking News: Victor Penlick Gunned Down In His Home." He felt like he was playing Jeopardy. The question was, "Who was Amelia K. Irons' boss?" It was a data point Amelia had given them when they had stripped her of her anonymity. *Dallas must be the epicenter of the cabal.* He looked at his hand. It trembled. *The crystal's master knew this happened, and it woke me up in the middle of the night to come and get it. Elowen is going to flip when I tell her what happened.*

He began a search on his phone for Victor's address. But he thought he heard a voice in his ear. It was as if someone had just whispered the word, "morgue." The plane lurched to a stop at the gate. He closed his eyes, and the word *MORGUE* flashed like a neon sign behind his eyelids.

Raven, Madison, and Senator Cockler stood in front of the vault in Victor's office. Raven held the open jewelry box in her hands. "This is a fake," she said as they looked at it.

The faces of the men on the big screen appeared troubled.

"I saw it in Amelia's home when we met there once, and this is not it."

"What's going on, Raven?" Hammerman asked.

"The director took it." All the pieces of the puzzle had just fallen into place for her. She and the other two sat down at the conference table. Raven said, "Gentleman, we have a problem. Last night you promoted me, knowing I had carried out the termination of my predecessor. I've done that kind of thing before, and that's not what's bothering me. My problem is with how I think it went down. The whole time I was lightheaded and foggy; it was like a dream. And I wrote it off as a mental lapse because of PTSD. Now, I believe the director manipulated me to carry out that mission."

"How can you be sure?" Justice Orden asked.

"Well, first, with that thing we know it's possible to manipulate people. We've seen Derrick Romano do that, and I'm certain the director got into my head. Second, when the cops showed up at

Amelia's yesterday, I was covered with blood sitting next to her body holding a five-inch blade and wearing her giant ring. They asked me if I was okay and if I'd seen who killed Amelia. No, I said, and they let me go. I should've understood what was going on then.

"And third, the director's dead. You all know about his son, Dakota?" Everyone nodded. "He's an engineer with a job somewhere in the Middle East. As we know, when the director put that crystal on, he shared its power with Dakota. Unfortunately for the director, his son hates him. And the twist to this strange story is that yesterday was the director's birthday."

"I'm not getting this at all," Adam Stone, the venture capitalist, said.

"I went by the director's house on my way here."

"They let you in?"

"My FBI ID is more than passable. There were two dozen black roses in the director's study with a birthday card. In the card there was a poem:

> 'Roses are black,
> Poppies are red,
> I hope you die
> With a bullet in your head.'

"It was signed 'Dakota.'"

"Shit," Skarlyle said. "If Victor was wearing the damned crystal when he died, then it's at the morgue."

"That's what I'm thinking," Raven said.

Unbelievable, Clayton thought. In a cab, he continued reading the article on his phone. *Victor Penlick was shot dead in his mansion the night of his birthday by a known homeless man, a retired vet.* The article provided the man's name, it described him, and it warned the reader not to approach him as he was dangerous. *Penlick was killed about 12 hours after Amelia Irons was murdered*, he realized.

The article said because a motive for the killing had not yet been established, the authorities were holding Victor's body at the city's medical examiner building. They would conduct a complete autopsy on receiving permission from the next of kin.

The Dallas Medical Examiner was only a 20-minute drive from the airport. Clayton had visited one in New York City for a book he wrote about a man who had a life-after-death experience. The place was sanitized from top to bottom, but that did not change what he would later call in his book "the super-unnatural feeling of death," which he went on to describe as a chill that pierced his bones and a strong desire to vomit. It was a feeling that hung with him for several hours after his visit.

The cabdriver was husky in the shoulders and bald. Clayton recognized his accent as Mexican. The man pulled the taxi into a parking slip in front of the morgue, which was three stories high and built with red brick set on a white concrete foundation. Tinted windows looked out over the parking lot. It was a nice building, but its backdrop was an industrial wasteland. Apparently, no one had wanted the city's holding tank for dead people as their neighbor. Clayton watched a woman wearing scrubs go to the entrance, wave a keycard, and pull the door open. There was a camera above the door.

"I need to get inside to have a look around without a lot of fanfare," Clayton said.

"You a journalist?" the cabbie said.

"I'm a writer."

"My cousin works here. She says people are dying to get in."

"That one never gets old. Is she working today?"

"I can call her to see if she can help you."

"That would be great."

The man took a cellphone out of his jacket pocket and made the call. "Hi, Grace," he said. "I'm good. How're you? Are you working? I'm sitting outside your building in my cab with a journalist who wants to take an unofficial tour. What do you think?" He paused for a moment and nodded his head. "Let me ask him." He looked at

Clayton: "She said she'll let you in, no questions asked, for a hundred bucks. If you want a tour, that'll be another hundred bucks."

Clayton pulled out his wallet and removed two hundred dollar bills.

"Grace, it looks like you just earned two hundred dollars," he said, and he disconnected. "She said she'll meet you at the service entrance in the back of the building in five minutes."

* * *

"Unfortunately," the senator said, "we can't just ask the medical examiner to retrieve the charm and hold it for us. The body and everything on it belongs to the county until the investigation's done."

"That's what I'm thinking," Greenbaugh, the CEO, said. "And even if he was able to do us that favor, there would be the risk that the crystal might draw him in. It would be a disaster if he put it on."

"We could send in a fixer—unofficial, of course," Skarlyle said. As an oilman, he had had to fix a lot of things, so to speak. "I've got a guy who can do anything you might ever imagine. And I mean anything. This guy could steal your grandmother's broach off her chest in the middle of church."

"He wouldn't want to do that with my grandmother," Greenbaugh said. "She'd shoot him in the gut."

"In church?"

"Yep, and in the name of God."

"But using a fixer would leave us with the same problem as asking the ME for help," Raven pointed out.

"We have no choice," Cockler said. "We'll have to set up a meeting with the medical examiner onsite."

"When?" Stone asked.

"Immediately," the senator said. "I'm thinking the longer we wait, the harder it will be to get our hands on the thing. I'll take Raven and Madison with me." He looked at the secretary. "Do you think you could set up a video call of the meeting for the others?"

"Of course," she said.

Grace wore green scrubs as she led the way down a blue and white tiled hallway. She was short, but she walked fast. Her ponytail bounced back and forth with each step. "How'd you meet my cousin?" she asked.

He did not detect a Spanish accent; she had probably lived in Texas since she was a kid.

"I got into his cab at the airport," Clayton said. He was dressed in jeans and a black overcoat. "How long have you worked here?"

"Five years."

"Do you like it?"

"It's more interesting than a retirement home, but not as good as a hospital. But everyone's dying to get in, you know?"

"That's what I hear. The first time I visited a morgue I had the creepiest feeling. I'm not sensing it now."

"I had that my first time, too. Really cold? Made you kind of sick?"

He nodded.

"But it passes, thankfully. So why do you want to see this guy?"

"He was famous in his industry, and I want to take a look at him for myself."

They came to a door marked "Examination Room." She unlocked it with her keycard, and they stepped in. There were sinks, soap, towels, gowns, facemasks, and latex gloves. "This is the prep room," she said. "Do you know how to do this?"

"I'll follow you," he said.

She proceeded to put on a gown and mask, wash and dry her hands, and she squeezed her hands into a pair of gloves. "Ready?" she said.

He gave her a thumbs up and a nod.

She opened the door. The room was all stainless steel and tile. Three exam tables on wheels were in a row in the middle of the room. Over each table hung an adjustable, swinging lamp. In one of the walls there were vaults, each one with a number on its door. Grace took a clipboard that hung on the wall. "Who're we looking for?"

"Victor Penlick."

After examining the clipboard for a moment, she put it back on its hook, went to a vault, opened the door, grabbed the edge of a metal table, and pulled it out of the wall. "Whoa," she said.

Clayton could feel the chill rising off the dead man's body. He looked like a perfect specimen of humanity until you got to his face. The gunshots had made him unrecognizable.

"Revenge?" Grace asked.

"Hatred," Clayton said. "Where's his stuff?"

"In the evidence locker."

"Do you have access to that?"

"For another two hundred bucks." He looked at her with a raised eyebrow.

"There's another person we'll have to pay."

He pulled two more bills from his wallet, and she pushed Penlick's vault back into the wall.

A security guard met them at the entrance. Madison got the video call going and filmed the group from behind as they made their way through security and down a long hallway. They came to a door with a nameplate: "Dr. Howard Peek, Medical Examiner."

The guard opened it and invited them in.

A woman sat at a desk. She was middle-aged and plump around the middle. Her eyes were baby blue, and her dark brown hair was styled with a short bob. "You're the group investigating the murder of Victor Penlick?"

"Yes, that's right," Raven said.

"Please have a seat, and I'll call the doctor."

They sat on a couch across from the secretary's desk. Madison sat on one end with her cell phone trained on Raven and the senator.

After a few moments the secretary invited them to follow her to the doctor's office, and they went in.

"Hello, Senator," the doctor said. He stood and held out his hand.

"How're you, my friend?" He was tall, well over six feet, and his head was crowned with short, thick, and dark curly hair.

"I'm well. Thank you for seeing us on such short notice," Cockler said as they shook hands.

"Of course. Please introduce me to your friends."

After everyone had shaken hands and taken a seat, the senator explained why Madison was filming the meeting.

"I don't have a problem with that," the doctor said. "Now tell me, how can I help you?"

The evidence locker was actually a whole warehouse attached to the medical examiner's building. There were two access points, which were an outdoor loading dock for incoming evidence, and an indoor office entrance. Grace opened the door for Clayton.

A police officer in a blue uniform with a gun on his hip sat at a desk behind a service counter. He typed on a computer. A badge over his left pocket read, "Sgt. Daniel Lopez." Behind him there was a window with a view of the warehouse. He looked up from the monitor.

"Hi, Grace. How're you today?" he asked.

"I'm just fine, Danny. How's your wife?"

"She's good. What can I do you for?"

"Evidence kit."

"Got the number?"

She had written it on her hand from the clipboard, and she read it to him.

After he typed in the number, he said, "We're due for a barbecue."

"José would love that."

There was the whirring and clinking of machinery working in the background.

"It's all automated," Daniel said, looking at Clayton. "With robots and conveyor belts, in a couple minutes the evidence box will appear right here." He pointed with his thumb over his shoulder at the window behind his desk.

Dr. Peek led them down a series of long hallways. "I probably should've gotten a cart," he said. "But I'm in the habit of using my visits to the locker to get some exercise."

"No problem," Cockler said. "A little exercise never hurt anyone."

Raven and Madison nodded.

Clayton tapped his fingers on the counter as they waited.

Grace watched him for a moment. "Someone else is looking for this evidence, too?" she whisper-asked.

"I'm afraid so," he said.

There was a beep and a greenlight blinked over the window behind Officer Lopez. He whirled around in his chair and slid it open. There was an aluminum box, one foot square. Lopez picked it up and put it on the counter in front of Clayton. Without saying a word, he returned to his desk and went back to work on his computer.

Clayton released the fasteners of the lid on the box and opened it. Inside there was clothing and three pieces of jewelry. Each thing was in its own sealed plastic bag. There was a wristwatch, a ring, and the black tourmaline crystal. Clayton soundlessly made the word, "bingo," and he grabbed the bag with the crystal and shoved it into his pocket. "Nothing here," he said, and he shut the box's lid.

The cop kept typing. "No problem," he said.

"Thanks, Danny. José will call you about that barbecue," Grace said as she slid a hundred dollar bill under the metal box.

"Sounds good."

Sergeant Daniel Lopez had just sent the evidence kit for Victor Penlick back to the warehouse when Dr. Peek and the senator, Raven, and Madison came into his office. He was lucky to get a visit once in a day. Two visits made a day extra special. He stood and met the group at the counter. "Hello, Dr. Peek. How're y'all doing today?"

"Very fine, son. Thank you. How's your wife? The kids?"

"They're all fine, sir. Thank you. What can I do you for?"

Peek took a moment to introduce the senator and the others. "This is Sergeant Daniel Lopez," he explained to them. "He's worked here for years and has a deep knowledge of the cases that're filed in the evidence locker." He redirected his attention to the officer: "We'd like to see the evidence kit for one Victor Penlick. He was last night's homicide in Bailey Pond."

"You got it," Lopez said, and he pulled a form from under the counter. "Please fill this out while I make the request. This'll take just a couple minutes. Y'all can have a seat."

Everyone sat as Peek filled out the form. When he was done, he sat with the others.

"It looks like a new system," Raven said.

"Oh, yes," Peek said, and he boasted about how the automated warehouse was cutting edge, the best in the industry for response time, ease of use, and security. As he spoke, there was a beep and the flash of the green light over the warehouse window. Sergeant Lopez retrieved the metal box, and the group went to the counter and looked at it expectantly as he undid the fasteners and flipped open the lid.

Raven rustled through the clothing and jewelry. "It's not here," she said.

"Damn it to hell," Cockler muttered. Madison followed his shaking head with the camera, which created a rocking ship effect for the others who watched on their computers. "Has anyone else had access to this kit?" he asked Lopez.

"No one else has formally submitted a request for it except for you," he said.

After the doctor escorted the group to the front door, they were outside again in the parking lot. They stared at each other. "I feel like it was just here," Raven said. "Do you guys feel that?" Raven said.

"I don't," Cockler said. Madison shook her head.

"Maybe it's because I was under the crystal's spell once."

"Are you saying the cop or Peek were lying?" the senator asked.

"What I think is that Clayton Lange beat us to the punch. We can keep looking for it. We should definitely go by Penlick's house again just to be sure. But I would be surprised if that thing was anywhere else but in Clayton Lange's possession."

Derrick looked at his hands. They tingled. He had been asleep for ten hours straight with all kinds of weird, vivid dreams, and in color. His dad, his real dad, was using the crystal, their crystal, again.

This is fucking awesome.

With his hand on Penelope's belly, he pulled her close from behind. She parted her legs. Her long, red hair smelled like mangos. He had been impotent for weeks with what his psychiatrist called situational depression. But that had just burned off like the morning mist from fresh blooms under a new sun.

CHAPTER 38

The upstate New York harbor town had a year round population of less than 2,000. But from Memorial Day to Labor Day thousands of people poured into it daily, shopping in the quaint stores, eating fresh seafood, and swimming and sailing. The main street was two lanes and lined with dogwood trees—the creamy white springtime blooms were full.

"I love the Hamptons," Elowen said. She and Clayton held hands as they walked past the shops. "The people are so friendly. It's so laid back."

"I feel it, and I like it, too."

They paused and gazed at lamps in the window of an antique store. "I saw Jocelyn's manuscript on your end table by the bed," Elowen said.

"It's really good. Lots of heart. I think I can see her parents with their musician friends in it. She has some really cool plot twists, and her dialogue is tight. I know an agent who might work with her."

"She'll be so excited." They ate lunch outside a deli across the street from the marina. Grilled paninis was their choice. Elowen took a sip of iced tea. "But I've been thinking about what we've learned about the crystal."

"Yeah?" he asked, and he took a bite of sandwich.

"Originally, you got rid of it because of the threat of the cabal and for our safety as a family."

"Right."

"But things got weird, people died, and now you have it again. I've been wondering if you're thinking what I'm thinking."

"That world domination is my destiny?"

"Not funny. When you told me about how the crystal—as in the devil—or maybe angels—it doesn't matter—called you to go to Dallas to retrieve it from the morgue, I was totally freaked out."

"I was, too." He took another bite. "This is probably the best panini I've ever had." He wiped his lips with a napkin. "But ever since I picked it back up, I feel better, healthier even, than I did before."

They finished eating, and Elowen paid the waitress. "Let's take a walk around the marina."

A light wind created a ripple across the water. They held hands with fingers intertwined. "Did you see the news that Derrick announced his tour schedule?"

"I missed that."

"His first concert for the season will be tomorrow, the fourth of July."

"Wow, that was quick. Where's it going to be?"

"Soldier Field in Chicago. He's calling the tour 'Fight Club.'"

Clayton shook his head. "He makes me sad."

"Me, too." She stopped walking and tugged on his arm. He turned and looked at her. "Clayton, this is what I'm talking about. Even though you've done good with the crystal—"

"Yeah, except for Charlie."

"Well, that's my point. And there's Derrick, who has intentionally done bad. I'm afraid of how easily this can get away from us. That dream or premonition or whatever it was you had before you went to Dallas, it wasn't a good thing."

He stared out at the water with pursed lips.

"Are you all right?"

"No. I wanted to be here for the holiday. But instead I've got to go to that concert tomorrow to figure out how to make this thing right."

Dazzle tapped out a rhythm on the snare and a tom. "Derr," he said, "I'm thinking the title for the concert and encore along with the graphics we're using for the posters are going to bring the heat down on us before we even begin."

The band practiced in a studio in Los Angeles. "We're totally stealing the title," Derrick said. "They'll think it's a PR stunt. The cities all want to give us a venue anyway—they love us."

"They love the money," TJ said.

"You know it." Derrick laughed and took the mic from the stand. "Let's do the whole set, beginning with 'To the Fire' and ending with the encore, 'Fight Club.'"

CHAPTER 39

A rap metal band had been warming up the crowd at Soldier Field when the fireworks began at 9:00 p.m. With the rockets soaring, exploding, and throwing ribbons of color across the sky, TJ played a bass riff, and Dazzle followed him on the on the drums. Rex came in with the first few bars of "To the Fire," and Derrick appeared at centerstage. He flipped everyone the bird and screamed, "I'm glad you're here!" And the audience gave it back to him, cheering wildly.

Derrick sang,

> To the fire, in the fire,
> All aflame
> Ain't no shame.
> To the light, in the darkness,
> Where it burns
> Everything turns to ash, baby.

The band played non-stop for two and a half hours.

Clayton had been a punk rocker in his youth, following the Ramones, the Dead Kennedys, and The Clash. They had been loud and rowdy, but nothing like this. Derrick and his crowd were deafening and violent. Clayton had had his share of bloody noses in the mosh pits, but the intensity in the pit tonight made his experience look like daycare playtime. Ambulance lights lit up the area throughout the concert.

With a final cymbal crash and an explosion of rockets, the stage blacked out and the band disappeared. The crowd chanted, "We ain't goin' home! We ain't goin' home!"

A single spotlight blinked on, illuminating Dazzle at the drums. He began tapping out something on the tom-toms, snare, and cymbals, and after setting the rhythm, he doubled the tempo. The people were stomping and jumping. Dazzle doubled his speed again—his sticks were hardly visible. The whole stadium was pogoing. And then, slowly, slowly he brought the audience down, and they landed softly. Collectively, they took in a deep breath.

TJ and Rex had picked up their instruments, and with the release of a rocket that exploded with a rainbow of colors, Derrick was again on stage. He shouted, "What do you want?"

"You!" the people screamed.

"Hell, yeah!" he screamed back.

"Hell, yeah! Hell, yeah!" they chanted.

Dazzle gave three quick beats on the kick drum, and Derrick sang,

> Ain't backin' down from the bout
> Not before I lay 'em out
> Bloody knuckles and broken noses
> Those I fought are pushin' up roses...

Holy hell, Clayton thought as he listened and watched. The pogoing and elbowing in the pit was heating up again. And in the stands, too. He was jostled in his seat, and he turned around. There was a man the size of gorilla staring down at him with a crazy grin.

"Come on, man," he yelled over the music. "Let's mix it up!" And he planted his two enormous hands on his shoulders and pushed.

Clayton fell into the row of seats below him. The guy he fell into bent down and punched him in the face. He could hear Derrick sing,

Let's get ugly and loud for the cops
Leave 'em with blood for their mops
Don't stop now, but fight, fight, fight
This is Fight Club, y'all, it's right, right, right!

Those were the last words Clayton heard before the man punched him in the face again.

Elowen had been able to sleep for only an hour. It was almost midnight. She got up and used the bathroom. Back in bed, she checked the news on her phone and found the headline, "Riot at Romano Concert in Chicago." She gazed at the crib where their baby would sleep. *Clayton, I don't want to raise this child alone.* She turned on the TV. There was live coverage of the aftermath of the riot on all the news stations.

A reporter stood outside a gate for the stadium. Behind her there were the flashing lights of a stream of ambulances and police cars. She said it was at the end of the concert when the whole stadium erupted with violence. She talked to two young men: "How do you feel about Derrick Romano after what happened tonight?" she asked.

"We got what we paid for!" said one who had a fresh blackeye. The other one added, "It was in the title of the concert. Duh." They laughed and walked away.

Elowen turned off the TV and called Clayton. His phone went straight to voicemail. "Where are you?" she asked. It had been a long time, but she remembered how her grandma had taught her to pray. She folded her hands and closed her eyes. "Dear Father in Heaven...."

The phone rang. It was five o'clock. She had fallen back to sleep. "Hello?" she murmured.

"Hello. May I please speak with Mrs. Elowen Lange?" a woman asked.

"This is she."

"I'm the patient advocate at Chicago Memorial Hospital...."

After the call, Elowen cried. Clayton had been admitted to the hospital at about 1:00 a.m. with a concussion. An hour later, in a cab on her way to the airport, she read on her phone about how during Derrick's encore fights had broken out across the stadium. There had been eye-gougings, head-stompings, stabbings, and lots of broken bones. The mayor told reporters Derrick would never be welcome in Chicago again, and that the city would sue him for damages. "We're lucky no one was killed," he said.

What's wrong with him? she thought.

"Which airline, ma'am?" the driver asked. He spoke with a sing-song Jamaican accent.

She told him, and she added, "I'm going to Chicago."

"Have you heard about the riot at the concert last night?"

"Yeah, my husband was there."

He looked at her in the rearview mirror and shook his head. "I'm sorry, ma'am."

It was noon when Elowen got to the Chicago hospital. Clayton was propped up on pillows. She looked at his face and shuddered. Obviously, the patient advocate had been trained to understate the facts: He had a concussion, but he had also been beaten hard. Both eyes were black and blue—one was swollen shut. His nose was bandaged, and his face was bloated like a melon, colored in different shades of red and blue. She kissed him on the lips.

"It was a helluva a concert," he mumbled.

"So I've heard."

"Would've been better on cable, though."

"I see you haven't lost your sense of humor." She noticed the crystal in a baggie with his wallet and watch on a table next to the bed. "That didn't help you."

"I wasn't prepared—it all happened so fast."

"What now?"

"I don't know."

"I ain't feeling it," Derrick said. He and Penelope lay in bed. It was early in the morning, still dark outside.

"Last night you were on fire," she said.

"Yeah, it was a great concert." He chuckled, but a gloominess quickly settled him. "Remember when I was blah?"

"Yeah."

"That's how I feel now. The old man's unplugged me again."

"Is it like a drug? You know, after you stop using it, you feel beat-up for a while as your body begins to heal itself."

"It's not like that. The feeling it gives me isn't like anything I can experience without it. I have to get that thing." He got out of bed and went to pee. His phone rang. "Go ahead and pick it up," he shouted from the toilet.

"Hello," Penelope answered. "Hi, George. What's up? Okay. Hold on." She put the phone on mute and shouted to Derrick, "It's George. He needs to talk to you about cancellations."

Raven met with Jake and Tarek in her home. With her promotion, she had bought a condo in uptown Manhattan. Her love for West African art was obvious with the bright colors and décor she had chosen. And she inherited Gus. Amelia, she had despised, but Gus, she loved.

As Tarek and Jacob took chairs at the dining room table, she admired her long acrylic fingernails and emerald ring.

"I read online that Clayton Lange was at Romano's concert last night and ended up in the hospital," Tarek said.

"I saw that," Raven said.

"I don't know what he was expecting," Jake said, "but he walked into a tsunami."

"He doesn't understand the crystal," Tarek said.

"Correct," Raven agreed. "After all this time he still doesn't see the obvious, that there's something behind it, possibly something evil, and it needs to be handled with care."

"Do you think Derrick intended for things to go as far south as they did in Chicago?" Jake asked.

"That's what I'm saying. I don't think he intended for the fighting to become a stadium brawl and for his whole tour to be canceled. Neither he nor Clayton know what they're doing."

"These guys are going to kill each other if they're not careful," Tarek said.

"That's what I'm counting on," Raven said. "And when they're done, we'll take possession of the crystal once and for all."

CHAPTER 40

The birthing room at the hospital was big and the colors were warm. Elowen's feet were firmly planted in the stirrups as the doctor examined her. "You're ten centimeters," the doctor said.

Clayton held Elowen's hand. "I love you, sweetheart," he said. She stared at him as though he spoke a foreign language, and she moaned.

Ten minutes later after much pushing and many more moans, the doctor announced, "Your baby is a girl!"

"Her name is Emily," Clayton said, and the doctor bundled her up and gave her to Elowen.

After the baby nursed, a nurse took her for her first examination. Elowen fell fast asleep. Clayton sat by the window in the room with a coffee, a Danish, and a notepad. "What can I do for Derrick?" he wrote. He closed his eyes for a moment, and then he jotted down, "I can build him up, take him out, or do nothing." *Those* are *my choices,* he thought. *Help him, kill him, or ignore him.* But he knew the last two choices were not going to happen. Derrick might be able to kill *him* for the crystal, but he himself did not have the gene that would even make that choice a relevant option.

Why is this kid so violent? he wondered. *He's angry because of his childhood. I get that. But this is more than anger. Is he a sociopath? Entirely possible. He's definitely narcissistic. But that doesn't explain the rage.*

Could the crystal have shaped Derrick in utero? He was six when he began to wear it. But it had been in Derrick's life even before he was born. *It's a part of him. He may even be the personification of the spirit of the thing.*

Helping Derrick—that would be a challenge. It would require turning the crystal back on itself—he was pretty sure that was the closest he was going to get to understanding it. If Derrick wanted to do evil, if that was his nature because of the crystal, then transforming him with the crystal was a fool's errand.

He was going to have to think this through. *I'm not going to put the baby or Elowen at risk,* he reflected. *But I'm not going to give the thing up to the cabal again.* That meant it was going back to the safe deposit box until further notice.

It was a sunshiny day in Malibu. Penelope climbed out of the pool and wrapped a towel around her waist. She watched Derrick through the sliding glass doors, lying on the couch in the front room.

He is absolutely manic when he has the crystal's power, she thought. *But without it he's so depressed.* There had to be something she could do for him. Otherwise the man she was looking at was not going to make music or love anytime soon. *I'm going to New York City.*

Derrick could feel Penelope staring at him. *I'm hollowed out,* he reflected. *I'd kill myself, but I don't have the energy to do it.* And he wondered if she was going to leave him. *She should.*

"I read that Clayton Lange's wife had a baby this morning," the senator said. He and the other men video-conferenced with Raven, who was at home.

"His celebrity status makes our surveillance easy," Raven said. She stroked Gus, who lay across her lap.

"Any idea where he's keeping the crystal?" the senator asked.

"No, but I got a report on Derrick Romano from our team on the West Coast. It sounds like he's holed up again at his place in Malibu with Penelope. So I'm going to say with a high degree of confidence that Clayton's not wearing it. It could be anywhere."

After the call, Raven continued to stroke the cat. He purred loudly. "You are a fickle animal, charming whoever feeds you," she said. *I guess we're all like that,* she thought, and she looked at a second monitor. Hacking the webcams at St. John's Medical Center had been easy—there was little security. Clayton was in his wife's room, and they talked about returning home tomorrow. *And are you going to make a stop on the way?* Raven wondered.

After another night at the hospital, Elowen was released with the baby, and Clayton drove them home.

She glanced over her shoulder at the baby in the backseat. "We were really blessed."

"Yes, we were," Clayton agreed.

"Are you still planning on going to the bank after you drop us off?"

"Yep," he said, and he patted the breast pocket of his bomber's jacket. "The sooner I get this thing to its new home, the better."

Minutes later, they were in the driveway, and Anna and Charlie met them with hugs and congratulations. They all went into the house, and after Elowen and the baby were settled in, Clayton was back in the car. The safe deposit box was at a bank in the village.

On the main thoroughfare, Clayton realized he had not eaten since the night before, so he pulled into a fast food drive-thru and got a breakfast sandwich and coffee. He parked to eat.

As he chomped into the sandwich, he looked across the street. There was a silver SUV, and behind the wheel was *that* girl, the redhead. *What's her name? Penelope, the one from the cabal.* She was staring straight at him. He choked on the sandwich and coughed.

He took a sip of coffee. This was disturbing. The cabal might also be around. They had been only one step behind him ever since he had retrieved the crystal from the morgue in Dallas. He finished the sandwich and pulled out onto the street. Penelope was still staring at him. He waved at her, and she shook her head.

About a block away from the bank, Clayton pulled up to the curb and parked. Penelope parked behind him. He could go talk to her. But what if she shot him? That would not be good. But she must know it would be almost impossible for her to do that, get the crystal, and escape. There was too much traffic to go anywhere fast, and there were cops all over the place. On the other hand, even if he could reason with her, what about the cabal? They must be insanely desperate to retrieve the damn thing, and he was certain they were mad as hell for how he got it from Victor. They, in fact, might shoot him.

He put the car into drive, pulled out into traffic, and drove the last block to the bank. It was on the other side of the street. Parked cars lined the curb. There was a yellow taxi across from him in front of the bank. *That's her,* he thought. The tall black woman—Raven—she sat in the back of the cab. He remembered her from the newscast he saw with Elowen the day Amelia Irons was murdered. "Shit, shit, shit."

He tapped his breast pocket again. "So you don't want me to die, at least not yet." He drove another block and took a left and parked. He grabbed his cellphone and tapped 9-1-1. "This is an emergency," he said. "There's a woman in a yellow cab waving a gun around in front of First Bank on Main Street in the village. Yes. That's right. She's still there, and she looks crazy."

He drove again. Taking the next left, he made a U-turn in the middle of the street. He took a right at the next intersection, and then another right. Slowly, he idled the car down the street until he was half a block behind the cab, and he double-parked. Penelope had followed him, and she stopped right behind him. Cars honked as traffic pulled around them. And then there were sirens blaring and blue lights flashing. Police cruisers came from both directions. Penelope's SUV jumped out into traffic, and as it sped by, Clayton saw her arm extend through the driver's window with her middle finger poking into the sky.

The police cars boxed in the cab, and a voice boomed from a PA system, "Yellow taxi in front of the bank, shut down your engine and roll down your windows!" The car's engine died, and the windows came down. "Driver and passenger, open your doors!" The doors opened. "Slowly, get out of the car with your hands above your heads!" In less than a minute the cabby and Raven were both on their knees with their hands in cuffs behind them. Each one was crowded by several officers. Clayton turned on his car's emergency lights and got out. The cops had bigger fish to fry—they would not be concerned about how he had parked.

Raven conferenced with the six men of the late Victor Penlick's cabal. Though she was released from custody quickly, she still felt humiliated for getting arrested for carrying a firearm without a permit. She should have been carrying her FBI ID. She had to give Clayton credit. Giving her up to the police was a genius move. She had underestimated him, and she had let her emotions take over when she heard him tell his wife he was going to the bank after he dropped her and the baby off.

"My friends," she said, "I saw Clayton, and I saw Penelope. I was within fifty feet of them. But Lange lucked out. Penelope was on his tail when he arrived at the bank. I have a strong feeling he had seen her and was spooked. I think he was looking for me when he got to the bank."

"What's next?" Adam Stone asked. "I feel like this thing is getting away from us, that this is money flowing through our fingers."

Judge Orden raised an eyebrow. He was always suspicious of people like Stone who made their living investing other people's money in other people's businesses.

"We're going to keep watching Lange for his next move," Raven said.

CHAPTER 41

Elowen cleared her throat in the doorway of Clayton's office, holding the 3-month old baby. He spun around in his chair. "To what do I owe the pleasure of this visit?" he asked with a smile.

She carried the baby to Clayton. "Your daughter wanted to say hi," she said, and he took her in his arms.

"I just finished my letter to Derrick," he said.

"Do you want to read it to me?"

"That would be great," he said, and Elowen sat next to him at the computer. She took the baby, and Clayton said, "Here goes."

Dear Derrick,

This is a long overdue letter, and I am sorry. But it was only recently I learned you were my son. Someday, I hope to have a conversation with you about my relationship with your mom, whom I once loved deeply.

Presently, however, there are more pressing issues, the principal one being that you and I share a superpower that has only been imagined in comic books. I didn't even know I had this power until my publisher revealed to me I was using it subconsciously to fulfill the plotlines in my books. It's the same power I used to free you from the cabal.

As you know, the source of this power is a black crystal. I acquired it from my late grandfather who stole it from Adolf Hitler. This and other stories concerning the path of the crystal to our family is for another time. For now, I'll only say that after a great deal of research and a series of tests and observations, I've concluded there is a force behind the crystal which has its own designs. I believe the source of the crystal's power intends for it to be used to create chaos on an unprecedented scale. For this reason, it is my intention to permanently retire it. I'm not sure what this means yet, but I believe it must be done.

I have been blessed with a lot of resources over the years through my artform, as have you. Perhaps we could be a team and use our God-given talents and other assets without the help of the crystal to make a difference in a positive way in the world, building a program to make big things happen.

I'm excited about talking to you, Derrick. Please let me know what you think at your earliest convenience.

Yours sincerely,

"I like how you appealed to his humanity," she said. "The association with Hitler, however, I'm not sure about that. Do you think that's necessary?"

"I'm guessing he already knows about it because of his time with Penelope. But either way, I think I need to be as transparent as possible with him. If he senses I'm hiding anything, he'll never open his heart to me."

It was two in the afternoon, and Derrick was still in bed. He had watched the news for half an hour, rolled over, and slept again. Penelope sat in bed next to him and read the letter from Clayton Lange. She looked at Derrick and then out the window at the ocean. She had come so close to getting the crystal from Clayton when she had been in New York a few weeks ago. But everything had gone sideways real fast with the appearance of that psychopath, Raven.

What Clayton wrote makes a lot of sense, she thought. *This is the way people like him think.* She looked again at Derrick. *But he's not going to go for it. Even when he's depressed, he wants to break things.*

An hour later, Derrick woke up, and he was hungry. She made him a bowl of chicken soup and served it to him in bed.

"This is really good," he said in between slurps.

"Thanks. You got a letter from Clayton Lange," she said, climbing back into bed.

He snorted a laugh. "Does he want to be my *daddy* now?"

"That, and he said he intends to get rid of the crystal because it's evil. But he wants to team up with you to make a positive difference in the world, using the other resources you guys have."

"He hasn't listened to my music, obviously."

"Maybe he's appealing to your better angels."

"Impossible. The demons killed 'em all. Here, let me see the letter." She handed it to him, and he gave it a glance. "There's a highlighter and pen in the desk in the other room. Could you grab them for me?"

"Sure," she said, and got out of bed. A moment later she returned with the writing utensils.

Sniggering, he marked up the letter in his lap, and he handed it back to her. "Send it to him, and we'll see how he feels about having a relationship with me after he reads it."

Elowen and Anna were out shopping, so Emily lay in a bassinet beside Clayton's desk as he wrote. A bundle of mail fell through the mail slot in the front room onto the hardwood floor with a thud. He got up and gathered the mail and went back to his desk to sort through it. There was lots of junk mail, a few bills, and a single hand-addressed letter. There was no return address, but the postmark was for Malibu.

Derrick's the only person I know there, he thought. He slit open the envelope and read the letter:

Dear ~~Derrick,~~ **Old Man!**
~~*This is a long overdue letter, and I am sorry. But it was only*~~

~~recently I learned you were my son. Someday,~~ **I hope to have a** ~~conversation with you about my relationship with your mom, whom I once loved deeply.~~

~~Presently, however, there are more pressing issues, the principal one being that you and I share a~~ **superpower that has only been imagined in the comic books.** ~~I didn't even know I had this power until my publisher revealed to me I was using it subconsciously to fulfill the plotlines in my books. It's~~ **the same power** ~~I used to free you from the cabal.~~

~~As you know, the source of this power is a black crystal. I acquired it from my late grandfather who stole it from~~ **Adolf Hitler.** ~~This and other stories concerning the path of the crystal to our family is for another time. For now, I'll only say that after a great deal of research and a series of tests and observations, I've concluded there is a force behind the crystal which has its own designs. I believe the source of the crystal's power intends for it to be~~ **used to create chaos on an unprecedented scale. For this reason, it is my intention** ~~to permanently retire it. I'm not sure what this means yet, but I believe it must be done.~~

~~I have been blessed with a lot of resources over the years~~ **through my artform** ~~as have you. Perhaps we could be a team and use our God-given talents and other assets without the help of the crystal to make a difference in a positive way in the world, building a program~~ **to make big things happen.**

~~I'm excited to talk to you. Derrick. Please let me know what you think at your earliest convenience.~~

Yours sincerely,

He had drawn a line through Clayton's signature and scrawled his own.

Plan B, Clayton thought.

That evening, after the baby had been fed and put to bed, Clayton and Elowen watched TV.

"I got a response from Derrick today," he said.

"That was quick."

"But it wasn't what I hoped for."

"I'm sorry."

"So am I."

"Next step?"

"He doesn't want to let go of the crystal's power."

"But he really doesn't have any say in the matter."

"That is true. However—and I know I sound totally co-dependent—but I have a bad feeling about what might happen to him if I make him go cold turkey."

"You're right. You are co-dependent. It's not on you to fix him."

"But I'm not ready to give up on him yet. I want to try to defeat his anger and hatred with love."

She scoffed, "Give me a break."

"Jesus, Mahatma Gandhi, and Martin Luther King, Junior all swore by it."

"Yeah, and look what happened to them."

"But their legacy lives on."

"I don't care about a legacy. I want a father for our daughter."

"So do I," he said.

In the morning, Clayton opened a blank document on his computer, centered the cursor, and typed, "A Father's Love for His Son." And he rested his fingers on the keys. He stared at the screen. Minutes passed. Nothing.

I need the crystal for this one.

An hour later, after a visit to the bank, Clayton sat back down at the computer. The black stone lay on the desk in front of him. *Is there a spirit or a demon in this thing? Or is it more like a power or force?* He shook his head as he picked it up by the chain. He might never know.

He dropped the chain over his neck, and when the stone touched his chest, he saw a flash of light that blinded him for a moment. He took a deep breath. As his vision cleared, the story came to him. And he typed.

It was going to be hard to give up the crystal.

Hours later, after lots of coffee and a chicken sandwich, he was well into the piece.

Elowen let him hole up in the office for three days without complaint, and Anna delivered sandwiches and coffee on request.

It's not Pulitzer material, he thought as he read through the finished work. *But it has a beginning, a middle, and an end.* It was a fictional story about real people, in this case, him and Derrick. In retrospect, this is what most of his novels had been: fictional stories about what he wanted or people he had envisioned wanted. But his telling of this story had a unique twist. He had figured out that the crystal gave the two generations a kind of mutual telepathy—he was going to use that to tell Derrick his story through his dreams.

His phone rang: "Hi, Elliot. I'm good. How are you? I've got a plotline for a hot romance I want to pitch to you. It's going to make Danielle Steele look like a Catholic school girl. Sure. Yeah. I'd love to come into the city. Tomorrow's great. See you then."

Elowen sat beside him with Emily at his desk. His eyes met the baby's—she was his reward for the sleepless nights.

"What's going on with Elliot?" Elowen asked.

"We're going to have lunch in the city tomorrow and talk about my next book."

"Sounds like fun. Did you finish your piece for Derrick?"

"I did."

"Congratulations."

"Thanks. I'm looking at his next concert. It's in Los Angeles in three weeks."

"I thought he was canceled forever."

"'Forever' can be measured in weeks when money is involved."

She shook her head. "Are you sure your plan will work?"

"I'm not sure of anything, but I have to try."

That night Clayton rolled around in bed, sleeping little. He got up early and made coffee. The house was dead silent. With a cup in hand, he went to his office and pounded out a few pages for the thriller-romance he had promised Elliot.

It was hours later when he joined Elowen and Anna in the kitchen. "I'll be leaving for the city in a few minutes."

"Are you driving?" Elowen asked.

"No. Taking the train. Why?"

"It might be safer to drive."

"Are you suddenly anti-train? Where's the city girl I married?"

"Your suburban housewife and the mother of your daughter buried her."

"I've taken the train and subway zillions of times without any trouble. I'll be fine." He kissed her and the baby.

He parked at the train station in the village and waited on the boarding platform. He surveyed the other patrons of city transit. There were just a couple of other people. Midmorning, it was slow. And it was quiet. There was no wind nor birds, but only ambient street noises.

The train squealed to a stop in front of him, and he flinched. "Where was I?" he asked himself. The doors of the car opened, and after a handful of people got off, he and the others got on. An androgynous voice gave the usual instructions about standing clear of the doors. He sat and looked around. The other people were all engrossed in their smartphones. As the train moved from the elevated tracks to underground, the lights flickered. There was the steady hum of metal on metal, and Clayton was lulled to sleep. Every couple of minutes the train stopped, but he slept through the ride until the voice announced, "Seventy-seventh Street." The doors opened, and two passengers got off in front of him. He watched them disappear around a corner in the corridor.

Behind him, there was the faint smell of whiskey and a gravelly voice: "Hey, is that you?"

Turning, he said, "I don't think I know—" and then he saw stars as his legs collapsed under him.

There was another voice. It was distant. It was saying, "Stand clear. Give the medics space." He opened his eyes. There was a blur of activity. Police were all around and there were two men leaning into him. He tried to raise a hand, but his arms were strapped down. He was on a gurney in the subway.

"He's conscious," one of the medics said. "Sir, you've been mugged. But you're going to be okay and we're going to get you out of here right now."

The next time he opened his eyes he saw a man in a white coat, who said, "I'm Dr. Dustin." He looked into each of Clayton's eyes with a penlight. "You're at Mercy Hospital in Manhattan. You were beaten up in the subway this morning. I think you're going to be fine. But I want to run some more tests."

"Is my wife here?"

"Yes, but a detective would like to have a word with you before you see her if you're up to it?"

"Yes."

The detective introduced himself and asked him three questions: "Did you see the attacker?" "Do you know anyone who might want to do this to you?" and "Have you been threatened by anyone recently?" His answers were no, no, and no.

"Hi, sweetie," Elowen said as she came through the door. She placed a hand on his arm. "Was this because of you-know-what?"

He turned his head to the side, and there on the end table was the black crystal. "I don't think so because I've still got it. This morning I bragged I'd never been mugged. I guess today was my turn."

"I talked to Elliot and told him you'd call him next week. He sends his and Sarah's love and prayers."

"Thanks."

Two hours later they were driving home. When they finally got into their neighborhood and were pulling into the garage, Clayton said, "I'm going to take a nap." She assured him that she would wake him for dinner.

In the bedroom, he lay down with his cellphone. There was a notification for a voicemail—no name, just a number with a Los Angeles area code. He opened the message. It was Derrick, and he was laughing:

Well, that was pretty damn exciting, wasn't it?! Yesterday, I wrote this song about an underground mugging, assigned your name and city to it, took a swig of tequila, went to sleep, dreamed, and *voila!* I read about you being nearly beaten to death in the subway in Manhattan this morning. There are no limits to this thing's power, are there? Not even the sky.

Clayton deleted it.

CHAPTER 42

They had finished breakfast and were sitting on the couch in the front room, Elowen nursing the baby. "Why do you have to go all the way to L.A.?" she asked. "I don't understand why you can't you do this from home."

"I don't know about you, but I've never been able to build a relationship from a distance. If anything good comes out of this, it's going to be because we made a connection up close and personal."

"How're you feeling, Derr?" Dazzle asked.

It was the middle of December in Malibu—the sky was clear, and the temperature was in the mid-70s. Derrick and his band members lay in swim trunks on lounge chairs around the pool. Penelope was in a microkini snuggled up next to Derrick.

"Like a rock star," Derrick said, and he took a sip of a Tequila Sunrise.

"That is what you are," TJ said. "Congratulations on the new bookings."

"All I have to do is sing about it and dream about where I want to go, and the calls come in."

"Tomorrow night's going to be dope," Rex said. "*We Are Family* is a sweet comeback theme."

"You know it."

"Any thoughts about Lange?" Penelope asked.

"Oh, yeah. He'll be there," Derrick said. "He's been sportin' the crystal. I'm sure he's planning something."

***

The taxi let Clayton off in front of the hotel. He had one full day before the concert. He had checked in with Elowen on the way in from the airport. There had been some tension between them over this trip when he left. But they were okay now.

"If it was just you and me, I'd feel differently," she said. "But we have a baby, and she needs you."

Elowen was right. This had to be it for him and Derrick.

The hotel receptionist checked him in, and a few minutes later he was unlocking his room on the thirty-fourth floor of the Biltmore in downtown Los Angeles. It was palatial. A little over the top, perhaps, but it was as quiet as a tomb, which would be necessary if he was going to get a good night's sleep before the concert.

He sat at a desk that faced a window with a bird's-eye-view of the city center. After setting out his tablet, he leaned back in the chair and let his eyes drink in the skyline. He would order room service and spend the evening reading and reflecting on the short story he had written, *A Father's Love for His Son*.

***

Derrick slammed a shot glass on the coffee table upside down. "Damn fine tequila," he said.

"The best money can buy," Rex said. "Are you good?"

"I'm excellent." He stood and took Penelope by the hand. "We're going to light up that stadium tomorrow night like nothing that's ever been seen before."

They went into the bedroom and shut the door behind them.

Clayton lay in bed after rereading what he had written. *I want to pray,* he thought.

He had not prayed since he was very young, and those prayers were the prescribed prayers of the church. He was a foxhole Catholic if there ever was one. As he reflected on his desire to pray, the words of a favorite passage from his story for Derrick tumbled through his mind:

Billy looked at himself in the bathroom mirror: He was changing.

For his whole life he had carried around in his gut an insatiable hunger to hurt people. He didn't know where that feeling came from. But he did know how to feed the monster. Now, however, ever since his father had reached out to him, that craving for violence had begun to dissolve. It was practically gone now; it was like a scene from a movie he had half-forgotten a long time ago.

He rubbed his cheeks and neck with his fingertips. The skin was soft. His muscles were relaxed. That's why he hardly recognized what he saw in the mirror. There was something in his body, in his heart that was changing.

And a tear rolled down his cheek.

Clayton knelt on the floor beside the desk, and he prayed, "God, you know what I'm trying to do with this story. Please bless it and help me to make things right with my son. Amen."

Imagining, tequila, and dreaming—not necessarily in that order— were the elements of preparation for a successful song-dream. Now, with Penelope, imagining, tequila, dreaming, and sex—definitely not in that order—were preparation for a successful song-dream.

She ran her hand down his chest. "What're you thinking?"

"I can feel the old man in my head. He'll definitely be at the concert." He got out of bed and stood naked at the floor-to-ceiling window of their room, and he looked out over the ocean.

"Do you have a song you wrote for him?"

"Oh, yeah. Actually, I have a whole bunch of songs I wrote just for him. I'm going to take him apart piece by piece."

"Why are you so angry, baby?"

"I don't know why. All I can say is that I'm angry at everyone except you and the band."

"Your fans?"

"They're only a mirror."

"And Clayton?"

"I want that crystal, and I'm going to squeeze him for it until he begs for mercy and gives it to me."

CHAPTER 43

Raven, Jake, and Tarek were in a hotel less than a mile from Clayton's. It was just before 8:00 a.m. the morning of the concert, and they were eating breakfast and drinking coffee outdoors at a rooftop café.

"What's our risk?" Tarek asked.

"We're only observers," Raven said. She took a bite from her omelet. "I doubt either man is giving us much thought right now. We're not in any greater danger than anyone else in the city." She asked Jake, "What do you know about security for the concert?"

"It's going to be tight. The powers that be are expecting the usual chaos, and so they've overstaffed EMTs, security guards, and police."

"And we'll have our own people inside," Tarek said. "If Clayton should find himself in a vulnerable position, we'll be able to snatch him up."

For breakfast, Clayton went down to the restaurant in the hotel lobby. Eggs benedict sounded good. He had dreamed his story, envisioning Derrick as the son and himself as the father. But he had had the strangest sensation: He had felt like Derrick had been watching him while he dreamed.

Derrick, Rex, Dazzle, and TJ were all on the stage, surveying the roadies' work.

"I had a vision of this stadium last night," Derrick said.

"Did you see *him*?" TJ asked.

"Yeah, he was sitting there." He pointed straight ahead at a row of seats that was eye-level with the stage.

"Sweet," Dazzle said.

Clayton was at the stadium two hours before the concert started. It had been warm during the day, but the temperature was dropping fast. It would get down into the forties before the end of the night. He was wearing a heavy coat and a Dodger's cap. Hopefully, it would give him cover from the cabal and Derrick's people—he was sure they would be looking for him.

Thirty minutes later he was in his seat on the 100-level without any mishaps. The stage was straight ahead, and he could take in the entire stadium. There were giant monitors on both sides of the stage for closeups of the band. There was a giant red neon sign with the words, "The Derr!" between the monitors.

Steadily, every one of the 77,000 seats were filled, and the pit was packed with people standing shoulder-to-shoulder. Clayton stuck out. It was his coat and his age—most of the crowd was 20-something, and nearly everyone's hair was black and combed forward. And they wore black jeans and only t-shirts despite the chill. Male or female, it did not matter, they all looked like Derrick.

Except Clayton.

The warmup artist was a longtime favorite of Derrick's fans. He was a true gangsta—his own words—who took pride in reliving his exploits in rhyme. Clayton watched the people rap his songs with him.

After 90 minutes of painting with vivid language the carnage the rapper had dreamed of inflicting on all the cops who had ever hassled him on the streets and the celebration he would have afterward "with the big booty girls, in his lap with their curls, who love to have fun with my gun," etcetera, the crowd was half-hoarse, demonstrably horny, and pumped up for a fight. When the rapper left the stage, the lights came down low, and a hush settled over the stadium. The energy level that flowed from the people's sense of anticipation was palatable.

It began with a soft, slow rumble—it was like thunder. Steadily the tempo and volume became harder and faster. Everyone was on their feet. And there was a burst of light like a flash grenade. Derrick was centerstage with the band behind him. He gave the double bird to the audience and said, "I'm glad you're here!" The people returned the gesture and screamed, "So are we!" Clayton stood with the audience.

Derrick sang,

> He got no creed
> And I let him bleed
> Let 'em bleed
> Cuz I gotta feed
>
> Good food for me
> Good food for you
> My daddy bleed
> Cuz I gotta feed

Is this about me? About us? Clayton wondered. His flesh crawled.

> Like the spider lone
> I eat my own
> Let 'em bleed
> Cuz I gotta feed...

He knows I'm here—he's trying to get into my head.

Derrick finished the song, but the band changed keys and kept playing. Derrick rapped,

You think you gonna mold me
These chains can't hold me
Momma don't scold me....

Clayton's ears were ringing—he could hardly make out the words. He sat down. The lights were flashing. *Is this all in my head?* He patted his chest through his coat. *It's still there, but why isn't my story working?*

The audience sang with Derrick,
It ain't so bad you see
To be on the street, a refugee
Where the bad motherfuckers decree
I'm the baddest motherfucker there ever be....

Clayton put his hand on his cheek—it was burning up. The men and women on his left and right sang, clapped, and stomped their feet. His shirt was soaked through with sweat—he was afraid.

The band was only an hour into its set, and Clayton thought, *How am I going to survive this? Is Derrick completely impervious to my dream?*

Derrick sang,

The pig's got me down
My face's on the ground
But I'll be back
Wit a counterattack

I'll have his mother
And his pretty wife, too
But nothin' be any better
Dan da pig's darlin' daughter....

Is he talking about raping a cop's mother, wife, and daughter? Clayton wiped his forehead with his sleeve, and he stood up. The song ended, and there was silence for a moment. And Derrick pointed straight ahead and whispered into the mic, "Old Man, I see you."

"How is this possible?" Clayton muttered. He saw Derrick's face on one of the giant screens. His black eyes drilled through him. Clayton looked around at the people—they were all staring at him. On the second big screen, Clayton's face appeared.

"Oh my God," Clayton said.

"This next one's for you, Daddy," Derrick said. And he rapped,

> You left my momma with a tear in her eye
> Left us in da ghetto with only a lie
> But you had it all as you took to the sky
> Fly, fly motherfucker to the sweet by-n-by
>
> My daddy weren't my daddy, and he had
>   to die
> Crushed by a bus and left where he lie.
> You all sad and broken up inside?
> Fuck you, motherfucker, you're the next
>   to fry.
>
> Everything's mine, from the earth to the sky
> You know why you can't, you can't deny—

Clayton scrambled into the aisle. He tripped on the stairs and fell to his knees. He struggled back to his feet. On the landing, he bolted through an opening into a wide, concrete corridor. A blast of cold air hit him in the face. He ran.

Derrick's voice rang through the passageway, but it was only static sound to Clayton. He imagined Derrick leering at him as he sang.

Emerging from the stadium, Clayton stumbled through the gate, and he fell. His head smacked the ground. And he dreamed: *Billy looked at himself in the bathroom mirror: He was changing.... That craving for violence had begun to dissolve.... There was something in his heart that was changing....*

Clayton opened his eyes. A medic—a big-chested black man—knelt over him. He pointed a flashlight in his face. "Sir, are you okay?"

"I think so. I tripped."

"Have you been drinking?"

"I wish I had."

Hundreds of people were passing by. A group of teenage boys were close, and Clayton overheard them talking. One of them asked, "What was that shit?"

His friend said, "It's like he had a fucking aneurysm or something."

"A fucking what?"

"You know, a brain explosion."

The other medic—a tall, gangly white man—told Clayton they needed to check his vitals. "My name's Jesse, and this is Rick," the medic said.

"Good to meet you guys."

Inside the ambulance, Clayton sat on a bench as Rick took his blood pressure. People poured out of the stadium.

"Is it over already? Was I out a long time?" Clayton asked.

"You were only out for a couple of minutes, sir," Rick said. "The concert ended early."

"What happened?"

"The singer collapsed in the middle of a song," Jesse said. "Seems to be going around." He raised an eyebrow. "Maybe it's a new variant."

"I don't think it's that," Clayton said.

"I'm sorry?" Jesse asked.

"I need to see him."

"The singer? He's already on his way to the hospital," said Jesse.

"Which one?"

"That's confidential, sir."

"He's my son."

The medics looked at each other.

Half an hour later the ambulance pulled up to the entrance of St. Mary's Medical Center. The medics and Clayton said goodbye to each other outside the vehicle with handshakes.

A woman greeted Clayton at the reception desk in the hospital, and he asked her for Derrick's room number. She typed some keys on her computer and gazed at the monitor for a moment. "I'm sorry, sir," she said, "but your name's not on the visitor's list. Because he's a high profile—"

"Please tell him I'm here. I'm certain he'll want to see me."

A couple minutes later Clayton was following a security guard down a long hallway on the fifth floor of the hospital.

"Old Man!" the tenor voice carried down the hall. There was a giggle.

Three men—two black, one white—emerged from the room just as Clayton arrived. They walked past him with their heads down.

"Those're my homeboys," Derrick said. He was in bed propped up with pillows, half covered with a sheet. He wore a blue and white-striped hospital gown. There was an IV in his arm.

"How are you?" Clayton asked.

"Seriously?" He held up his arm with the IV. "What did you think of my song about you and my momma?"

"It was sad."

"But it's true. Why did you leave the concert?"

"I had to. Why are you so angry, Derrick? Where's this coming from?"

"What, are you a fucking psychoanalyst? Good luck with that. But I'll tell you what, that little story of yours was awesome! When it hit me—" He patted his chest. "I felt like my heart was going to explode. You could've killed me, man. You know that?"

"That wasn't my intention. I was appealing to your soul, that part of you that still believes in love."

"Impossible."

"How did you become so callous?"

"Love is a figment of the imagination. It's a thing invented by poets and teenage girls. It's shit."

"It's the alternative to the rage, Derrick, to the anger and hatred."

"Are you kidding me? Those things are jet fuel for me. They make me what I am. The songs I write are fed by my rage. It's what makes me, me. And if I don't have that, what am I? You?" He chuckled.

"Derrick, you've hurt a lot of people. Why are you doing this?"

"Okay, I'm going to tell you something. But I'm going to say it only once. So listen carefully: Everyone dies. Most people fall into the abyss randomly—they don't see it coming, and they're totally surprised by the darkness when it swallows them up, and for that reason they're usually content with their dumb lives. Others do realize their mortality before it kicks them in the head, but they don't do anything about it, and they're generally miserable until they die. And then there's a handful of people who see the same thing, but they begin to work hard to create a sense of purpose for themselves. Are you following my argument?"

Clayton nodded.

"I find fulfillment in expressing my purpose, which is to show everyone that there is no purpose for their lives."

They stared at each other for a long moment.

"You don't really believe that," Clayton said. "I know you don't. Like me, you believe we all have an eternal destiny."

Derrick's eyes sparkled as he threw back his head and laughed. "Shit, man, you wouldn't be coming around if that's all you wanted to tell me. You're just trying to protect your bitches."

Clayton glared at him. "Fuck you."

He laughed again. "Getting under your skin? This is my offer: Give me the crystal, your home, and your money, and go far, far away. Go to Oklahoma! I love it. If you do that, I'll let you all hang around for a while. And leave me your dog, the Frenchie. My pit bulls, Annihilator and Typhoon, would love him as a playmate."

Clayton shook his head. "Son—"

Derrick laughed. "Really, when have you ever been my daddy? When did you rescue me from that psycho who beat on me and my momma? When did you help anyone but your sorry ass self? I made you an offer. Give me everything or, you know, there're consequences."

"You're going to kill me?"

"I'm going to show you how dark and deep the abyss really is." His grin was wolfish.

"Derrick—"

"Winner takes all." And he rolled over, pulling the covers over his head.

CHAPTER 44

"It's a week ago today when Derrick Romano passed out on stage during his concert in L.A.," Raven said to the men she viewed on the monitor.

She was at Amelia's old office that overlooked Central Park. Tarek and Jake sat on either side of her. "Clayton had left the stadium right before that happened. Two of our people were following him and were going to pick him up when he collapsed in the parking lot. The EMTs got to him first."

"What do you make of the relationship between the two men?" asked Justice Orden.

"I was able to watch their interaction via an unsecured webcam in Derrick's hospital room. I recorded it, and I'll share it with you now." The monitor switched to a video of Clayton and Derrick talking—they could see the men's profiles. After Clayton left the room, Raven switched the monitor back to the video-conference.

"It sounds like they used the crystal's powers to attack each other during the concert," Adam Stone said.

"It's a war of the gods," Hammerman said.

"And we'll wait to see who the winner is," Raven said.

Clayton and Elowen sat next to each other on the couch.

"You're lucky you weren't hurt," Elowen said.

"I know."

"You've got to get rid of it."

"But how? I can't give it away, and I can't destroy it. I mean I could try, but I'd probably die in the process."

"I don't know, but you've got to figure this out. You can't sit on it forever."

"Maybe I could, in a sense. We could create a trust that would ensure that it was kept in a vault for an indefinite period of time."

"But will you be able to resist the temptation of using it again?"

"I'm not sure I can." He released a sigh. "And to be honest, I don't think I'm done with it quite yet."

"Seriously? Think about everything we've been through, all the risks you've taken—you've been beaten twice. You could've been killed."

He cleared his throat nervously.

"Clayton, you promised us that if I let you go to the concert in L.A., that would be the end of it."

"But I have an idea."

"Of course you have an idea. You're a writer. You probably have a thousand ideas a day. And that's great for a novel. But not for our life together!" She stared at him.

He said nothing.

She stood. "You need to make a final and definitive decision about what you're going to do."

"Is that an ultimatum?"

"We can't live like this, not knowing from one day to the next where we stand with you. I'm trying to build a home. But this lunatic you feel so attached to wants to tear us apart. You can't give him the crystal, and you can't keep using it. It doesn't get much simpler than that, Clayton. Use that big creative brain of yours to sort this out. That's *the idea* I want to hear about. So, to answer your question, yes, I guess it is."

"'Yes,' what?"

"Yes, it's an ultimatum. Choose Derrick or choose us."

"But Elowen—"

"I'm going to give you some space to work through this. I'm going to take the baby and go stay with my mom for a few days." And she turned and left the room.

CHAPTER 45

Anna stood at the sink washing pans from breakfast. "Is Charlie watching the news?" Clayton asked. He drank coffee and read the newspaper in the nook.

"Yes, he is, Mr. Lange."

"He's more than welcome to come over here and watch it on the big screen."

"Thank you, Mr. Lange. But he loves the cottage." She grabbed the coffee pot and refilled his cup. "Do you miss them?"

"A lot."

"If you apologize, I'm sure she'll come back."

"That's not it. She's angry and afraid because I'm still trying to do something with Derrick. She feels like I'm putting her and the baby at risk."

"Are you?"

"I think what I'm doing minimizes our risks in the long run better than anything else I could do."

"Mr. Lange, please don't risk your life for that boy. The baby needs you a lot more than he does."

"You're right, Anna." He folded the newspaper and got up from the table. "I'm going to write through the rest of the morning. Could you please bring me a bowl of soup and half a sandwich for lunch?"

"Of course, Mr. Lange."

He went to his office, sat at the desk, and looked out the window to the yard. A rabbit was in the garden nibbling on the leaves of a marigold plant. Clayton powered up the tablet and opened his story, *A Father's Love for His Son.* Glancing out the window again he saw that Herodotus had appeared and put the rabbit to the chase. *The rabbit's plan was to eat,* Clayton reflected. *But it was his ability to improvise that saved him. That's a perfect allegory from nature that demonstrates what life is really like.*

The story he had written was solid, but Derrick was writing his own story at the same time. Like the rabbit, Clayton would adapt, which for him would take the form of an epilogue: In his story, the father would give his son everything. Money can't buy you love, as the song goes, but it can be a sign of what one believes and hopes for another person. A life filled with joy and happiness—that was his hope and dream for his boy.

The story revolved around a family that had made its fortune on Texas crude two generations earlier, and now the father would officially bequeath ownership of the oil wells to his son. As a sign of the inheritance, he would give him a ring. It was a family heirloom and a source of pride for the one who wore it. It had been designed by the founder of the company, his great-grandfather. In its center was a giant diamond, on one side was the emblem of the company—a rig spouting oil—and on the other side was the letter "T" for the family name.

A smile formed across Clayton's lips as he imagined the scene unfolding. He wrote,

As a token of his desire for reconciliation with his son, Jonas placed on Billy's finger the ring his granddad and his father had worn. It was something he himself valued more than anything he had ever possessed. It was as though the ring itself had the power granddad had wielded during his reign as the king of Texas crude. Billy would now wear it, and with it he would inherit the estate. But he would also be filled up with his grandfather's greatest virtue, which was honor.

He reread the whole thing and finished it with, "The End."

It was hours later, and the house was still and dark. But Clayton's sleep was restless. He looked at the clock—6:20 a.m. He had been dreaming the epilogue. But while he dreamed, he sensed he was not alone.

The phone rang. "Hello?" he answered.

"Hey, Old Man, did you have sweet dreams last night?"

"Dreams, yes. Sweet, no."

"I felt you in my head telling me a story. Kind of foggy now, but it had something to do with an old fart trying to lure his boy back into the family by giving him his inheritance, which had something to do with oil and a ring, yada, yada."

"That was it, more or less."

"This is so romantic, you telling me stories, and me singing you songs."

"It would be a true father-son story of reconciliation if you weren't trying to bust my balls."

He laughed. "I can't deny that. So what's going on? Are you going to give me the damned crystal?"

"'*Damned* crystal'? You're probably closer to the truth than either of us will ever understand."

"Where is it?"

"You need to promise me one thing."

"Here we go."

"I want you to leave me and my family alone."

"Even little Emily?"

"Especially little Emily. And I want you to guarantee this arrangement with a poison pill."

"Let me guess: You want me to sign a contract that'll reward you with the ownership of all my recording contracts if any danger ever befalls you or members of your family which can be traced to anything I've ever said, written, or performed. Is that about right?"

"That's what I want."

"Well, I just might have to think about that for a while."

"And I just might have to throw this *damned* crystal into the sea. It'll find its way back someday, but not during your lifetime."

He could hear Derrick breathing.

"All right, I'm in, Old Man. Where shall we make this happen? I've got a condo in Midtown where I hang out when I'm in the city. It's dope. I could fly out later this morning and be there this afternoon, and you could meet me there."

"We're going to meet underground. Text me when you get into the city, and I'll tell you where to go." He disconnected.

It was just after three in the morning. "Man, this guy is a clever bastard," Derrick said.

Penelope and the band were in a hot tub on the deck at his house in California. They had been drinking beer and snorting coke all night. The stars glittered against the water.

"A poison pill, huh?" Dazzle said.

"It's a cryin' shame," Rex said.

"But nobody outwits the Derr," TJ snorted.

"So true," Derrick said. "But that was a smart move. And to tell you the truth, I don't blame him. And what the hell? What're his wife and kid to me anyway?"

"You're going to do it?" Penelope asked.

"Hell, yeah. When I get the crystal, in fact, the last thing that's going to be on my mind is Clayton Lange and his family." He quaffed his beer. "Probably," he added, and everyone laughed.

Clayton was on his way into the city when he called Elowen late in the morning. She let her guard down for a moment as he explained his plan. But when he finished, there was a long silence.

"Clayton," she finally said.

He sensed tension in her voice.

"Why did you call me?"

"I, um—"

"What you just said is not a plan. I'm going to be honest with you.

You sound like a kid who has a book of matches and a can of gasoline, and you want to see what happens when you set it on fire!"

She was becoming louder.

He should have thought about how he was going to talk to her a little more thoroughly. He assured her everything was going to be okay. But cringed because he knew he sounded phony.

"Clayton, you're talking about giving that little psychopath the key to living out his dream of manifesting hell on earth."

"Not exactly. I mean, I know that's what it sounds like, but that's not my end game."

"'End game'? What is your 'end game'?"

"To save his life, to secure our safety, and to keep the crystal out of the hands of the cabal."

"You're talking in circles!" she said, and then she accused him of mansplaining and not respecting her. She hung up.

He had lived with only Herodotus and Anna for years, and he had never experienced loneliness. But now he did. And if Elowen had called him back, he would have told her exactly what he was going to do—anything to get her to come home with the baby. Thankfully, she had not called. No one except him could know exactly what he was going to do without risking everything.

It was just after 2:00 p.m. when his phone dinged with a text message. It was Derrick: "I'm at LaGuardia. Where are we meeting, Old Man?"

He texted back: "Take the A-line to Canal Street downtown. I'll be on the southbound side. Come by yourself."

It would take Derrick about 90 minutes to get to the stop if he took the subway, or an hour if he grabbed a taxi. Himself, he was drinking coffee at a shop just above the subway stop.

It was three o'clock, and Clayton sat on a bench underground. He watched passengers discharge from a train. Derrick was not with them. The doors slapped shut, and the train rumbled down the tunnel. He heard the squeak of sneakers on the concrete, and he glanced at the stairs.

"Hey, Old Man," Derrick said.

"Have a seat. You left your boys behind?"

"They went to the condo with Penelope."

"That's cool she's still with you."

"Yeah, sure, pretend to care."

"I do care." He pulled a sheet of paper from a manila envelope. "This is the contract we talked about."

"The poison pill?"

"I prefer 'the promise of preservation.'"

"That's why you're a writer," he mocked. He took the paper, and Clayton gave him a pen. He signed it in his lap and handed it back.

"Thanks," Clayton said.

"Where's the damned crystal?"

"I don't have it."

"Give it up, Old Man." Down the tracks, a train squealed. He nodded in that direction. "Or else."

"Or else you'll kill me? You'd never get the crystal."

"Kill you? That'd be murder. What kind of man do you think I am?" he scoffed. "I have a vision of you and your pal, Charlie Kravets, in the Special Olympics together."

"It's in a safe deposit box."

"Where?"

"Washington Federal Bank."

He looked up and over his shoulder at the stairs. "Is that the bank I saw on the corner?"

"Yeah," Clayton said. He rifled around in his jacket pocket and pulled out a key. "This is for the box." He handed it to Derrick. "Goodbye, Son."

Derrick stood and grabbed Clayton by the arm. "Oh, no, you don't. You're coming with me. You know, just in case it isn't there." They came up out of the tunnel. Across the street was the bank. "Come on, let's go get my inheritance."

"Derrick, you do realize this thing will make you the most powerful man on earth," Clayton said, "more powerful than the first men who used it, the great kings and emperors, men like Alexander the Great, Augustus, and Constantine, for you'll have more opportunities and greater resources than all the richest men on earth combined."

"A lot more." They stood in front of the bank's doors. "You know, that's the thing I don't get about you. You had this charm for so long and even after you understood what it could do, you never did anything worth a shit."

"Actually, I—"

"What you did was a drop in the bucket compared to what you could've done. Now, with my imagination and vision, we're going to see some action. Let's go." He pulled open the door and invited Clayton to precede him.

A woman who wore a bright blue dress like a tent sat at a desk. The title "Associate Manager" was on her nameplate. "How may I help you gentlemen?"

"We'd like to open our safe deposit box," Clayton said.

After gushing over how wonderful it was to have such famous clients entrust the bank with their treasures, she walked them to the vault. Derrick walked next to her and whispered in her ear, "If I had any say about it, your fat ass wouldn't be entrusted with a cow turd."

Her face turned red as she escorted them into the vault. After unlocking the crypt, she slid the box out and set it on a table in the middle of the room. She scuttled from the vault without saying a word.

The two men sat next to each other. Clayton turned to Derrick. "Look at me," he said. Derrick's eyes were filled with amusement. "I heard what you said to that woman. That was inappropriate and meanspirited."

"I don't give a shit," he said, and he put his hand on top of the box.

Clayton placed his hand on top of his. "Son, I want to tell you something before you open it."

"These may be your last words, Old Man. Go for it."

"With great power comes great responsibility. It's a responsibility not only to the people over whom you'll use it but also to your family, especially your mother. But perhaps most profoundly you have a responsibility to care for your own soul."

"You're a little late with this kind of lecture, don't you think?"

Clayton lifted his hand, and Derrick opened the box.

In the box was a photograph. Derrick grabbed it and yelled, "What's this?" It was the picture of his mom and Clayton with their arms wrapped around each other at the frat party. There was nothing else in the box.

"This is all I have for you. Your mom still loves you, and I love you, too. If you can take hold of that love, you'll have more power than a thousand crystals."

Derrick released a scream that was primordial, and he lunged for Clayton. They tumbled to the ground, and Derrick sat on Clayton's chest. He pulled a blade from a sheath on his ankle. "Now you're going to die."

A metal screen which separated the safe deposit viewing area from the rest of the bank swung open. "Put the weapon down!" shouted a security guard with a gun trained on Derrick. He was a big man, filling the door's opening. The associate manager whom Derrick had just humiliated was his girlfriend. She had a tear in her eye as she looked over his shoulder. "Put it down very slowly!" the guard said.

Derrick's eyes were crazed, and he growled. With a grin that matched the insanity in his eyes, he looked down at Clayton, and he lifted the knife to his shoulder for a sweep across Clayton's throat. As his hand came down two shots from the gun exploded. They echoed through the bank like a cannon, and Derrick fell back onto the floor.

Clayton rolled over to him. "I'm sorry," he said.

Derrick gurgled through blood, "Fuck." And he was dead.

When Elowen returned with the baby, she was furious. She didn't take off her coat as they stood face-to-face in the front room. "Clayton, you could've been killed!" she yelled. "What was going on in your head?"

"All I can say is that I had to try."

Shaking her head and without a goodbye, she left him again and returned to her mom's house.

For the past week it had been cold and generally miserable on all fronts. Clayton gazed out the window from his office. Derrick had not left a will nor told anyone whether he desired to be buried or cremated. Clayton thought he probably would have preferred to have been immolated in a pyre surrounded by his groupies. But Clayton had always believed funerals were for the living not the dead. So he would bury him in a plot next to his own parents and grandparents. But before proceeding he had to make a phone call, one which he did not want to make.

The phone was picked up on the sixth ring. "Yeah?"

"Hi, Serenity. This is Clayton."

"No shit? Mr. Superstar Novelist Clayton Fucking Lange? You're calling the mother of the man you murdered to offer your fucking condolences?"

"I didn't kill him, Serenity. He was about to kill me, and a security guard shot him."

"I could tell the press so much shit about you."

"Why are you mad at me? I should be mad at you. You're the one who hustled Joe Romano with *our* baby. I loved you, Serenity. You were my light, and you broke my heart."

There was silence on the other end of the line for a long time. "I gotta go," she said, and she hung up. He wished there was an easier way. But he was going to have to go to Detroit.

The next day the cabbie drove into the East Detroit projects and parked in front of a rotting duplex. For a fat tip he agreed to wait for Clayton.

Clayton's senses were on high alert as he walked up to Serenity's place. There was a dead rat in the gutter. The smell of trash and dog urine hung in the air. Gunshots were not far away.

As he surveyed the block, a little girl with cornrows in her hair—maybe five years old—grabbed his leg. She had the biggest, brightest eyes. "Hey, Mister, my momma wants to talk to you."

He looked across the street and saw a woman who wore only a dress slip standing on the porch of her duplex. She winked.

"Tell your momma that's very nice of her, but I have a meeting. Okay?" he said, and he patted her on the arm.

Serenity's door was open, and he walked in. "Serenity?" he called.

She appeared in the doorway to the kitchen holding a large glass that was filled with ice and a pink beverage, perhaps vodka with a splash of cranberry juice. She had pulled a brush through her hair and smeared some rouge on her cheeks. In college, she was perfect at 115 pounds. Now, she was less than a hundred. Maybe she thought her legs were still sexy, but the short skirt she wore showed only spindles.

With a devious grin, she revealed missing teeth. "Hey, stranger," she said. "Wanna drink?"

He swallowed. He did want a drink, but not with her. "We need to talk about the funeral," he said.

It was two weeks later when he buried Derrick in the family plot in Queens. Serenity was there, in addition to Derrick's band, Elowen and the baby, Elliot and Sarah, Anna and Charlie, Clayton's aunts, and a handful of others. The weather was the same as it had been for his mom's funeral a little over a year ago—it was a rainy and gray afternoon. It suited everyone's mood.

It was an open casket service, and the priest sprinkled dirt on Derrick's chest as he recited the blessing: "We now commit his body to the ground; earth to earth, ashes to ashes, dust to dust...."

After the ceremony, the priest invited everyone to place a rose in the casket before the lid was shut. Clayton was last in line, and he set the black tourmaline crystal with the chain on Derrick's chest. "Rest in peace," he said.

———

It was weeks later when the sun shone on the Lange's home, and Clayton and Elowen grilled BBQ hamburgers with Elliot and Sarah and Anna and Charlie on their patio. Emily crawled in the grass—she was enthralled with Herodotus who romped around her, nudging her with his pug nose.

"They grow up so fast," Charlie said.

"They sure do," Clayton said. "I'm going to get more lemonade," he said, and he grabbed the pitcher and went up into the house to refill it.

Elliot followed him. At the kitchen counter, the publisher said, "I'm really proud of you, Clayton."

"Thanks. That means a lot."

"You made a whole bunch of lemons into lemonade."

Clayton held up a full pitcher. "Literally," he said.

"And I'm looking forward to your first alternate history novel."

"I've learned so much about emperors, sultans, kings, and dictators over the past few months, the writing comes easily."

"It'll be brilliant, I'm sure."

They went back outside, and Clayton refilled glasses, beginning with Elowen. After their confrontation immediately after Derrick's death, he was not sure how or when they would reconcile. But when she saw him bury the crystal with Derrick, she decided the relationship was worth another try.

"How's Serenity doing?" Sarah asked.

"She finished rehab last week," Clayton said as he refilled her glass. "And she's starting an outpatient program."

"I have a toast," Elowen said, raising her glass. "To the master of the art of fiction: May you enjoy many more fruitful years of scribbling." Everyone clinked their glasses. "And to honor that toast, we have prepared a special gift."

Charlie slid a box out from under the table, and he set it in front of Clayton.

"In this box," Elowen said, "are elements of the past which have given witness to the words, ideas, visions, and dreams of two men who have catapulted people from the dreariness of their everyday lives into new and exciting realms filled with adventure, intrigue, suspense, and surprise. This afternoon, we dedicate this device to the future work of Clayton H. Lange, writer extraordinaire."

Clayton screwed up his face; his eyes were filled with bewilderment.

"Well, open it," Elowen said.

He stood over the box, tore it open, and lifted out an antique Underwood typewriter. "This typewriter," Elowen said, "is the same year and model as the one Dr. Edward Freiwald gave you. But it is more than that. Its carriage is the one we saved from Dr. Freiwald's typewriter."

Tears streamed down Clayton's cheeks.

There were polite titles for his job, but he preferred the old school title, gravedigger. It was accurate. It was true. In fact, the only thing truer than his title was death itself. That was how ole Caleb saw it, anyway. His body was lanky and strung with long, hard muscles from years of labor. He was a clean cut man well into his 60s.

It was 3:00 a.m. at Glen Cemetery in Queens. Several people watched as Caleb pulled up shovelfuls of dirt with a backhoe and then cleared the casket with a hand shovel. He had exhumed a lot of bodies over the years but never at this hour.

He had no idea why this exhumation was happening now. Was it the fear of publicity? Did this have to do with a murder investigation, and somebody was in a hurry to get to the truth? Was there another party competing for information which the dead might provide? Was it legal? It did not matter to him; it was not his concern. He got paid double overtime, and it was on management to sort through this sort of thing.

Back in the seat of his machine, he powered up the diesel engine, engaged the gears, and slowly lifted the casket up and out of the hole. Shifting the transmission into reverse, he pulled the rig back, and set the casket on a stand.

He climbed down and released the straps that bound the casket. He crossed himself. Taking a camelhair brush from his belt, he swept dirt off the lid. When he was done, he put the brush back, and he grabbed the casket key from the cab of the backhoe. He inserted it into the hex bolt at the foot of the casket and cranked on it until the gasket around the edge was released. There was the familiar hiss of the escaping gases—the small group that had come for the exhumation collectively gagged at the putrid odor. But not Caleb. He had opened caskets many times.

He lifted the lid of the casket on its hinges. The scene was one of contrasts. There was Derrick Romano, formerly a musical revolutionary, but now only a voiceless memory. He was dressed in a fine cashmere wool suit—something he would never have chosen for himself—a garment which was ruined by the boy's heavy state of decay—largely liquification. In the center of his suitcoat were roses—once lush, but now as dead as their cohabitant. And there was the object which lay just as it had been left by Clayton Lange months ago: a black tourmaline crystal on a white gold rope chain.

For a long moment, all was still.

But then a black hand with long acrylic fingernails and a ring with a ten-carat step cut emerald hovered over the crystal and snatched it up.

9 798990 527706